RUTHLESS BEAST

LYDIA HALL

Copyright © 2023 by Lydia Hall

All rights reserved.

No part of this book may be reproduced in any form or by any electronic or mechanical means, including information storage and retrieval systems, without written permission from the author, except for the use of brief quotations in a book review.

❧ Created with Vellum

ALSO BY LYDIA HALL

Series: Spicy Office Secrets

New Beginnings || Corporate Connection || Caught in the Middle || Faking It For The Boss || Baby Makes Three || The Boss's Secret || My Best Friend's Dad

Series: The Big Bad Braddock Brothers

Burning Love || Tell Me You Love Me || Second Chance at Love || Pregnant: Who is the Father? || Pregnant with the Bad Boy

Series: The Forbidden Attraction

My Mommy's Boyfriend || Daddy's Best Friend || Daddy Undercover || The Doctor's Twins || She's Mine || Tangled Trust

Series: Corrupt Bloodlines

Dangerous Games || Dangerous Refuge || Dangerous Obsession || Dangerous Vengeance || Dangerous Secrets

BLURB

The death of my brother brought me face to face with a commanding mafia leader.

Lucas had all my attention from the moment our eyes met.

He saw the sadness in mine and embraced me.

I felt protected.

But Lucas is way older… *and* dangerous.

Still, he's not the one I have to be afraid of.

My brother's death was, in fact, murder.

And my own life is in the hands of the rival gang.

Lucas has always felt like a protector.

But his mystery sends shivers down my spine.

He's anything but innocent.

And he would go to any lengths to ensure my safety.

Even if that means taking me in without my will.

But there's one thing that even Lucas has no control over.

A secret – a baby that's growing inside my belly who would call him daddy.

1

EMILY THORNTON

"Oh, wow! That's amazing, Ems. You are such a fabulous artist."

"Ooh, fabulous, hey? Thanks, Dannie. You're my biggest fan," I coo in appreciation of my best friend, Daniella's encouragement.

"It's true. Next to yours, my drawings look like something a two year old would deposit on a canvas with pureed broccoli."

"Funny."

"How's the assignment coming along?"

"I'm almost done. This is the last in the collection I have to submit by Friday. I'm nervous."

"You're crazy. You're always nervous when the truth is that your art professor would be so lucky to have more students like you in his class. You're going to ace it. No sweat."

My one-woman fan club smiles brightly at me. Dannie and I couldn't be more different if we tried. We are polar opposites in every way, but we are cut from the same cloth when it comes to friendship and loyalty.

Daniella is a math nerd. With her eyeglasses and pullovers, she'd be perfectly at home on the set of The Big Bang Theory. I zone out when she starts waxing lyrical about equations and stats. She may as well be speaking a foreign language, for all the sense it makes to me. The light dances in her eyes, and I swear her voice goes up a few octaves as she chatters on about all things mathematical. I nod my head and pretend to be interested, but truthfully, I'd be happier watching paint dry.

I painted a canvas for Dannie for her twentieth birthday. It was my artistic interpretation of an equation she'd been particularly fascinated with at the time. I have to say it was pretty damn impressive. Even I was amazed at how good the end result was. The canvas hangs over her desk now. Dannie insists that it serves as her inspiration when she's feeling a tad unmotivated.

"Are you working this afternoon?" she asks, a red gummy worm dangling from her lips.

"No. Pierre is working an extra shift. He's going to visit his parents next weekend, so he asked if I'd swap shifts with him."

"Uhhh, Pierre. That man is too beautiful for his own good," Dannie gushes.

"That he is. Pity he bats for the other side."

"Hey, give me one night with him, armed with a bottle of wine, and I'll change his mind."

"You're far too horny for a math major, Daniella Freeman."

"It might interest you to know that apparently old Einstein got around quite a bit in his day," Dannie grins. "Genius is horny work, my dear woman," she says, staring mockingly down at me over the rim of her glasses.

"Is that so?"

"Yup. Speaking of horny work, How's your love life? What happened to that tall drink of water you met at the gallery? Paolo, was it?"

"Ah, yes. I'm afraid the delicious Paolo went back home to Italy."

"Oh, darn it. Never mind. It's a good thing you have a best friend who has your back."

"You're referring to that enormous vibrator you bought me for my birthday, aren't you?" I sigh, rolling my eyes.

"Don't knock it til you've tried it, hon. Not all of us have access to lovers of art with deep pockets who enjoy lazy afternoons filled with champagne cocktails and oodles of rampant sex."

"Do you even know what I do at the gallery?" I laugh.

My phone rings, cutting our conversation short. It's David.

"Hi, Big Bro."

"Hey, Ems."

"What's up?"

"I was just wondering if you were free for dinner."

"Hey, gorgeous man!" Dannie yells out loud. "The answer is yes. Yes, I'll marry you!"

"David says hi," I say as she cackles and leaves the room.

"That girl is one fraction short of a whole number," David laughs.

"And the horse it rode in on," I add. "Anyway, I'd love to join you for dinner. Where are we going?"

"You decide. I'll swing by at 6 p.m. and pick you up. Okay?"

"Great. See you then."

David's and my parents died suddenly when I was twelve and he was twenty. For the last twelve years, my older brother has been dad, mom, brother, best friend, bodyguard, guardian, and all the other things my parents aren't able to be for me. I'm so proud of him.

David is handsome and very clever. He's done well for himself when it comes to finances. And the most impressive part is that he did it all while raising his little sister like a boss.

It's 5:55 p.m. when I hear his car engine's telltale roar outside my apartment.

"I'll see you later, Dannie!" I call out in the direction of her bedroom.

"Have fun!" she calls back. "Give my future husband a sloppy kiss on the cheek for me!"

"Will do!"

Dannie has a serious crush on David. They have a very playful relationship where he pretends it's annoying, and she embarrasses him at every opportunity. It's cute.

"Hiya," I say, jumping into the passenger side of the Mustang.

"Hey, Sis. You look lovely."

"Thanks, Davy. Let's make some girls jealous," I giggle.

"You're not going to pretend you're my hot girlfriend again, are you?"

"Of course I am. It's the least I can do to pay you back for all those times you scared the crap out of my dates."

"Hey, thanks to my vigilance, you were never disrespected, were you?"

"Yeah, yeah. I also never had a serious boyfriend until college, thanks to you. Moving on, what's new with you?"

"Nothing much. I work too hard to get into any trouble. How's school?"

"You mean university. I'm twenty-four just in case you missed it," I smirk. "School is school. I'm looking forward to getting my last assignment in. It's almost time to dust off the old tux, Bro. Your baby sister is graduating soon."

"I can't believe the time has gone by so fast. I'm super proud of you, Ems."

"Thank you, David. I couldn't have done it without you. I love you so much, you old stinker," I smile and slap him playfully on the knee.

"Woah! Don't get me all misty now. You'll ruin my reputation as a tough guy."

"Tough guy! Oh, please. You're a softy, Mr. Thornton. And don't let them tell you anything different."

"Where would you like to go?"

"I'm in the mood for Mexican."

"Then Mexican you shall have, young lady."

"Do you ever wonder what our lives would be like if Mom and Dad were still alive?" I say after a few moments of silence.

"All the time."

"Do you think you and I would be this close?"

"I'd like to think so."

"I miss them, Davy."

"I miss them too, Ems. They'd be very proud of you, you know."

"What about you? You've done incredibly well for yourself. You're so young, and look at the life you've made for us."

David is far away. I can see that he has something on his mind.

"What is it?" I ask, resting my hand on his knee.

"Nothing," he says after a while. "Just thinking about work stuff."

"Are you sure?"

"Yes, of course."

"You'd tell me if something was wrong, wouldn't you, Davy?"

"Probably not," he grins.

"Come on. I'm an adult now. You don't have to protect me from everything anymore. I'm tougher than I look."

"Don't I know it! Trust me. It's nothing serious. I'm just preoccupied. Come on. No more talk of work or studies. It's tequila and loaded nachos time."

"You don't gotta tell me twice, Amigo."

"It's a good thing you're not a language major," David chuckles.

"Oh, come now. I talk English so very deliciously."

David is making light of things, but I sense there's something he's not telling me. I hope that in the course of the evening I'll be able to pull out of him whatever it is that's bothering him.

I don't know much about David's work. He doesn't speak much about his clients, but I understand that. Client confidentiality is key when you're an accountant, and my brother is nothing if not honorable.

The restaurant is packed, but the owner always makes a space for David and me. It used to be our family's favorite place to eat, so after the owners learned of our parents' accident, David and I were pretty much guaranteed a permanent table no matter what.

"Hello, you two. So nice to see you."

"Hi, Pedro. It's always good to see you," David smiles.

"It smells heavenly in here as always," I chime in.

"The usual for my special friends?" Pedro asks.

"Oh, yeah. And keep 'em coming," I grin.

It isn't long before I'm in Mexican food heaven.

"I could so die deliriously happy right now," I grin after licking the habanero sauce off my fingers and washing it all down with a healthy glug of margarita.

"No one wears habanero better than you, little sis," David laughs.

"Ain't that the truth? Are you going to eat that?" I ask, pointing to a perfectly untouched chili popper.

"Go ahead," he says. I eagerly scoop up the treat before he changes his mind.

It isn't like my brother to leave food on his plate. What's more, he's been absent minded all evening. I try one last time to get it out of him.

"Davy, what's wrong? You're not yourself. You know you can talk to me, right?"

"I'm fine, Ems. Really. It's been a busy week. I'm tired."

I raise one eyebrow while sipping on a margarita.

"Don't give me the hairy eyeball, Inspector. I'm serious. I'm just tired."

"Okay. I'll let you off the hook this time. What's keeping you so busy?"

"A new client. They're a big deal. I'm snowed under."

"Well, you can relax. I'm sure they know, as do we all, that you're the best. You don't have to work yourself to death to prove anything, David."

"You're sweet."

"Okay, now I know there's something wrong," I cackle. "You never call me sweet."

"Haha. Are we having dessert?"

"I am. No dessert for you, Davy-boy. You didn't finish your meal. Mom will turn in her grave if I allow you to break that golden rule."

"You're in a good mood. I take it you're excited about graduating next month."

"I can't wait. I'm done with studying. It's time to make some money."

"My poor starving artist sister," David winks. "Are you going to work at the gallery full-time after that?"

"Yes. They've offered me good money. Also, Adam told me I'm free to paint while I'm there, and I can display my work."

"Of course he did. Having you there is a winning scenario for him. Your art is stunning, Ems."

"Ahhh… Thanks, Davy. Why don't you have dinner with Dannie and me next Saturday? I know she's dying to perv over you," I tease.

"As much as I'd love to fulfill Dannie's fantasies, I'm afraid I'm busy next Saturday."

"A girl?"

"No, I'm afraid it's much less exciting. My new client invited me to his place for a function."

"You know who to call if you need a date," I tease some more.

"Thank you, Cupid, but I've got this."

"I'm just saying. I have a team of friends who are all more than willing to keep you entertained."

"So, what you're saying is that you don't believe that I can scare up a decent date? When did my little sister lose faith in her stud of a brother?"

David pulls a face of mock devastation. He's so handsome. I love my brother so much.

"No doubts here, Bro. You're da man."

The waitress comes over and asks if we'd like to see the dessert menu. I watch her eyes as they explore David's body. I'm used to it. I'm very proud of him.

"Two shots of Tequila, please," I say, snapping the cupcake out of her lascivious thoughts. "Don Julio."

She smiles bashfully at me, as if she forgot for a moment that I was there.

"That's telling her," David says, laughing once she's out of earshot.

* * *

It's 11:48 and I'm in bed with a lovely little buzz, courtesy of faithful old Don. Dannie raps on the door twice before she pokes her head inside the room.

"How's my future husband?" she grins.

"Still as handsome as ever."

"Did he ask you for my hand in marriage?"

"Not yet. Any day now."

Dannie giggles and plops herself down at the foot of the bed.

"Did you have a good time?"

"I did, thanks."

"What is it? Your mouth is saying one thing, but your eyes are telling a different story."

"You know me far too well."

"Spill it, Mildred."

"I'm worried about David. I get the feeling he's keeping something from me."

"Did you ask him?"

"I did. He waffled on about a new client and being very busy, but I know it's more than that."

"Woman's intuition is a curse."

"It is when you can't put your finger on the problem."

"You know what men are like, Ems. I'm sure David will tell you if it's serious. They don't like to talk about feelings and shit."

"I guess not."

"Well, I'm paste. Sleep tight, Ems."

"Good night, Dannie."

I decide to send David a text before I turn off my nightlight.

Hey, Davy.

Thanks for a lovely evening. I miss you. Let's do this more often. Sleep tight.

Love ya.

2

LUCAS LUCCHESE

"Congratulations on your promotion, Lucas. I can't think of a better man for the job."

"Thanks, Andreas. Sometimes I wonder if this job is a promotion or a one way ticket to the grave."

"So somber? This isn't like you. What's up?"

"Oh, just thinking out loud," I remark, flipping through the folders on my desk.

"You wanted to see me. How can I help?"

"Yeah. I need background checks on a few people. George was old school—you know, handshakes, trust based on friendships, and the like. I'm more of a wanna-see-you-coming kind of guy."

"I hear ya, Boss. Far too many trigger happy wannabes out there looking to get themselves into trouble. We don't need that kind of heat."

"Agreed. Here," I say, handing my resident snoop the files.

"I'm on it."

LYDIA HALL

"Thank you, Andreas. Oh, and I want info on family members and significant others too."

"Sure thing, Boss."

Taking over after George's passing is something I've coveted for many years. It's almost unheard of for a man of my tender thirty-six years to be promoted to the head of the mob organization. But I can't think of anyone more deserving. Not to toot my own horn, but I've worked my ass off to get to the top, and I intend on staying here.

George had collected good people over the years—loyal people—but I want to make certain that the men I entrust my life and business to are worthy of their position. If there's a snake, I'll sniff it out. So far, I'm happy with the team that is now working directly under me. There are just a few guys I need Andreas to check out.

He is my Consigliere—my most trusted advisor. We've been working together for a long time. We've come through the ranks together, except where I'm less muscle and more management, and Andreas prefers to be behind the scenes as the ace sleuth. I trust him impeccably, plus the man is a savant when it comes to digging up dirt.

One man I am very happy to inherit from Geroge is David Thornton. His excellent reputation precedes him. A whiz with numbers, David has made himself indispensable to our organization, and in the mob world, that's no easy feat.

I check the clock against the wall in my office. It's 4 p.m. David should be here any moment now. I want to have a quick look at the finances, cash flow, investments, and projected income for the next six months.

There's a knock at the door.

"Come in."

"David is here to see you, Mr. Lucchese."

"Thank you, Samantha. Show him in, please."

David is roughly my age, but he has the eyes of a man who has learned a great deal in his life. I read in his file that his parents died when he was in his early twenties and that he brought up his sister on his own after that. I find that commendable. Family is the most important thing, and I admire a man who honors his commitments.

"Hello, David," I say, shaking his hand.

"It's good to see you again, Mr. Lucchese."

"Please call me Lucas. Take a seat."

"Congratulations, Lucas. According to the murmurings, you're the best man for the job."

"So I hear. Thanks. Shall we get down to discussing some figures?"

"Of course."

He and I spend the next hour going through the finances of the LA division. I'm impressed. He seems to have his finger on the pulse.

"It all looks good, David. From now on, you report directly to me, and only to me. I plan on running the show slightly differently than George."

"Of course."

"Okay, great. Thank you. You're doing a good job. Keep it up."

"Thank you."

"Oh, before you go," I say while David is heading for the door.

"Yes?" he says as he turns to face me.

"I'm having a small get together at my place next weekend. It would be good if you would attend. I'd like to introduce you to a few people."

"Thank you, Lucas. I'll be there."

"Needless to say, David, I assume you understand that you will be working exclusively for our organization from now on. Of course, I'll compensate you if there are private clients you have to let go of. We're going places, and I need your undivided attention."

"I understand."

"Good. Samantha will send you an invite for the weekend. Bring someone, if you like."

He nods and leaves the office.

"Sam!" I call through the open door.

"Yes, Mr. Lucchese," she says when she enters the office.

"I need you to take a few notes, please."

"Of course."

"Please contact this catering company," I say, handing her a business card, "and arrange a few menu options for roughly a hundred people for next Saturday. I'll email you the guest list I want you to send invitations to."

"Of course. Do you have a theme in mind?"

"Let's keep it semi-casual."

"Yes, Sir."

"Thanks, Sam."

It will be my first function as the new boss. I prefer to keep things on the down low. In my experience, people feel more comfortable that way and are more likely to let slip what's on their mind. A smart leader keeps his ear to the ground. That's where the watercooler gold's at.

I'll ply my guests with good food and expensive drinks while I sit back and watch. I didn't get here by missing a damn thing. Managing people is what I do best.

* * *

It's been a few days since Andreas and I met in my office, and he's delivered the info he's collected on a few of the people as I had requested.

I shake my head as I page through the files. Let it never be said that mobsters are altar boys. There are a few sketchy customers in this pile, but at least there are no major surprises.

I reach for my coffee, and my shirt's cuff catches on one of the files, which consequently falls to the floor, spilling its contents.

"Damn it."

A face catches my eye when I bent down to retrieve the scattered photos. It's that of a young woman, whom I reckon to be in her early twenties. She's stunning, and I can't help but give the photo a second look.

Who is she? I look at the outside of the file. It's the Thronton folder. This must be his sister. She's exquisite. I collect the photos and place them on my desk so I can look through them at my leisure.

I see the resemblance now. The woman has David's piercing blue eyes and full lips. In one of the photos, she's wearing her hair up in a bun, exposing her sleek, olive skinned, swan-like neck. I can't stop staring at the photo of this rare beauty.

This isn't like me. I'm not the kind of guy who gets obsessed with women, but there's something about this girl that has me spellbound. I look through the notes Andreas provided on the Thornton siblings.

Emily Thornton. Twenty-four years old. Art major.

Impressive. I read on and spot the name of a gallery where she works part-time.

So, what's the plan, Lucas? Are you going to do a drive by perv session? The girl is twelve years your junior. What are you going to do? Pack her lunch for school every morning?

Okay, so she's a little younger than I am. No big deal. According to the info from Andreas, Emily is single, so I'm not threatening to break up a happy home here.

Get over yourself. David Thornton works for you. It behooves the boss of a mob organization to remember not to dip his pen in the company's ink. No matter how irresistible that ink may seem.

"You're right, you annoying, pain in the ass voice of reason," I relent softly, talking to myself like a madman.

No good can come from pursuing Emily. I stare at the photo for a while longer before I place it back in the file and set it aside.

* * *

"Nice shindig you put together, Lucas."

"Who doesn't like a party?"

"The house looks great. The reno must have set you back a bit," Andreas smirks.

"How would it look if the new boss lived in a hovel?" I chuckle.

"Indeed."

"Thanks for the detailed reports, by the way."

"My pleasure. Anyone worrying you?"

"No surprises, thankfully. There was one face that surprised me."

"I bet I can guess which one," he smiles.

"Okay, smartass. Let me have it."

"Emily Thorngton. Am I right?"

"So, it isn't just me?"

"Hell, no. That girl stops traffic wherever she goes. I'd be worried if you hadn't noticed. Hell, even I had a second take."

Andreas' sexual orientation was one most would find surprising. Being gay didn't always gel with the idea of being a tough mobster.

"If anyone could turn me, it would be that stunner," he chuckles.

"Yeah, I'm thinking I'd better stay away from that powder keg."

"I haven't seen Tamara around. Are you two not together anymore?"

"No. Tamara wants a picket fence with all the trimmings, and I'm not there yet."

"Especially not now. You're going to have your hands full for the foreseeable future. Not that I have any doubts; you'll pull it off without a hitch."

"How's Peter?"

"He's well."

"Why didn't you bring him along?"

"You know I prefer to keep my personal life separate from work."

"I respect that. Remember, though, that if anyone gives you shit about your choices, I'll be sure to clean their clocks with pleasure."

"You're a good friend, Lucas."

"Right. Time to mingle."

"Is that code for snooping?"

"Uh-huh."

"Go get 'em, Boss."

I make my way to the bar, where a group of guys are chatting away. One of the benefits of working yourself up through the ranks is that you gain excellent working knowledge of those around you.

I will now keep an eye on the ones I know are prone to fucking up. I haven't made too many changes since taking over from Geroge, but I have no issue with culling if it's necessary.

I spot David, so I make my way over to him. I don't ask him about Emily, even though the image of her beautiful face is burned onto my retinas. I wonder if she's as stunning in the flesh as she is in photos.

Focus, Lucas.

"Hi, David. I'm glad you could make it. Are you alone?"

"Hello. Yes, I'm afraid my date dropped me at the last minute."

"Woman, hey. What can you do?"

"Pretty little puzzles."

Oh, screw it. I have to dip my toe in forbidden waters.

"I understand you have a younger sister. An artist."

"Yeah. Emily."

"I respect the fact that you cared for her after your parents died, David. That says a lot about your character."

I wonder if this conversation is appropriate. Most men who work in my industry prefer to keep their families out of it. I hope David doesn't think I'm meddling. Or worse, I hope he doesn't see through the gossamer veneer and spot a man commenting on matters that don't concern him. Matters like a very hot sister.

"That's kind of you to say, Lucas. It's been a challenging journey, alright."

""Your parents would be proud of your commitment."

I decide to change the subject before I put my foot in it and focus on something less personal and more business-like.

It's after 11 p.m. when the last of the stragglers leave. All in all, it was a successful party with just the right amount of ass kissing on the part of my employees. I don't suffer fools and suck-ups lightly. Say what you mean and do as you say, and you'll go far with me.

It's been a long day and I'm exhausted. If only I could fall asleep. My mind is preoccupied with all sorts of things. Mostly, I'm thinking of my future. George made life very difficult for himself and those around him. He was far too reactive for a Mafia Don. I'm amazed that he lived to his ripe old age. I always thought his odds of dying young and brutally were substantially high. But apparently, he had nine lives.

I close my eyes. It's quiet. I like quiet. LA can be a very busy place, which is why I live out in the mountains. I bought an old place and revamped it. I have everything I need out here. A gym, a squash court, an indoor Olympic size swimming pool, and as many mountain trails as my legs can carry me along.

My thoughts head in an unintended direction. Emily Thornton. There's no point in trying to fight this. I'm intrigued. I haven't felt this way in a long time, so I'm just going to go with it. What's the worst that can happen?

3

EMILY

What is that noise? I'm somewhere between asleep and awake. Is that my phone ringing? I open one eye and look around the darkened room. What's the time? I feel for the phone on the nightstand and look at the time on the face before answering the call. 4 a.m!

What the hell? Who's calling at this hour? I don't recognize the number.

"This better be serious," I answer groggily.

"Is this Emily Thornton?"

"Yeah, this is she. Who is this?"

"I'm sorry to wake you, Miss Thornton. My name is Detective Cox."

Detective! What? I sit bolt upright.

"What's happened?"

"Could you meet me down at the precinct, Miss Thornton?"

"Look, what the hell is going on? Why? Am I in trouble?"

"No, you're not in trouble. I'd prefer to discuss the matter at the precinct, though. I can send an officer to collect you if you like."

"Uhm. No. Thanks. I can drive myself. I'll be there in a bit."

"Ask for me at the front desk."

I end the call and wipe the sleep from my eyes. What the hell is going on? I get dressed at lightning speed after I'm more awake. The last time we got a call in the middle of the night, David and I learned that our parents had been killed in a car wreck. So, naturally, I'm not a fan of late night calls.

"Ems? What are you doing up so early?"

Dannie is standing at the door in her nightgown, her hair all over the place. She always looks like she's just stepped out of a wind tunnel when she wakes up.

"Sorry, Dannie. I didn't mean to wake you."

"That's okay. Is everything okay? Who called?"

"A detective. He wants me to meet him at the precinct."

"A cop? Did he say why?"

"No."

"I'm coming with you," she says, heading for her room. "I'll be ready in four minutes."

Ten minutes later, Dannie and I are on our way to the police station. The streets are quiet. My heart, however, is racing like a greyhound rounding the track.

"I don't like this, Dannie. I have a terrible feeling."

"Whatever it is, we'll deal with it together."

Daniella takes my hand in hers and squeezes it.

The precinct is busy despite the early hour. I guess crime doesn't keep a regular nine to five like the rest of us. I park outside on the curb. Dannie and I exchange glances before we get out of the car and walk into the building.

"Can I help you?" an officer behind the counter asks me.

"Uh, yeah. I'm here to see Detective Cox."

"Is he expecting you?"

No! I make it a habit of driving down to the cop station before dawn!

"Yes. He called me."

"Your name, please?"

"Emily Thornton."

"Please, take a seat. I'll tell him you're here."

I nod and move over to a row of seats against the wall.

"Thanks again for coming with me," I say and squeeze Dannie's hand.

"Hey, if you're about to get busted for anything, I'm here to defend you."

A few minutes later, a tall man with sandy hair and kind eyes walks toward us. He looks more like a surfer than a cop. He must rock undercover work. The cop looks straight at me. I wonder how he knows what I look like.

"Emily?"

"Yes. This is Daniella, my friend."

"Hello. Please come with me."

"What's going on?" Dannie demands. "Is Emily in trouble?"

"I'll explain in a minute."

My stomach is in a knot, and my breathing is shallow at best as Dannie and I follow Detective Cox into the belly of the precinct. He stops outside a small room and gestures for Dannie and me to enter.

He starts talking once we're all seated.

"I'm terribly sorry to tell you this, Emily, but your brother has been killed."

Cox keeps talking, but I can no longer understand a word he's saying. It's white noise. Then, the darkness starts closing in from the corners of my eyes and gradually grows until all I see is a faint light. Then, nothing. Is that my voice? Am I screaming?

"Emily!"

I recognize Dannie's voice. I feel her shaking me, so I open my eyes very slowly.

"What…where am I?"

"We're at the police station, Ems," she says softly.

She's crying. I wonder why. Then it hits me.

"David!" I cry out.

"It's okay, Ems. I'm here," Dannie says, hugging me tightly.

"What happened?" I demand with a shaky voice from the cop.

"David was killed earlier this morning. Murdered. I'm very sorry, Emily," he says.

"Murdered? Are you sure?" Dannie asks.

I'm unable to speak. All I can manage is to stare into space.

Murder! What is he talking about? Who would want to harm my brother?

"We're sure. It was definitely a homicide."

"I don't understand," I whisper. "Where is he? I want to see him."

"Of course. I'll take you to him in a few minutes. But first I need to ask you a few questions. Perhaps you can be of assistance."

"No! I want to see David now!" I yell at him in anger.

"Please, Detective," Dannie says softly to Cox, who relents, nods, and takes us to the morgue.

"I'll leave you alone with him for a few minutes," Cox says and nods at the mortuary attendant before he leaves.

Dannie is pale. I've never seen her like this.

"Are you okay?" I ask.

"Don't worry about me. I'm so sorry, Ems. Go. Be with David."

My brother's body is covered with a sheet. I can see only his head. I'm afraid to pull back the cover for fear of what I might find, but I have to. This is my brother. I must see him. I must know.

I never had the opportunity to touch my parents' bodies after they died. The family and the doctor thought I was too young at the time. I hate the lack of closure I've suffered all these years. I won't make the same mistake with David.

His skin is cold to the touch. No! He can't be dead! It's a mistake. David isn't dead. He's just sleeping.

Dannie is standing behind me, against the wall. She doesn't come any closer, but I can hear her crying softly. I suppose it's her way of giving me some privacy so I can say goodbye.

"Open your eyes, Davy," I whisper.

His cologne wafts into my nostrils as I place my warm cheek against his cold one. What is that smell? Is it blood? I pull the cover down slightly. That's when I see the crimson stain across his chest where the bullets had ripped through his perfect flesh. I take in a deep gasp of air as the shock sets in.

David isn't sleeping. My brother is dead. He's been murdered! I have no idea where to go from here.

"Davy," I whisper. "I'm here, Davy. I'm here."

I take his cold hand in mine. My legs are shaky and I'm trembling all over. He's so cold. Instinctively I wrap the sheet around his body and tuck it in on the sides, like a mother does to her child in the cold of winter.

"Please, you can't leave me alone, David. How can I go on without you?" I whisper again.

Tears are streaming down my cheeks as I drop my head onto his cold, still chest. Dannie comes over and places her hand on my back. She's crying as loudly now as I am and I know her pain is as real as mine.

"I can't do this, Dannie," I turn around and howl into her chest.

"I'm here, Ems. I'm here."

Detective Cox is standing next to us now.

"I'm sorry, Emily, but we have to talk now."

I don't want to leave David's side because I know from experience what it means. He's not coming back. Like my parents, he'll be gone forever. I'll never hold him again or hear his laughter at my stupid jokes. He'll never give me advice again or tell me he loves me.

David is dead, and he's never coming back.

"Emily," Cox says again, gently touching my shoulder.

"Okay," I whisper, knowing that my time with my brother is over.

"Let's have a chat."

I don't know what he expects from me. If it's answers he's looking for, he's barking up the wrong tree. Why David is lying on a slab in the morgue is as much a mystery to me as it is to him.

"Come with me. Can I get you a cup of coffee?" he offers.

Coffee? I need whiskey.

"No. Thank you."

Dannie and I follow Cox to his office. My best friend has her arm around me, no doubt concerned that I'll hit the floor again. The initial shock has passed, leaving behind a numbness that's hard to describe to someone who's never lost a loved one.

Once we're back in his office, Cox closes the door and sits down on the edge of his desk while Dannie and I settle on the couch.

"Where did you find him?" Dannie asks.

"In his car outside his apartment."

"Who called you?" I want to know.

"Someone who lives in his building—a neighbor. She was suspicious when your brother had been seemingly sitting out there in his vehicle for a few hours."

"Was it an attempted mugging or something?" I ask again.

"If it was, the attacker must have been interrupted because all of David's valuables were still on him."

"This is insane," Dannie says incredulously. "David lives in a gated community. It's safe out there. How could this happen?"

I'm trying to keep myself from falling apart, so I don't say too much. The shock of it all is still coursing through my veins.

"Do you know of anyone who would want to harm your brother, Emily?"

"No," I answer simply.

"Please call me if you think of anything that may have bearing on this case."

"I thought you said this was a mugging gone wrong," Dannie interjects.

"That's what it appears to be," he answers. "But we have to consider all possibilities."

"Can we go home now?" I ask, feeling completely deflated.

"Of course. I'll be in touch."

"Come, Ems. Let's go home. I'll drive."

Dannie and I leave the precinct as the sun peeks over the horizon. My first day without David. I don't know how I'm going to do this.

* * *

It's been two days, and I cannot bring myself to get out of bed. Daniella is clearly concerned about me, as she hasn't been to any of her classes and won't leave me alone in the apartment for longer than half an hour or so.

"I'll be fine, Dannie," I say when she checks in on me.

"I'm not leaving you, Ems."

David's death is a terrible shock for both of us. Dannie has been in love with Davy since the moment she first saw him when he picked me up from high school. My best friend is taking his death almost as badly as I am. I'm grateful for her comfort.

"We have to make funeral arrangements, Sweety," she says once she's sitting next to me on the bed.

"I know."

"I'll help you."

I burst into tears at the thought of David's lifeless body buried in the ground. Another Thornton gone forever. I'm all alone now.

"It's going to be okay, Emily. You're going to get through this," she says, rocking me.

"I just don't understand, Dannie. Who the hell would do this? And why? David has never hurt a fly."

"You said he didn't seem himself when you saw him a week ago. Do you think something happened at work? People can be real assholes when it comes to money."

"I don't know. I don't even know who to ask."

"What about Simon? Perhaps he can help."

Simon called this morning. He was away and had only just heard of his best friend's death. I was so upset that it hadn't occurred to me to ask him if he knew of a reason anyone would want to hurt David.

"What if it was a burglary gone wrong?" Dannie asks. "David was a wealthy guy. That's reason enough. Perhaps he fought back and surprised the thief."

"I don't know. The detective has been utterly useless."

"I suppose the cops don't like to jump to conclusions."

"They'd better try a little harder. It's been two days, and still they are clueless!"

"Come on. Let's go to the kitchen. You need to eat something."

"I'm not hungry."

"I don't care. You're going to get up and come to the kitchen."

There was no point in arguing with her. Daniella was right. I have to pull myself together if I'm going to survive this.

"Okay. But, please, no wheatgrass shots."

"Lasagne. I promise."

"I love you, Dannie. Thank you for being here."

"I love you too. We're going to survive this. You're strong. This is what David would want."

After lunch, Dannie and I start on funeral arrangements.

I'm going to find out who did this, Davy. I swear I am. And when I do, the son of a bitch will rue the day he set eyes on you.

4

LUCAS

"What?! David Thornton? When? How?"

"Last night. It looks like it was a hit."

"Damn it! Any idea who's behind this?"

"Not yet, but we have our ears to the ground."

I can't believe this. David is, or rather, was, an integral part of my future plans. That, and he wasn't a dick. It's almost impossible to find someone in my world who doesn't make me want to run in the opposite direction while screaming profanities. And now he's dead. This is a serious setback. I liked David.

"No one sleeps until this man is found. Understand?"

"Understood, Boss."

"F.U.U.U.U.C.K!"

I don't know what has me more enraged. The fact that I just lost a key person in my organization or that some bastard out there thinks he can meddle in my affairs. Either way, I'm ready to rip someone's head off and shove it down the gaping, bloodied hole left behind.

I have to call a meeting. Someone has to know something. I refuse to believe that David's murder was anything but a strategic move. I did just take over as head of the most powerful business in the state. I don't believe in coincidence.

Emily. Her captivating face suddenly flashes in my mind's eye. What must she be going through right now? First, she loses her parents, and now her brother is dead. Why is this bothering me so much?

I did consider David an honorable man—a rarity amongst mobsters—so it isn't too big of a stretch to feel responsible for his beloved sister. I have to check on her. David would have done the same for me, I imagine.

I have to be cautious, though. I don't know how much Emily knows about the work her brother did. He seemed to me to be a private sort. I don't want to sully Emily's opinion of her brother now that he's dead.

* * *

It's the day of the funeral. The church pews are full, so I sit at the back, flanked by my bodyguards. Everyone is on edge at the moment, so my appointed muscle accompanies me wherever I go.

I don't want to be conspicuous today. David's killer may be here, and me making a big scene about losing him may attract unwanted attention.

I look ahead at a figure in the front pew. Emily looks every bit the part of a grieving woman. She's wearing her long, black hair down, so it covers her face when she looks down at the hands. She sits very still. I imagine that her mind is racing. Mine would be too if my brother, and sole protector, was suddenly ripped from my side.

Emily is so beautiful that I find it almost impossible to look away. It's obvious that she's spent a fair amount of time crying. Even so, her beauty is spellbinding. It's time for the eulogy, so she gets up and moves toward the pulpit. A reverant hush falls over the mourners. She takes a few moments to compose herself before she speaks.

"Thank you all for coming today to celebrate David's life," she says in a shaky voice. "I don't really know where to start. My brother was such an amazing presence in the lives of those he cared for that it's almost impossible to express the extent of our loss."

Emily looks up at the ceiling for a few moments, as if she's drawing strength from an invisible source. Her big, blue eyes glisten when she looks out over the mourners. I feel sorry for the beauty. Clearly she's struggling to talk.

"Uhm…David was…he was…"

Oh, for fuck's sake! Why doesn't someone else step up and help this poor wounded soul? I would if I could.

A young woman stands up and starts to move toward Emily, but David's sister isn't ready to give up just yet. Emily smiles and gestures for the other woman to sit down again.

"Sorry," Emily says and smiles. "The past week has been incredibly difficult. This must seem a little out of character for those of you who know me. I am after all the family nutter."

A wave of muted amusement moves through the church.

"Anyway. I could wax lyrical about my big brother, but that will keep us here indefinitely."

Emily talks for the following twenty minutes about the love she and her brother shared and she even throws in a few anecdotal tales from their childhood. I marvel at her inner strength and determination to make this day about David.

After the body is taken to its final resting place, the mourners gather in a hall adjacent to the church where they mill about and share war stories. I want to talk to Emily alone, so I wait for an opportunity. It comes when I see her leave the room and wander into the garden.

Emily is standing under a large Norfolk Island Pine tree. She looks so small and frail suddenly. She jerks when I speak.

"Oh, sorry, I didn't mean to startle you," I apologize.

"Hi, yeah, I didn't see you there," she says.

"I'm Lucas. We haven't met. David and I used to play squash together."

"Hi, Lucas."

"I'm truly sorry for your loss," I offer.

"Thank you, Lucas. And thank you for coming."

"Of course. I was very fond of your brother. I'm so sorry, Emily."

I didn't mean for my words to sound so personal. The last thing I wanted to do here was to interject myself into Emily's life. She doesn't need to know the full extent of my relationship with her dead brother. Worst of all, I'd hate for her to find out that his and my association was possibly the cause of his untimely death.

"What do you do, Lucas?"

"I'm in finance."

Not exactly the whole truth, but it's close enough.

"David was always bragging about his talented baby sister," I say. This too is a lie, but I have a burning desire to please this woman. I'm happy to meet you. I'm just sorry it's under such awful circumstances."

"Thank you," she smiles.

Emily looks me dead in the eyes. Her confidence is attractive. I wonder what it would be like to kiss her. My body tingles at the thought of her touch.

"Emily!"

It's the woman who attempted to come to Emily's rescue during the eulogy.

"Would you excuse me, please Lucas?"

"Of course. My condolences again."

She smiles briefly before she leaves my side. I watch as she and her friend go back into the hall. I have to get to know this beautiful creature better. The least I can do is keep an eye on her. I'm responsible for her mystery.

Uh-huh. How very magnanimous, Lucas. Why don't you just stop lying to yourself and admit it? You want this woman.

* * *

It's been a week since the funeral and all I can think about is Emily. It's ridiculous, I know, but I can't help it. I have to find a way to get to know her, but how?

I know where she works. It wouldn't be hard to take a drive down to the gallery to say hi. I could use the concerned-acquaintance motivation as my justification. Isn't that what a concerned human being would do? Surely, Emily wouldn't see through the facade. It's a chance I have to take or I'll go nuts.

It's around noon when I pull up outside the gallery. After having done my homework, I know what Emily drives. Her car is parked on the curb.

The gallery has large window frontage making it fairly easy to see what's going on inside. I spot the object of my obsession soon enough. She's wearing white cotton pants and a pale blue shirt, perfectly complimenting her olive skin. My chest tightens at the thought of touching that perfect flesh.

What would David think of me? Here I am, lusting after his sister like a crazed stalker. I really need to get a grip.

Either get out of your car and go talk to Emily, or get the hell out of dodge, Lucas. You're acting like a child.

It's too soon. Besides, what will I say to her? Is it a coincidence that I happen to visit the very gallery in which she works? It's a little too obvious—seeing her so soon after meeting her at her dead brother's funeral.

No. I have to stop this madness before she gets hurt. Then again, I don't know who killed David. The same person may be targeting Emily next. Vengeance is big in the mob. I owe it to Emily to keep an eye on her.

I retrieve my phone from my pocket and scroll through my contacts until I find who I'm looking for. I press dial and wait for an answer.

"Lucas? Is everything okay?"

"Hi, Ben. Yes, I'm fine."

"Nasty business, David's murder."

"Yeah. I need you to do something for me, Ben."

"Of course. Anything."

"I want you to keep an eye on Emily Thornton. Whoever killed David may have it in for her too."

"Sure. I'll do that."

"I'll send you a pin location. How soon can you get here?"

"You're there now?"

"Yes. I'll be leaving in a few minutes."

"Okay. Send me the pin, and I'll come right over."

"Thanks, Ben. Appreciate it."

"No problem, Lucas."

I feel better now that I've spoken to Ben. I decide to wait until he gets here before I leave. In the meantime, I watch Emily through the glass. She's talking to a portly woman dressed in Chanel. The two women

LYDIA HALL

are standing in front of a large painting displayed on the wall, and Emily is gesticulating. Her movements are deliberate as she mimics the artist's brush strokes. The portly woman nods and smiles while they chat before moving onto the next piece.

It isn't long before Ben arrives. He parks before he climbs into my car.

"Good to see you, Lucas. Is that our girl?" he asks, nodding his head in Emily's direction.

"That's David's sister, yes."

"Wow. She's gorgeous."

I find Ben's comment irritating. I don't mean to, but I snap at him. Something about keeping this professional and being respectful over the loss of such a valued member of my organization, and so on. Ben stares at me as if I've just accused him of being a traitor or something, but he doesn't retaliate, leaving me feeling like a gigantic dick.

"Keep me informed on her whereabouts," I bark before Ben gets out of the car.

"Of course."

"And, Ben. This girl's been through enough. Don't fuck this up."

I drive away feeling better about keeping Emily safe but uneasy about the effect she seems to have on me.

It's been two weeks, and Ben assures me he hasn't seen any unsavory characters lurking about. It's Friday morning, and I find myself parked outside the gallery once more. This is ridiculous. Perhaps if I go in and say hi, I'll get over myself. It's worth a shot. Trying to put Emily out of my mind has been wholly unsuccessful, so I may as well try a different approach.

She's the only one in the gallery when I enter and look around. Will she recognize me? Our introduction was rather brief. I don't expect her to remember much about me. The poor girl had just lost her brother in a violent manner. I was surprised at how collected Emily was on the day. She's clearly a strong character.

The woman dressed in Chanel points to the painting she and Emily were discussing and nods. Emily smiles brightly at her before the two head toward a desk, where I assume the purchase is ultimately finalized.

I watch as the portly woman waddles off on stilettos that are honestly not a smart choice considering the load bearing issue. She drives off in a luxury SUV. It's now or never.

I can see Ben sitting in his car. I nod surreptitiously at him, and he nods back. Emily is alone in the gallery when I enter. She is breathtakingly beautiful.

Okay, Lucas. Stop stalling. This is it. You're here. Now what?

5

EMILY

It's been two months since I buried my brother, and somehow life carries on. I have good days and bad days, and I'm grateful to everyone around me for bearing me up. My work at the gallery keeps me sane.

I'm not looking forward to graduating. I was so excited about it when David was alive, but now it's just another milestone without him. One of many to come.

It's just after 5 p.m., and I'm about to lock up the gallery. Mrs. Fouché just ordered two paintings, so I'm a happy bunny. I hear footsteps just as I'm about to call it a day. I look up to see who it is.

I know that face. Honestly, who could forget it? Lucas is the perfect specimen of a man. I thought so even when I was in the throes of heartbreak at David's funeral. In fact, I felt almost guilty about the direction my thoughts had taken when he and I stood talking outside under the trees.

I wonder why he's here. Is it a coincidence? Is he here to check up on me?

"Hi, Lucas. So nice to see you again."

"Hi, Emily. I was in the neighborhood."

I'm lost in his green eyes. I can't help but wonder why David never mentioned Lucas. He's not exactly forgettable.

"Are any of these yours?" he asks, looking around.

"As a matter of fact," I say, pointing to a large canvas, "I hung this one just this morning."

Lucas takes his time looking it over before he speaks.

"David was right. You are very talented."

His words excite me. Others' opinions on my work seldom affect me. I'm not sure why Lucas' comment strikes at the core of my being. Is it because he's so ridiculously handsome? I'd have to be blind not to notice.

"Thank you. Do you enjoy art?"

"I do indeed."

"Who's your favorite artist?"

"I know it sounds lame, but I don't have a favorite. I'm a firm believer in allowing my gut to dictate on the day."

"Smart. Art appreciation is definitely connected to one's mood. Some days I paint dark and foreboding pieces. Other days, I'm all butterflies and candyfloss."

"I take it you were in a good mood when you painted this," he smiles as he studies the piece on the wall.

"I was. Who knows what tomorrow will bring?"

Lucas says he's here by happenstance, but my gut tells me he has other intentions.

"I like it. Will you deliver it to my home?"

LYDIA HALL

"You want to buy my painting?"

I wasn't expecting this.

"Of course. It's an excellent investment, I'm sure. One day, when you're a famous artist, I'll be able to boast that I knew you way back when," he smiles. "What else are you working on?"

"You're not pushing for a discount if you buy more than one piece, are you?" I tease.

"Damn straight," he grins.

"Come on. I'll show you."

Lucas follows me to the back of the gallery. I'm acutely aware of his presence so close behind me. It's intoxicating.

"This is my newest creation. It's a little darker than the other one."

"Brooding. I like it. An interesting face in the background."

"I'm surprised you noticed. Most people miss it."

"I don't miss much," he says, his green pools resting on me.

There's something about this man that has me all thumbs. Perhaps it's his intense stare. It could be the way he looks into my soul. Whatever the reason, Lucas has me intrigued.

"I'd love to see it when it's completed," he says.

"I'll let you know when it's done."

Lucas stares at me for a long while, making my knees a little weak in anticipation of what he's about to say next.

"Would you like to have dinner with me?"

"I'd like that."

"Good. Are you free tomorrow evening? Let's say around 7 p.m."

"Sure. Where?"

"Do you have a preference when it comes to food?"

"I'm not fussy. I'll eat it if it's tasty. I must warn you, though. I'm not the kind of girl who pushes salad around her plate. I have a healthy appetite."

"Good. I like a woman who enjoys having a mouthful."

Lucas is definitely flirting with me. It's working too. I'm suddenly very turned on.

"Hello, is anyone here?" a voice from the front of the shop interrupts us.

"Saved by the bell," Lucas grins. "See you tomorrow evening. Would you like me to pick you up?"

"No. That's alright. I'll meet you at the restaurant."

"I'll forward you the address."

* * *

"Wow! You look stunning, Ems."

"Thanks, Dannie. I don't know why, but I'm nervous."

"Really?"

"Yup."

"Well, I suppose it is a little intimidating going out with someone as drop dead gorgeous as Lucas."

"He's sexy AF, alright. But that's not it. There's something about him. I don't know what it is, but he makes me all giddy and nervous. I feel like a schoolgirl with a crush on a sexy teacher."

Dannie laughs.

"Oh, yes, please. I got a really wicked mental picture just now."

"Behave yourself, Daniella. I saw him first."

"Fine," she laughs. "It's good to see you smiling again, babes."

"I almost feel guilty for living my life while David is dead."

"Don't you dare, Ems," she says softly, pulling me into a hug. "David loved you more than anything in the world. He'd want you to be as happy as you can be. You have nothing to feel guilty about."

"How are you doing, Dannie? I know you were in love with David. You and I have lost someone so dear to us."

Dannie's eyes tear up.

"I still can't believe he's gone," she says, wiping at a tear as it rolls down her cheek.

"We're going to be alright, Dannie."

"I know, but, fuck it, it hurts!"

"Go have some fun, Ems."

I've cried so much that I cannot imagine that there are any tears left inside of me. Besides, I don't want to look like a train wreck tonight.

Lucas is meeting me at the new Italian Trattoria in town. I'm looking forward to tonight. I haven't been on a date in ages, and as a student, I always look forward to getting a good meal where I can.

David refused to let me starve. He used to give me an allowance every month so that I could focus more on studying and less on trying to keep the wolves from the door. My loving brother left me a substantial amount of money when he passed, so I doubt whether I'll have to worry about money ever again. Even so, some habits are hard to break, and I feel that frugality is now entrenched in my being.

"I'll see you later, Dannie."

"Don't do anything I wouldn't do," she yells as I leave the apartment.

"I wouldn't dream of it," I yell back.

* * *

Lucas is at a table in the back of the restaurant. He stands up when he sees me following behind the waiter.

Holy…he's gorgeous! My date is wearing a black shirt and dark jeans. His dark hair is slicked back, which makes his green eyes seem even greener. Lucas' cologne lingers in my nostrils as he kisses me on the cheek.

"Hi," he says, smiling. "You look beautiful."

"Thank you. You clean up nice, too."

"Can I interest you in a glass of Champagne?"

"Ah, my Achilles heel. I'd love one, thanks."

Lucas nods at the waiter, who leaves the table immediately and returns a few minutes later with a bottle of champagne and two flutes.

"Dom. Very nice," I comment.

"If you're going to do something, you may as well do it right."

"I agree. What a lovely vibe," I say, looking around the restaurant.

"It is, isn't it?"

"Any recommendations?"

"I haven't had a bad meal here yet. What are you in the mood for?"

"You can catch me in a trap with pasta. Tomato base with lots of chili and capers."

"Sounds good."

Lucas orders a pizza bread starter, and we chat while we pick at it. By the time the main is served, it seems as if we've known each other for years.

"You're easy to talk to, Emily," he says in between bites of perfectly cooked pasta.

"So are you. I was nervous about tonight," I relent.

"Why?"

"I'm not sure."

"And now?"

"Now I feel like I can tell you anything."

"That's good news," he grins.

"How long did you and David know each other?"

Something in Lucas' eyes shifts as a result of my question. I find it a little harder to read him now. Is he sad?

"David and I met about four years ago. He was a great guy. I'm sorry he's gone. I miss him."

Lucas' heartfelt sentiment seems genuine. It makes me feel closer to him. I suppose the fact that he knew and loved David is comforting to me.

"Yeah. It's been difficult. My brother's death has left a gaping hole in my life."

"Do the police have any suspects yet?"

"No. Not a clue. It's so infuriating. I feel so helpless. At least I could get answers if I knew where to look. But I have no idea who killed David or why. I don't know if we'll ever know."

Lucas reaches across the table and places his hand over mine. His skin is warm, and the simple kindness sparks inside me an intense desire for him. The chemistry between us is electric. Corny, but unmistakably genuine.

"I'm here for you, Emily. I know I can never replace your brother, but please know that I will do anything to protect you," he says while looking deeply into my eyes.

"Thank you, Lucas."

"Could I interest you in dessert?" the waiter suddenly asks, shattering the intense moment Lucas and I are caught in.

Damn it!

"Gelato?" Lucas smiles.

"Yum," I grin.

"Chocolate?" suggests the waiter.

"Is there any other kind?" I chuckle.

"Two, please!" Lucas laughs.

* * *

It takes all manner of self restraint not to wrap myself around Lucas' beautiful body like a pretzel at the end of the evening. We say our goodbyes, and soon I'm on my way back home, fantasizing about having crazy sex with him.

Dannie is still out with friends when I get home. I notice something on the floor once I unlock the front door. It's a business card. I read it once I've switched on the light.

It's Detective Cox's card. He wrote on the back.

Hi, Emily.

Please call me when you get this. Thanks.

LYDIA HALL

. . .

I check my watch. It's just after 11 p.m. I wonder if he's still up. I'm wide awake. Even more so now, so I dial his number and wait while the phone rings.

"Detective Cox."

"Hi, Detective. It's Emily Thornton."

"Hello, Emily. Thank you for calling me."

"Do you have news about David? Have you arrested a suspect?"

"No, not yet, I'm afraid."

"I see," I say, my words dripping with disappointment and irritation.

"I do have a theory I'd like to discuss with you when you have a moment," he says.

"What is it?"

"Could we have coffee tomorrow? I'd like to talk to you face to face."

I'm growing weary of the cops and their theories. Why don't they just get it over already and catch the bloody killer?

"Uh, okay. Tomorrow at noon at the coffee shop near the precinct?"

"Okay."

My good mood is shot to hell. What a crappy ending to a spectacular evening. I get into bed, but who knows if I'll sleep now?

* * *

"Thank you for coming, Emily," Cox smiles.

"Hi. Sure. What did you want to talk to me about?"

"How familiar were you with David's work?"

"What do you mean?"

"Do you know if he worked for any unsavory clients?"

"Unsavory? I'm sorry, but you're going to have to be more specific."

"Well, we know David was a skilled accountant…"

"Chartered accountant, actually," I blurt out, interrupting the detective. David wasn't just any accountant. He was brilliant.

"Sorry, yes, chartered accountant. My question is this. Do you know if he had any interactions with organized crime syndicates?"

What? How insulting. What is this cop trying to say?

"David would never get involved with such people. Why would you even ask me something like that?"

"I'm sorry, Emily. I'm not trying to offend you or sully the memory of your brother. But it does look to me like David's death may have been a hit. At this stage, I'm investigating all the angles."

"The mob," I say softly. "David was always very private about who he worked for. I took that as a sign of his loyalty and discretion. An admirable quality when you're dealing with such a sensitive subject as someone's wealth."

"I agree. No one wants an accountant with a loose tongue, I suppose," Cox says, slurping his coffee. "So, he never discussed his client list with you?"

"No. And I didn't ask."

"Do you know if he talked about his work with anyone?"

"I'm sorry, Detective. I can't help you."

What the hell is this cop trying to tell me? Was David involved with the mob? Surely not. Not the man I knew and loved. It's impossible!

"What makes you think it was a hit, Detective?"

LYDIA HALL

"When you've been a detective for as long as I have, you get a feel for this sort of thing."

A feeling? This guy is telling me he thinks David was involved with the mob because he has a feeling! What? Does he get a sore knee before it rains, too? Is he joking?

"I know what you're thinking, Miss Thornton. This cop is full of it. Right? And I don't blame you. But believe me when I tell you that this was more than likely a professional killing."

I don't know what to say after a bombshell like this.

"Okay. I'll call you if there are any developments in the case. Until then, please feel free to call me if you have any questions or if you remember anything that might be relevant. Even if it's a small thing."

"Okay. Thanks."

6

EMILY

"Sooo, how was last night?" Dannie asks, grinning from ear to ear.

"Amazing," I gush.

"Did you ravage his sexy bod?"

"Honestly! What kind of girl do you take me for?"

"Oh, come now. Lucas is absolutely worth the off chance of coming across, let's call it, available. I'd be all over him like white on rice if I were you. The man is beautiful."

"I hear ya! I did have to focus really hard on not ripping off his shirt so I could check out whatever he's hiding under there," I chuckle.

"Shirt! I'd be keen to see what sort of weaponry he's hiding in his chinos. I have a feeling it will be well worth the effort."

"You're incorrigible!"

"Uh-huh. Are you seeing him again?"

"I don't know. We'll see."

"What is it? Is something wrong? You're not acting like a woman who's just been out with a Greek god."

"I had coffee with Detective Cox this morning."

And just like that, the mood turns somber.

"I see. Okay. And? Any news?"

"Yes, actually. The great detective has a theory."

"A theory? Surely cops deal with facts and evidence rather than theory? Or did I miss something?"

"Cox seems to think that David's murder was mob related."

Dannie stares at me with a look of utter surprise that soon morphs into confusion.

"What? Mob? Are you serious?"

"He seems to think so."

"But that doesn't make any sense. Why would David be involved with criminals? No. I don't believe it. Cox is full of crap. If you ask me, *Columbo* has seen one too many detective movies."

"That's what I told him. Not the bit about him being full of it, but certainly the part where David would never get mixed up in anything to do with the mob."

"Do you want to know what I think?"

"Always."

"I think you should talk to Simon. If anyone knows what David was or wasn't into, it's his best friend."

"I don't get it, Dannie. Why wouldn't David tell me himself?"

"Are you serious? You're his baby sister, Ems. There are some things family members don't like to share with each other. Simon is, sorry, was David's closest friend. He knew your brother best. If David was involved in anything like that, he would have discussed it with a bud."

"I guess it's worth a shot."

Dannie has a point. If anyone knows anything it would be Simon. He and David have been friends since kindergarten. I sit down on the couch in the living room and scroll through my contacts until I find his name.

"Hey, Ems. Is everything okay?" he says when he answers the call.

"Hi, Si. I'm okay, thanks. Can we meet for a drink? I wanted to talk to you about something."

"Uh, sure. When?"

"How about tonight?"

"Of course. I'll meet you at the club. Sevenish, okay?"

"Sure."

My mind is a maelstrom of questions. Does Simon know anything about David that I don't? And if he does, will he tell me?

"What did he say?" Dannie asks.

"I'm meeting him tonight at the club."

"Good. Do you want me to come with you, Ems?"

"No, it's alright, Dannie. I'll be fine. Besides, don't you have a hot date tonight?"

"I sure do. He's no Lucas, but he certainly gets my motor racing," she grins.

"Did you say he's a professor?"

"Yup. A stand-in for Clark, who's getting married, so they got this cutie pie in to sub for him."

"Isn't that frowned upon? A professor dating a student?"

"Nah. I'll be done with my masters by next month. It's not as if he's seducing a newbie."

"Well, I expect a full report when I get home."

"You got it," she smirks.

I'm happy that Dannie is seeing someone. David's death was a terrible shock, and she took it pretty hard. I know my best friend secretly pinned her hopes on dating my brother some day. I, too, thought it would eventually happen. There was an unmistaken chemistry between them, but I suspect David held back for fear of upsetting my friendship with Dannie. Not that it matters anymore.

"I need some shuteye before tonight. I think I'll take a quick nap."

"Sure, Ems."

I've been a bit tired and rundown. I remember taking frequent afternoon naps after my parents died. I guess it's just my body's way of coping. I don't cry anymore the moment my head hits the pillow. Progress, I suppose. Today, I fall asleep quickly. Thank God.

It's 7 p.m. on the dot and I can see Simon waiting for me at his and David's regular table at the country club as soon as I walk in. He stands up in anticipation as he sees me approaching.

I've always liked Simon. He's one of the good ones.

"Hi, Emily," he says, kissing me on the cheek. "It's so nice to see you."

He and I haven't spoken much since the funeral. I suspect the pain we're trying to deal with makes it hard to see each other. He does call once a week to check on me, though.

"Hey, Si. It's good to see you too."

"Please, sit. Can I get you a drink?"

"Yes, thanks. A vodka cranberry will hit the spot."

Simon gestures to the waiter, who comes over and takes the drinks order.

"How have you been, Emily? Is everything okay?"

"Yeah. I'm okay. I'm still in shock, but I'm sleeping better. How about you?"

""I've been better."

Poor Simon looks so dejected. I feel for him. He and David were practically inseparable. This must be as hard for him as it is for me.

"So, what did you want to talk to me about, Emily?"

"I spoke to the detective on David's case this morning."

"Oh? Any news?"

"No, not exactly. He did tell me something alarming, though."

"What is it?"

"Cox has a theory. The cop seems to think that David's murder was an execution rather than a mugging gone awry."

Simon's face grows pale.

"What? What do you mean by execution?"

"He asked me if David had any ties to the mob."

Simon just about chokes on his drink.

"What? What did you say?"

"I told him David would never be that stupid. But, then I started thinking about it. David was very secretive about who he worked for and he did lead a lifestyle that most guys his age would envy. Did I miss something, Simon?"

The look on his face alludes to the fact that my brother's best friend knows something he's not telling me.

"Please, Simon. David is dead. I need to know why. If you know anything, anything at all, I beg you to share it with me."

Simon stares past me into the distance. He definitely knows something. I give him time to formulate his explanation. I reckon whatever he has to tell me won't be easy to relay.

"David didn't want you to know."

His words send a chill down my spine.

"Didn't want me to know what?"

"At first, after your parents died, David had to do what he did to ensure that you have a future. Money was tight before the estate was eventually settled. Then, I guess the money was so good that it made no sense to stop."

"I don't understand, Simon. What are you saying?"

"It's true. David did work for the mob. But he was strictly an accountant. He never got involved in anything shady. The books he took care of were legitimate businesses. Your brother was a good man."

My legs are lame again. Too many shocks in one lifetime will do that.

"Why didn't he tell me?"

"Two reasons, I'm guessing. One, he was ashamed, and two, he wanted to keep that world as far away from you as possible. You know your brother would have done anything for you, Emily. Above all, David wanted to keep you safe."

"He told you, didn't he?"

"Yes, he did. He needed someone to talk to. I was the least likely to be affected by it. Davy wanted to tell you, Emily. He and I had dinner together two nights before he died. We talked about it, and I told him he should tell you everything. I know you're strong enough to handle it. He promised me he'd think about it."

"I don't know what to say. Is that why he's dead?"

"I don't know. He spoke about working exclusively for one of his clients, but he never said who."

"Is there any way of finding out who this client is?"

The realization of what Simon just shared with me suddenly hits me like a shovel. If David was working for the mob and he's dead, how long will it be before someone kills me too? That's how it works in the mob, isn't it? That is, if Hollywood movies are to be believed. Am I about to come to a tragic end too?

"Are you alright, Ems? You're very pale."

"It just occurred to me that I may be next, Simon. Or you. Who knows what will happen next?"

"Why would they hurt you?"

"Who the hell knows? They may think I know something. It's the mob, Simon! They don't need an excuse to kill."

I down my drink without pausing.

"I'm going to need something with a bit more firepower," I say, waving the waiter over. "Whiskey, please. Neat," I order when he comes over.

He smiles, nods, and then walks in the direction of the bar.

"Why don't you go away for a while?" Simon suggests.

"How can I? I have commitments. I can't just quit my job at the gallery. And how can I leave poor Daniella high and dry with the rent?"

"None of this is more important than staying alive, Emily. If this was indeed a mob hit, then who knows? You may very well be next. I think you should consider carefully before dismissing the idea so quickly."

I empty the whiskey tumbler as soon as the waiter hands it over.

"More," I breathe.

I don't care if I get drunk off my ass. My life as I know it has just changed, and something tells me it will never be the same again.

"Where will I go?" I say after a long, awkward silence.

"You can go to my house in Spain if you like. No one will look for you there. You can stay as long as you like, Emily."

"Spain! Are you nuts? I don't speak Spanish. Where will I work? I don't know anyone there. I'll be all alone. No. I can't, Si. I just can't."

Simon places his hand over mine.

"It's going to be okay. I'm here. We'll think of something. I know this is scary, but you have to think about going somewhere safe. Even if it's just for a short while. Until this all blows over."

"I can't believe this is happening."

I'm crying softly now. Not because I'm afraid of the future, but because I just imagined how afraid my brother must have been when he realized what was happening to him during the last moments of his life. The fear must have been crippling.

"We have to find the man who did this, Simon. I want him dead."

"I agree. But we have to let the cops do their work."

"Oh, please. The cops couldn't find their asses with a mirror. You know how seldom they find hitmen. David's murder will be another one in a long line of cold cases by the end of the year. We'll be lucky if they learn anything."

"You can't think like that."

"I have to go," I say, getting up.

"Can I drive you home?"

"No. Thanks, Simon. I'm fine. I want to be alone."

"Are you sure?"

"Yes."

"I'm going to follow you home anyway. Just to be safe."

"Thank you for telling me. I know it must have been hard for you."

"I'm sorry I didn't tell you earlier, Ems. I know that David would have told you himself had he been given the chance."

"Yeah."

Simon settles the bill before we leave. I have a lot to think about, and I have a feeling I won't be sleeping much tonight.

Dannie is still out when I get home. I'm glad. I need a bit of time to myself before I talk to her. My best friend will no doubt want to comfort me and reinforce the fact that David was a good person.

I know all of that, but I'm mad. I'm mad at my brother for keeping this from me. I'm mad that he felt that I wasn't strong enough to hear it. But, most of all, I'm guilty because I'm angry with a dead man. How will I process this anger?

It's hard when you're mad with the dead. They can't explain themselves. After anger comes guilt. Guilt because he's dead and I'm alive.

Damn it! I need whiskey.

I'm out cold by the time Dannie comes home. I know this because when I open my eyes again, the morning sun is radiating through the slit in the drawn curtains and my head feels like it's about to implode.

7

LUCAS

"Hi, Emily. This is a nice surprise. How are you?"

"Hello, Lucas."

"What's wrong?"

"Can we talk?"

"Of course. I'm listening."

"No. I mean in person."

"Sure. When?"

"Could you meet me at the gallery after six tonight?"

"Okay. I'll see you later."

"Thanks, Lucas."

I can tell by Emily's tone that something is wrong. I check my watch. Another four hours to go before I find out what's bothering her. I have an awful feeling in my gut that it has something to do with David's death. I hope she hasn't learned the truth about me because I don't know how to explain that to her.

I still have no idea who killed David, and it's frustrating the hell out of me. I have shaken all the branches in every tree I can think of, and still no one has any ideas. No intel on the streets. It's almost unheard of. Maybe it wasn't a mob hit. No one knows what goes on behind closed doors in anyone's life. Perhaps David was into something that caught up with him. It's not impossible, although highly improbable in my estimation of the man.

For the first time in my life, I'm stumped, and I don't care for it. What kind of mafia boss doesn't know what's going on on the streets? I have to do something about this before my men lose faith in me. That's as good as a death sentence.

It's 6 p.m. when I knock on the locked gallery door. I can see Emily through the glass. She looks nervous. Not a good sign.

"Hi," she smiles when she opens the door for me.

"Hey."

She locks the door behind me as soon as I'm inside.

"How are you, Emily?"

"Not so good."

"What's wrong?"

"Come sit. I need to talk to you about something."

I follow her into the belly of the gallery, where there are no windows. Yeah, something is very wrong.

"Okay," she says when we're both seated.

"What's going on, Emily? Is this about David?"

"Yes."

"Did they find the person who killed him?"

"No."

"It's okay. You can talk to me. What is it?"

"The police think that David was killed by a ..."

"A what?"

"They think it was a mob hit."

SHIT!

My mind is racing, but I manage to keep a straight face.

"The mob? Are you sure? That's ridiculous. Why would they think that?"

"Apparently David did some work for them."

"How do you know that?"

"A friend confirmed it to me."

"I see. So, you didn't know who he worked for?"

"No. David never discussed his clients with me. I had no idea."

"This must be very shocking for you, Emily."

"I'm floored. I can't believe my brother would get involved with criminals."

"David was a good man, Emily. I imagine he did what he had to do."

Emily pulls up her knees and hugs them tightly as she stares into space.

"Are you okay?" I ask.

"No. I'm scared, Lucas. What if they come after me?"

"Why would they? You don't know anything."

"I know that, but they don't."

She's quiet for a while, then she sighs.

"I have to leave. I've got to get away from this place. It probably isn't safe."

"But where would you go?"

"I don't know yet. All I know is that I have to get the hell out of here."

"I can help you."

"How?"

"You can stay with me."

"No, Lucas. David is dead. I can't put your life in danger too. I'm a target, and I refuse to drag you into this."

"But.."

"No, Lucas! My mind is made up. I'm leaving."

This is a disaster. Emily has no idea how far the mob's reach is. If she is a target, she has no chance of getting away unless someone who knows what they're doing helps her. Someone like me.

"Please, Emily. Let me help you."

"No, Lucas. I just wanted to tell you that I'm leaving. I don't want you to worry. Okay? I'll be fine."

I can see that this discussion is getting me nowhere. Emily is stubborn. I don't see how I have any other choice but to take matters into my own hands.

* * *

"Are you sure you want to do this? If the girl is a target, then you could become one too. We don't know for sure why David was murdered."

"Don't question me, Andreas. Just get it done. Okay?"

"You're the boss."

"Yes, I am. Be careful who you use for this. I don't want this girl in any danger. She's already lost her entire family. She's fragile."

I know what Andreas is thinking, but he has the good sense to keep it to himself. He knows it's pointless to argue once I've made up my mind.

"I take it she isn't onboard with the idea of staying with you until this blows over."

"Emily doesn't know who I am or that David worked for us. I'd like to keep it that way for now. I do know that if she tries to run away, she's going to get herself killed."

"Do you want me to keep her at the safehouse?"

"I think it's best if she stays as close to me as possible."

"The main house?"

"Yeah. I'm not ready to explain myself to her, though. So I need you to pick her up for me."

"Is that a euphemism for knocking her out and bundling her into the trunk of my car," Andreas smirks.

"Yup. Just make sure you don't hurt her."

"I wouldn't dream of it."

"Thanks. I owe you one."

"No sweat. I'll let you know when it's done."

* * *

Emily

I have to talk to Dannie about leaving. I've been putting it off for days now. She's not going to be happy. I'm not exactly bubbling over with excitement either, but what can I do?

I'm at our favorite pizza joint, waiting for a takeaway. The best I can hope for is that a slice of Dannie's favorite cheesy snack will placate her while her best friend drops the bombshell that she's running away.

"Honey, I'm home," I call out once I've unlocked the front door to our apartment.

"In the bedroom!"

"Hey," I say from the open doorway of Dannie's room.

"Is that pizza?"

"Yup. Your favorite. Pepperoni with extra cheese."

"Okay, what have you done?"

"It's what I'm about to do."

"Uh-oh. Come on. I'll get the wine," she sighs and leaves the room.

I join her in the living room, where I flop myself down on the sofa. Dannie places an unopened bottle of red wine and two glasses on the table next to the pizza.

"Right. The doc is in. What's ailing you, princess?" she says, pouring the wine.

"I'm scared, Dannie."

"Why, Ems?"

"If David's death was a mob hit, then I may be next."

"We've talked about this, my friend. It's been months. Don't you think that if you were next, they would have done something by now?"

"I can't take that chance."

"What do you want to do?"

"I have to leave LA."

"And go where?"

"I could go stay with my cousin in Texas for a while. Just until I'm on my feet. I can get a job there and a place of my own."

Dannie is upset. I can see it in her face.

"I'm sorry, Dannie. I really am."

"I don't want to lose you, too."

"That's why I have to do this."

"Please don't go," she pleads softly.

"Don't cry, Dannie. Please. You're breaking my heart."

"I'm coming with you," she says suddenly, wiping away the lone tear that escaped her eye.

"That's crazy. You can't give up your life for me. I won't let you."

"I'm not giving up anything. We can start over somewhere else. Together. Come on, Emily. Two are better than one."

"Where would we go?"

"I have family in Minnesota. My aunt lives on a stunning lake. No one will look for you there."

"I don't know, Dannie."

"Come on. I'll call her. She adores me. I'm sure she'd love to have us for a while. Please. Just until the cops catch the guy."

I would prefer going with Dannie. Heading out into the unknown all on my own is a bit daunting. This could work.

"Are you sure?"

"Of course, I'm sure. I'll call her."

"Now?"

"Yes, now."

Dannie leaps off the couch and fetches her phone from her bedroom. She scrolls through her contacts, then calls her aunt.

I listen to the conversation as Dannie skates around the real reason for her sudden hankering to move in with her aunt. I must admit, I'm feeling more optimistic about all this. This is going to be good for me—getting away from everything that reminds me of David.

"All set," she announces with a grin once she ends the call. "Aunt Ruth is happy to have us."

"Wow. I don't know what to say except thank you, Dannie."

"As if I'd leave my best friend high and dry, of course."

"How soon can we leave?"

"How soon can you pack?"

"Don't you have things to finalize at the university first?"

"Nope. All done and dusted."

"What about the cute stand-in professor?"

"He's a dildo. I don't see a future there. Besides, he can't kiss for shit."

"That's too bad."

* * *

Saying goodbye to the gallery is harder than I thought it would be. I arranged to take leave—I don't tell them I'm not coming back, of course. It's better no one knows about my sudden change of address.

It's my last shift. Dannie and I are packed and ready to hit the road in the morning. My last night in LA. It feels odd. It's been my home for so many years now. There's so much history here.

I grew up here. This is where I graduated from high school and university. My parents and David are buried here. But I have no choice. I have to leave it all behind and start fresh.

I'm not angry at David anymore. He did what he thought was best for us. How can I hold that against him? He had no way of knowing what would happen. All I have for him now is gratitude and deep love.

"I guess this is goodbye for now," Sandra, one of my colleagues, says, coming over to me to hug me. "We're going to miss your beautiful art around here."

"Thanks, Sands. I'll be back."

"I hope so."

I look around one more time at the walls that hold the art I've grown to love.

This is it, Emily. It's time to say goodbye and leave the past behind.

I hear the sound of the gallery doors opening.

"Did you forget something, Sands?" I call out into the darkened gallery.

She doesn't answer.

"Sandy. Is that you?" I call out again.

Silence.

"Who's there? Hello?"

I don't see anyone. Perhaps the wind blew the door open. It happens sometimes. I've been telling them for months now to replace that flimsy lock. It will be a disaster if the paintings get damaged by a gust of wind.

I make my way toward the front. The door is open, just as I suspected. It's pretty windy outside. My cell phone beeps. It's a message from Dannie. She wants to know if I'd be okay with Chinese takeout for dinner. As if she even has to ask. I'm a sucker for a good dumpling. I type my response and then head for my desk to fetch my purse and keys.

My heart stops when, out of the corner of my eye, I see a shadow moving near the front desk.

"Who is that? I have a weapon," I lie.

Am I seeing things? I have been on edge lately. It's entirely possible that my mind is playing tricks on me.

I don't hear anything except for the wind howling outside. I hate that sound. It's creepy.

"Come on, Emily. Stop being a drama queen and lock up," I say out loud to myself, the way I usually do when I'm being silly.

I get as far as the front desk when I see the figure of a man standing in the shadows. I can't see his face, but he's tall and muscular. An electric shock shoots through my hands and feet at the sight of him. I know I have to run, but my legs won't move for a few seconds.

By the time my body recovers from the initial shock, it's too late to run. He's right behind me. I scream, but it's no use. Before I can react, the man grabs me, and I feel a sharp pain in my upper arm.

I flail about for a few seconds, my arms and legs doing their best to free me from his iron grip. It's no use. I do manage to get a few swipes in with my nails, and I hear my attacker yelp when I dig out some of his flesh with my nails. Yeah, take that, you bastard! I hope that hurts.

So, this is how it ends. I was so close to getting away. One more night, and I would have been in Minnesota, skiing on a lake, soaking up the mountain air. Instead, I'm the prey, and the hunter has just snared me in his trap.

The night becomes darker than it should be. Before long I'm floating in a sea of nothingness. This can't be the end. Can it?

8

EMILY

Ugh…ouch…my head…

What the hell happened? Where am I?

I open my eyes very slowly. The last thing I remember is rushing for the front door of the gallery. Then…

I sit bolt upright. I remember now. The tall man rushed me, and then my world went dark. My arm hurts, so I run my fingers over it. Is that a needle mark? What the hell!

My heart is racing out of my chest. Is this the same man who murdered David? Why did he kidnap me? Why not simply shoot me like he did to my brother? I don't understand what he wants from me. This isn't good. Oh, Lord. Help me!

I look around the room. It's rather plush. Not the type of accommodations you would drag someone to if your intentions were to kill them anyway. What the hell is going on? Where am I?

I try to stand, but I feel a bit squirrelly, so I stay seated for a while longer until the dizziness passes. That's better. I get up so I can assess my dilemma better. The room has no windows, just a door. Not a good sign. I walk over to the door and bang on it a few times. No response. I hammer it harder.

"Hello! Is anybody there? Hello!"

Damn it! Now I'm pissed. How dare he, whoever he is, do this to me? Isn't it bad enough that he ripped David from my world? Now he has to torture me. What the hell did David get himself mixed up in?

Dannie. Oh, no! Poor Dannie is waiting for me. She's going to be gutted if anything were to happen to me too. No. This is bull! I'm going to get out of this alive if it's the last thing I ever do. This son of a bitch isn't going to get away with this. I'll scratch his eyes out. He got the jump on me the first time, but he won't catch me like that again. This time, I'm ready for him.

I'm not feeling great, so I walk back to the bed and sit down. The cocktail of whatever my attacker jabbed into me has me all loopy and nauseated. I hope it passes soon, or I'll be incapable of fighting back when the bastard comes for me.

I don't understand this. Why not kill me at the gallery? Why would he drag me here? Is it information he wants? Does my kidnapper think that I hold secrets that David wouldn't reveal? Will he kill me when he finds out that I know less than nothing about whatever David was into?

I check my watch. It's 11 p.m. Poor Dannie must be frantic by now. I hope she's called the cops. Someone must be looking for me. Please let someone be out there looking for me.

I'm suddenly very drained, so I lay my head on the pillow for a few seconds. I'll close my eyes for a moment. I'm listening intently for any noise, but it's dead quiet.

It's okay, Ems. You're going to be fine. You've got this.

* * *

It's 7 a.m., and I'm still here. I must have fallen asleep again. Am I going nuts, or can I smell Lucas' cologne? That's it. I've finally gone stir crazy. It must be the drugs. Talk about the power of positive thinking.

I wonder if Dannie called him. I wish now that I'd taken him up on his offer to help me. If I hadn't been so stubborn in my determination to go it alone, I would have been tucked away safely now. Instead, I'm in a stranger's bunker with no clue as to whether I'm going to live or die.

Oh, my word. I'm so hungry! All I can think of is the Chinese food that Dannie bought for us last night. I can't believe I didn't get to enjoy it. I would kill for a dumpling right about now. Is my kidnapper planning on starving me to death? Does he know that I'm one of those people who becomes hangry when I haven't eaten? Good luck to him if he doesn't feed me soon.

Is that a key I hear rattling in the lock? My heart leaps into my throat, and I'm instantly high on adrenaline. Fight or flight? It would seem like after yesterday's flight, my body has chosen fight mode this time around. Come on, you bastard. This time, I'm ready for you!

I jump off the bed and take on a defensive stance. The door opens slowly, and in steps a man I haven't seen before. He's not the same one who ambushed me last night. This man is stocky and bald. He's carrying a plate with a sandwich on it in one hand and a set of clothes in the other.

Perhaps I can get past him. But where would I go? I don't know what's on the other side of that door. I could be in the middle of nowhere, for all I know. No. I have to employ a different tactic here.

"Who are you? Where am I? What do you want from me?"

I'm trying to stay as calm as possible, but my voice is a little shakier than I'd like. Even so, I push out my chest and act with as much gusto as I can. The image of a feral cat challenging an elephant springs to mind. I'll be lucky if he doesn't bust a gut laughing at all five feet, two inches of me and my bravado.

"Here's something to eat. I'm sure you must be hungry," he says in a voice that is far too soft and refined for a man of his physical stature.

"Where am I?"

"You're safe."

"Safe? From what?"

The man ignores my question and places the food on a table in the corner of the room. There's no point in attacking him because he'll probably swat me off like a fly. I glare at him when he turns around, but he ignores me and heads for the door.

I grab a glass from the nightstand and throw it at him out of pure frustration. The glass misses his head and shatters against the wall.

"Calm down," he growls at me before he closes the door and locks it.

"Argh!" I scream out loud before I sink back onto the bed, defeated.

Food! I have to eat as I'm growing faint, so I head for the table to inspect the sandwich. Steak! Oh, thank God! I don't care if the meat is laced with poison or barbiturates at this point. I'm sure the muscle bound man would have hurt me already if he wanted to, and I'm bloody starving, so I take a big bite. It's delicious.

There isn't much I can do at this point, so after I devour the sandwich, I lay down on the bed. I could use a shower. I am worried, though, that someone may come into the room while I'm in the bathroom. I could barricade the door while I'm in there.

I look around for something with which to jam the door. The chair next to the table will do the trick, so I carry it to the bathroom and shove it under the door handle. The clothes are my size. Curious. It's as if my kidnapper knows me well enough to dress me perfectly.

LYDIA HALL

Has he been watching me? The thought of it sends a fresh batch of chills down my spine. I guess I was a sitting duck at the gallery with its large wrap-around windows. I should have paid more attention to my surroundings, but I was too preoccupied with David's tragedy. Now I'm paying the price.

With the bathroom door secured, I decide to have a long soak in the tub rather than a shower. My body aches, and warm water will surely help with that. I don't know what the brute did to me when he bundled me into his car, but I feel like I was pretzelled into a small space. I guess that's what you get when you're in the hands of the enemy. I don't understand why he didn't just kill me. Why prolong my agony?

My arm hurts where the needle went in. I rub gently over the spot where a bit of blood has crusted over. The bathroom cabinet is stocked with basic items. Toothpaste—my host clearly prefers victims with minty fresh breath while he kicks the snot out of them—toilet paper, a toothbrush, an assortment of feminine hygiene products, a hairbrush, and a few other essentials. Was this all bought for me?

I pull a bottle of body wash and a washcloth from the cabinet and place them on the edge of the tub while I run the water. None of this makes sense to me.

I slip into the water once the tub is full. The warmth is wonderful for my aching body. I close my eyes, the rising steam enveloping me. Am I weak because I'm so close to tears? I've always considered myself a capable, feisty woman, but this situation has me feeling ridiculously vulnerable. The worst of it all is that I'm all alone now without David. I'd hate to think that my inner strength was a consequence of knowing that my brother always had my back.

Now that he's gone, I'm truly alone. So much for inner strength and resilience.

You can't think like that, Emily. You are strong and perfectly capable of getting through this.

Of course I am. If growing up without parents has taught me anything, it's that I can keep going even when everything around me is telling me that I cannot. I will get through this. I don't care what I have to do to placate this enemy. David's death won't have been in vain. I refuse to lay down and die. This is bullshit!

I dry myself off with a newfound determination to face my enemy. As I pick up the clean clothes, a pair of lacy panties falls to the floor.

"You've got to be shitting me!"

How dare he? Now he's buying me underwear! In my size, to boot! Who does this pervert think he is? I'm going to shove this skimpy piece of material right down his mobster throat.

I brush my teeth and brush my hair. I refuse to look like a victim when he shows his face.

"Okay, asshole. Let's dance."

* * *

I check my watch for the hundredth time. It's noon. So, what's the plan, I wonder. Am I to rot away in my lonely tower like Repunzel? Is this man ever going to appear so I can confront him? This is ridiculous. I should damn well…

Voices. I hear voices outside the door. I leap off the bed and take on a bulldog-like stance to show that I'm not afraid. Actually, I'm crapping myself, but that's my secret and will remain so.

"Who's out there?" I yell out as loudly and calmly as I can.

The voices stop.

"I said, Who's out there? You can't keep me here forever. I demand to know what's going on!"

Oh, come on. Just open the blasted door so I can see who I'm dealing with! It's quiet now, and it's driving me scatty. I listen intently from my perceived stronghold, intent on sniffing out the enemy's plan. Any moment now, the door will open, and I'll be face to face with the man who'll rue the day he jabbed me in the arm.

The voices are back. I brace myself as I hear the sound of the key turning in the lock.

Okay, here we go. It's go time. You've got this, Emily. Don't back down!

The door opens slowly.

What the...

I stare at the man standing in the doorway. I can't believe it! How is this possible? How did he find me? Did Dannie call him? How did he know where to start looking? This is crazy!

"Lucas!" I gasp and run over to him. "I don't believe it. How did you find me?"

I throw my arms around my rescuer's neck. My hellish fate is at an end. It's over! I'm free! I cling to Lucas as though my life depends upon it. I don't know how he did it, and I don't care at this point. All I know is that this beautiful man in my arms is here for me, and I couldn't be happier.

9

LUCAS

This is rather awkward. What do I do now? Emily thinks I'm here to save her. I suppose I am, but she's not going to like my methods or the reasons behind them. She feels so small and vulnerable in my arms. She's trembling, which makes me feel even worse!

"Hey," I whisper into her soft, lush hair. "Are you okay?"

"I've been better," she says, relaxing into my arms. "Where am I? How did you find me?"

"It's a long story. Come, let's sit down."

"Sit down! Are you nuts? Get me the hell out of here, Lucas!"

"Please, Emily, sit down. We need to talk."

The look of confusion on her face stabs at my heart. She's like a vulnerable child, and all I want to do is hold her in my arms and kiss it better. But that is going to have to wait, as I have a lot of explaining to do, and this isn't going to be easy.

I take a trembling Emily by the hand and walk her toward the bed. We sit down on the edge of it while I formulate my words. There's no sense in beating around the bush. I just hope she doesn't hate me after this.

"What's going on, Lucas?"

"There's no easy way to say this, so I'm just going to go ahead and tell you."

"I don't understand."

"I'm the one who had you taken, Emily."

She doesn't say anything at first. I watch as the cogs in her head come to a grinding halt at my admission. Then, slowly, the realization of my revelation kicks in, and before long, the wheels are spinning again at full speed.

"What? What the hell are you talking about? Why would you do such an appalling thing? Is this your idea of a joke? Because if it is, it isn't funny."

"No. It isn't a joke. Perhaps I need to start at the beginning."

Emily is glowering at me. She's even more stunning when she's mad. And I can tell that she's about ready to scratch out my eyes.

"Is this about David?" she asks. "Are you keeping me here because you figure you owe my dead brother something?"

"Yes. And no."

"What the fuck, Lucas?!"

"I'm sorry. I didn't mean to scare you. This really is the best place for you right now. Please, you have to trust me."

"Trust you? I barely know you! I thought I did, but it turns out I really have no bloody idea. Do I?"

"You're right. You have no reason to trust me. But I promise you, this is for your own good."

"And who are you to make that decision for me? You think because you knew my brother, it gives you the right to make decisions about my life? I don't think so. You *will* let me out of here right now!"

"I'm sorry, but I can't do that."

"And why the hell not?"

"Because David worked for me, and I can't be sure, but I think that's the reason he was murdered."

Emily's silence is painful. She's staring at me as if she caught me whipping a puppy. I wish she would say something. Anything would be better than the death stare I'm getting from her.

"You? You're his new client?"

"No. Actually, David started working for me—well, for our organization—years ago."

"Organization? I don't understand... Oh, my goodness. You work for the mob. Don't you?"

How does one answer a question like that? It's a multifaceted issue fraught with pitfalls and hidden explosives. I swallow hard before I answer.

"Yes."

Way to go, laying it out so succinctly for her there, genius.

"Wait a second. Did you kill my brother?"

"No! Of course not. I was very fond of David. He was a bright and loyal man. I would never hurt him."

"Do you know who did?"

"No. I don't. Not yet, anyway. But I'm working on finding out."

Emily sinks into the mattress. With her shoulders drooping, she places her head in her hands.

"How is this possible?" she whispers.

"I'm sorry, Emily. I didn't want you to find out like this."

"What's that? That *you* are the reason a good man died, or that you lied to me about who you are?"

"Both, I guess."

"I don't believe this. So, the whole time we were together at dinner and at the funeral, you were lying to me about who you are. How can you live with yourself? You're a monster!"

Emily's words hurt like a son of a bitch. This is not the direction in which I wanted this conversation to go. I was hoping she'd understand why I did what I did, but I can see that I was being naive. There's a lot of hurt locked up inside this woman, and I've done nothing to ease her pain.

"I'm sorry, Emily. About everything."

"What did David do for your *organization*?"

I take the obvious swipe on the chin like a man.

"He oversaw our finances. David was really very talented. I'm going to miss him very much."

"I'm sure you'll find another unsuspecting idiot to handle your dirty money."

"I'm going to let that one go because I know you're upset."

"How gracious of you," she snaps and gets up.

I watch as Emily paces the room. I know I have to give her some space, so I stay where I am.

"So, what's the big plan, Lucas? Is that even your real name? Keep me locked up here until you sort out your shit?"

"Yes, Lucas *is* my name, and I want to keep you safe until I know for sure that you're not in danger."

"I have a life, Lucas. You can't keep me locked up like some sort of prized possession. Besides, I'm perfectly capable of taking care of myself."

"Oh, really? I got to you without much effort. You have no idea how ruthless the enemy can be, Emily."

"I'm starting to get an idea," she snaps at me again, her eyes ablaze with rage and sarcasm.

"Okay, I deserve that."

"You can't keep me locked up in this box, Lucas. I need fresh air and sunlight."

"I don't intend to keep you here. I wanted to talk to you first before I moved you. It's important that you cooperate."

"I have to know. Why do you care what happens to me anyway? I'm nothing to you. A stranger. What's with the Big Brother act? What do you want from me?"

"I told you. I was very fond of David."

"So, you're doing this out of a misguided sense of loyalty to a man whose death you're responsible for? Do you imagine that you're going to redeem yourself by kidnapping and forcing me into a situation I didn't ask for?"

"That's a little harsh. Don't you think?"

"Harsh! I think I'm more than justified in my assessment of the situation. Now, thank you very much for *keeping me safe*, but I'd like to go now. I'm officially letting you off the babysitting hook. You're not responsible for me."

"Yes, I am. I know you're not happy about this, but it is what it is."

"It is what it is! How dare you? Let me out this instant! I'm not kidding around, Lucas. You let me out, or you'll be sorry."

I'd laugh if the situation wasn't so serious. There's no way Emily would do any physical damage to me. She's so tiny compared to me that she couldn't hurt me if she tried. Emotionally? Now, that's a different story. I have no idea why I care so deeply for a woman I barely know, but I do.

"You're not thinking straight, Emily."

"Oh, yes, I am!"

"Let me go, and you'll never see me again. I'll disappear. That way, you don't have to work out your guilt over David anymore."

"That's not what this is," I blurt out, regretting the words the moment they're out.

"What do you mean?"

Emily stares at me for a while, and then the penny drops.

"Oh!" she mocks. "Oh, I see. You think there's something between us. Ha! That's ludicrous. We went out for one dinner, and we shared one kiss. In what universe do you imagine I would ever be with a man like you? Especially now that I know who you really are."

Her words are cutting. Spiteful. Emily's sentiment is clear. I'm scum, and she hates me.

"You're not going anywhere," I say as I get up and head for the door.

"Lucas!" Emily shouts out in frustration.

I keep walking.

Out of nowhere, she rushes me and starts beating my back with her fists.

"No! You can't do this to me," she yells.

I swing around and grab her by the wrists. I don't hurt her, but she tries violently to break free from my grip.

"Let me go, you bastard!"

"Not until you calm down," I order, but Emily is like a bull rushing the red flag.

I pull her in closer to get a better grip on her. Her body is right against mine, and I'm aware of every one of her beautiful curves.

"Stop it," I insist, but she is too mad to hear me.

In the chaos, I do something that takes me by surprise. I lift her off the ground and kiss her. At first, she struggles and kicks against me. But soon, my crazed captive stops fighting back. My head is spinning as my tongue darts in and out of her warm, perfect mouth. Emily kisses like she fights—with every ounce of passion she has.

My body is reacting with such passion that I find it hard not to carry her across the floor to the bed, rip off the clothes I bought for her, and make raw, frenzied love to her. The argument is now all but forgotten as the two of us lose ourselves in the most spectacular kiss I've ever had.

I pull back for a second and stare into Emily's eyes. The passion I see in them only eggs me on, so I kiss her again. I realize that I'm still holding onto her wrists, but she doesn't seem to mind. Emily isn't fighting it. This woman is driving me crazy.

I put her down so that her feet are firmly on the floor before I reach down and kiss her left breast. The nipple is hard under my tongue, so I bite down very gently. Emily moans softly and throws back her head.

"I want you," I whisper.

I'm still holding her wrists behind her back. What started as an act of self preservation has quickly morphed into a delicious game of dominance. I'm hard with excitement.

"I want you, Emily," I say again, a little louder and more forcefully this time.

The object of my lust doesn't say a word, but her eyes are challenging me—daring me to take what I want. Do I do it? Is this a good idea? My mind is swimming in a sea of endorphins. I cannot trust myself to make the right decision here.

Don't do this, Lucas. This is a mistake.

My mind is telling me that this is wrong, but my body is dancing to its own tune. I'm at a crossroads, and I have to make a decision pretty quickly.

A knock on the door makes up my mind for me.

"Boss! I'm sorry to interrupt, but I need to talk to you."

Damn it!

The words snap me out of the dreamy state I'm in. I let go of Emily's wrists and step back.

"I'm so sorry," I stammer. "I have to go. We'll talk later."

Emily doesn't say a word. She's breathing heavily. So am I. I'm aware that my erection is visible for all to see, so I shift my shaft to the side as best I can before I leave the room.

"This isn't over," she says calmly before I close the door behind me.

Yeah, no kidding! I know it isn't. In fact, I have a feeling that this is just the beginning. Of what, though, I have no idea.

"Sorry, Boss. I didn't mean to interrupt you."

"It's okay, Donny. What's up?"

"I thought you might want to know that our ears on the ground have learned some info on David's murder."

"Okay. Who did it?"

"Well, we're not sure who the shooter is yet, but we know who's behind it all."

"Gallo?"

"Yeah."

"I had a feeling."

"Do you want us to do something about him, Boss? Just say the word, and he's history."

"No. I don't want to start a gang war now. Let me give it some thought. Thank you, Donny."

"Sure thing, Boss."

"I know what you're thinking, Donny, and I assure you we will show our strength very soon. Gallo is no fool. He'll be expecting retaliation, so he'll be ready for us if we attack. The time isn't right. You make sure no one, and I mean no one, does anything to the Gallo family. If he gets as much as a paper cut without my say, there'll be hell to pay. You got me?"

"Yeah, Boss."

"Okay. Thanks."

Fucking Gallo. I knew it. He's trying to start something between our families now that the old man is dead. Well, he's got less than zero chance of pulling me into an ill conceived attack. I'll bide my time and strike when the moment is right. This isn't over.

"I'll be coming for you, Gallo. And when I do, you're going to be sorry you screwed with me. That's a promise."

10

EMILY

What the hell just happened? What am I doing? If I had any hope of being in control, I just pissed it away. Now Lucas has the edge over me, and I'm screwed. I hit the pillow in frustration, furious with myself for being so weak.

So much for scratching out my enemy's eyes. Sticking my tongue down Lucas' throat was tantamount to thanking him for kidnapping me and keeping me here against my will. Ugh! Fool!

It was a spectacular kiss, though. I've never felt like that in a man's arms before. Lucas is perfect. Everything about him makes me want to beg him to rip off my clothes while I submit to him. Which is ridiculous because I'm not the kind of woman who takes kindly to being told what to do or how to do it. But damn if I didn't enjoy every second of our brief and unexpected dalliance.

I should be focusing on getting the hell out of here. Instead, I can't help wondering what would have happened if that knock at the door hadn't interrupted us.

Stop it, Emily. Focus on the big picture, please. Remember where you are and why you're here. David is dead because of Lucas!

Okay. So, I forgot myself for a moment. It won't happen again. From here on out, I'm going to focus on getting as far away from my captor as humanly possible before I end up in an early grave like my brother. Nothing good can come from being involved with someone with this lifestyle.

The mob. I would never have guessed, not in a million years, that this kind of thing was going on right under my nose. I should have pushed David when I knew he was keeping something from me. Woman's intuition and all that. I may have failed as a sister, but I won't fail myself.

* * *

Lucas

"What is it about this woman that has you all bent out of shape, Lucas?"

"I feel responsible for her. Andreas. It's because of me that her brother is dead."

"That's bullshit."

"Is it?"

"You have no way of knowing that for sure."

"Oh, yes, I do. You know Gallo and his men have had it out for me since the old man died. Killing David was a personal attack on me."

"Are you sure?"

"Of course. The timing is too perfect for this to have been a coincidence, Andreas. Gallo has a bone to pick with me, and he's chosen to hit me where it hurts. David was the best accountant we've ever had. With him dead, Gallo figures I'm going to hurt. And' he's not wrong."

"Okay, I get that. But what about Emily? Why would he even care about her?"

"He probably doesn't. Not yet. But I can't take that chance."

"Dominick says she's a handful."

"She's no wallflower, that's for sure. I can't blame her, though. Emily is scared. Fear makes people do crazy things."

"I take it she had no idea that David was working for us."

"No, she didn't."

"The news must have been a shock."

"I'd say. We're not exactly known for our humanitarianism, Andreas."

"So we are in the mob. David made his choices. You're not to blame for that."

"No. I guess not. But I am going to make sure I keep Emily safe."

"How long are you planning on keeping me here?"

"As long as it takes."

Andreas laughs.

"What's so amusing?"

"The fact that you think you can appease a woman scorned without losing a limb."

"Haha. Funny."

"Can I tell you what I think?"

"Can I stop you?"

"Probably not."

"Okay, let me hear it."

"I think this feisty stunner has bewitched you."

"You do, do you?"

"Uh-huh."

"I owe her brother. That's all."

Andreas grins and gets up.

"Okay. If you say so."

Smartass. He always did read me too easily.

I know I can't leave Emily locked up in the basement for too long. The accommodations are pretty plush, if I have to say so myself, but even so, she'll need to move upstairs into the main house. She's pretty pissed at me right now, so I'll have to charge one of my men to keep an eye on her so that she doesn't do anything reckless, like run away. Emily is a feisty, independent girl. I wouldn't put anything past her, including scaling down a drainpipe to get away from me.

I have an idea to keep her mind occupied. Hopefully, Emily will see my intentions more clearly if she can quiet her mind and the rage she must have right now. I decide to take a drive to an art supply store close to the house.

The sales assistant watches me as I comb the aisles, looking for the right supplies. I'm clueless, really. I haven't done art since preschool, and even back then, my creations were less arty and more splodges.

"Can I help you, Sir?" the assistant smiles, eagerly looking to help me out of the pit.

"I think you'd better, yes."

"What are you looking for?"

"I have a friend who's a painter. I'd like to buy her a few supplies so she can paint, but I don't know what I'm doing."

"I see. That's very sweet of you. Don't worry, I'm sure between the two of us we'll figure it out."

"I'm glad you're confident," I smile.

"What is your friend's medium?"

"Medium?"

"I see. You truly are a newbie," she chuckles sweetly. "Okay. Does she use acrylic, watercolor, oil, gouache, or ink?"

"I'm not sure. Perhaps you can give me a bit of everything. Just in case."

"Okay. I can do that. How much were you wanting to spend?"

"Price isn't an object. I want her to enjoy this gift."

"Your friend is a very lucky lady."

Yeah, I think so, but I know Emily will disagree vehemently.

"I have a few other errands to run. Would you put something together for me in the meantime? I'll be back in an hour to fetch it."

"It will be my pleasure."

"Thank you; you're very kind."

I leave the assistant to it and make my way to a clothing store. Emily will need new clothes. The one outfit I arranged for her isn't enough, taking into consideration that she's going to be with me for a while.

It's easy to buy clothes for her. Emily's body is perfect, so she will likely look spectacular in whatever I give her. Underwear is a challenge. It's such a personal item. I hope my choice won't piss her off even further. I'm already in the doghouse.

Why do I care, anyway? I'm doing my best. If she can't see that, then it's not my problem.

I spend a good hour choosing jeans, shirts, sleepwear, undies, fragrances, and shoes I think will look good on her. The bill is substantial, but I don't care. It's not like I have to budget anyway.

The art supplies are wrapped up and ready for me when I get back to the store. I thank the assistant, pay for the supplies, and leave her a generous tip for her expert assistance. Now the hard bit. I have to give all this to Emily and hope she doesn't throw it at my head.

I suppose I could have done this the easy way. I have people who would gladly do all this crap for me, but I feel I owe my captive the respect of delivering it myself. It's been a full day since the kiss, but I swear I can still taste Emily on my lips. I rap softly on the door before I enter her room.

"Can I come in?" I ask, lingering in the doorway.

"Why are you asking? This is your prison. You can do as you like."

Ouch. It's official. Emily is still angry. I enter with my meager offerings and set the bags down on the table.

"I brought you a few things."

"Unless there's a ticket to Tahiti somewhere in there, I'm not interested."

"I'll just leave it here for you. Let me know if you need anything, and I'll see what I can do," I say before I turn to leave.

"I want to go home, Lucas."

"I'm sorry, but you can't."

"I wish I'd never set eyes on you."

That was unnecessary. I leave the room feeling dejected and just a tad offended.

* * *

Emily

LYDIA HALL

I'm spitting mad. Does this thug truly believe that he can placate me with a few gifts? Like a petulant child, I stay on the bed long after Lucas has left the room and locked the door behind him.

I'm well aware that I'm acting like a brat, but what other options do I have? I want Lucas to know how angry I am with him. I want him to hurt like I do. He may not have pulled the trigger on the weapon that killed David, but he's responsible nonetheless. If it weren't for him and his shady business, my brother would still be alive. How can I act as if everything is fine?

I sit and stare at the bags for at least half an hour while feeling sorry for myself. But, ultimately, the boredom gets to be too much, so I amble over to see what's in the bags.

I look at the contents of the first bag. New clothes. After my shower this morning, I put on the same clothes as I had on yesterday. I hate wearing the same clothes two days in a row, but I didn't have a choice. Now I can at least change into fresh, clean clothes. Oh, thank heavens! Clean underwear. Lucas has good taste in clothes; I have to give him that.

Next, I open the other bags. Art supplies. And not just any old crap. Expensive stuff. Again, I'm impressed. My captor has good instincts. On paper, Lucas is the perfect gentleman and host. It's a pity this isn't a typical scenario. Lucas is generous. Most women would be fawning over him for that. But not me. Not this time around. I will not be elevating this mob boss to hero status anytime soon.

I gather from the various outfits and the generous amount of art supplies that Lucas plans to keep me here for quite some time. I have to wonder whether Dannie or Simon will ever find me here. Are they even looking, or have they given up?

Poor Dannie. She must be frantic. Damn Lucas for putting her through this so soon after the shock of David's death. Does he realize what he's doing to us? I have to get word to her somehow. My best friend has been through enough.

I'll have to play along and behave, or I won't get what I want. If it means that I'm going to have to swallow my pride, then so be it. I can play nice. Up to a point.

At least I have my art to distract me. I take out the supplies and lay them out on the floor before I choose a canvas. I know exactly what I'm going to paint. A portrait from memory.

The next time Lucas comes to see me, I'll have David's face on this canvas. If he thinks I'm going to make it easy for him to forget what he's done, he's got another thing coming.

"I won't let you forget about my brother's death, Lucas. Never!"

11

EMILY

I'm expecting to see Lucas when there's a knock at the door. It's been two days since he gave me the art supplies and clothes, and I have seen neither hide nor hair of the man since then.

"Come in," I snap, ready to give my best performance yet.

But it isn't Lucas at the door. It's the bulky henchman who brings me food every day.

"Where's your boss?"

"We're moving you," he announces. "You don't have to pack. We'll bring your things for you."

Moving? Where to? Am I finally getting out of here? And why isn't Lucas here to tell me himself?

"Moving me?"

"Yes. The boss wants you upstairs."

"I see."

I should throw my toys out and make a scene. No one will blame me if I do that. The cheek of it all! But I have to get out of this dungeon first if I have any chance of escaping, so I'll play along.

"Well, I guess the boss gets what the boss wants," I snap and get up.

"This way, please," he grins.

"What is your name?"

"Dominick."

"Where is Lucas, Dominick?"

"He's busy."

"Too busy to talk to his captive?"

The musclehead shrugs his shoulders.

"My job is to follow orders," he says matter of factly.

"Well. Do me a favor, Dominick. Please tell your boss I'd like to have a word with him when you see him, will you?"

"Yes, Ma'am."

He's unexpectedly polite. I guess it's pointless taking out my frustration on him. It's Lucas I'm mad at.

I follow the man-mountain up a flight of stairs, and I'm utterly gobsmacked when we reach the landing leading to a large living space. This must be the inside of Lucas' home. It's spacious and opulent. Not the kind of show-offy opulence of a gangster, but rather that of a man with excellent taste.

I wonder where in this mansion I'll be staying now that I've been upgraded from prisoner to houseguest. I don't have to wonder for long.

"This is where you'll be staying from now on," Dominick says as he leads me into a cottage adjacent to the house.

If I didn't know better, I'd say it was a luxury chateau where I'm to enjoy a free, yet unplanned, holiday for a while.

"I take it; I can move around freely in here."

"Of course. Just don't go outside until the boss has spoken to you."

"I wouldn't dream of it," I answer, my words dripping with sarcasm.

Dominick smirks before he leaves me to explore my new digs. The first thing I notice is that the external doors are locked, and there are no keys in sight. So much for the don't go outside speech. The cottage has two en-suite bedrooms on the far side, away from the kitchen and living room. It's all very modern, with the finest decor and finishes that gangster money can buy.

The interior designer should have painted the walls red. It would be more fitting than the soft green and white trim it has now, seeing as this place was no doubt bought with blood money.

How long before Lucas makes his grand appearance? Am I going to have to wait another two days before the mob boss graces me with his presence? I hope not. I have to talk some sense into him. Convince him to let me go, or I'll go crazy. I hope to at least talk him into allowing me to call Dannie and tell her that I'm not lying dead in a ditch somewhere.

The sound of footsteps on the tiles in the entrance yanks me from my internal dialog. I look up expectantly, but once again, my hopes are dashed. Instead of Lucas, a young woman enters, carrying the clothes that Lucas bought me. Hot on her heels follows a young man carrying art supplies in bags.

"Good morning, ma'am," they greet me politely.

"Hi."

"Have you decided which bedroom you prefer?" the young woman asks me.

"Uhm, yeah. The one overlooking the ocean. Thanks."

I assume that's where she takes the clothes.

"I'll put this in the studio for you," the young man says.

"Studio?"

"Yes, Ma'am. There's a large room upstairs."

I follow him up a staircase into a large open area with a large window overlooking the ocean. I don't know how I missed it. I assumed the closed door was a guest bathroom. This is a nice surprise.

"Is it okay if I put it over here?" he asks.

"Yeah. That's great. Thank you."

I feel like a bitch for having been so snippy with the staff. It's not their fault that I'm here. They're just doing their job. I make a mental note to cut the sarcasm with them. I am nothing if not a polite human being.

"My pleasure," he says with a bright smile before leaving the room.

It's beautiful up here. The view of the ocean is spectacular. It's the perfect place for an art studio. I wonder what Lucas had in mind when he built this room.

Lucas. Where the hell is he?

"Do you like the view?"

I jump at the sudden voice behind me. It's Lucas.

"Geez! Didn't your mother teach you that it's rude to sneak up on people?"

"I'm sorry. I thought you would have heard me coming."

"Where the hell have you been?" I snap at him without thinking first.

"It's good to see you too."

"That's not funny, Lucas."

"You're right. I'm sorry, I haven't seen you in a while. I had things to take care of. Are you okay?"

"No. I'm a hostage. How is that okay?"

"You're not a hostage, Emily. You're a houseguest."

"Oh, really? I don't lock the doors when I have houseguests. We must have different interpretations of the word."

"Is that David?" Lucas asks, pointing to a canvas on an easel nearest to the window.

"Yes."

"It captures him perfectly. You're very talented, Emily."

Lucas' compliment takes me by surprise. And now I'm annoyed because the painting was supposed to serve as a reminder to him of his misdeed rather than garner his admiration for the artist.

"David had such kind eyes."

"A fat lot of good it did him," I retaliate.

"Are you okay, Emily?"

Why is this man being so nice to me? What does he want?

"Do the clothes fit?" he asks, changing tactics when I don't answer his previous question.

"Yeah."

"The kitchen downstairs is state of the art. Would you prefer preparing your own meals? Or my chef can do it for you. Feel free to write up a list of items you need, and I'll see to it that you have them."

"So, I'm here for the long haul."

"I'm sorry, Emily. But, yes. You're safe here with me until I find the man who killed your brother. After that, you are welcome to leave."

"What if you never find him?"

"Oh, I'll find him. I promise you that much."

"What will you do to him when you do?"

"You let me worry about that."

"More bloodshed."

"I don't expect you to understand the way things work in my world, Emily. Just know that I'll do whatever is necessary to keep you from harm."

"Against my will."

"I'm sorry, but it's the only way."

"You should have let me leave on my own. I'd be far away from this place by now."

"Or not."

"Do you really think David's killer is looking for me? And if so, why? I don't know anything."

"It's not about what you know as much as it is about who you know."

"Stop talking in code. What are you saying?"

"David's murder was meant to ruffle my feathers."

"Ruffle your feathers! A man is dead because of you. And that's the way you see it?"

"No. I'm sorry. That's not what I meant. Damn it, Emily. Why are you making it so hard for me to apologize to you?"

"Because it's all just words, Lucas! David is dead. What am I supposed to do? What did you expect from me? Kind words of thanks for locking me up?"

"No! But a little gratitude would be nice. David was a grown man. He knew the risks. I didn't force him into this business. He came willingly."

"Oh, don't you dare! Don't you put this on him. I'm sure that if my brother knew the full extent of your *operations,* he would have chosen to leave."

I'm super pissed right now. My face is warm, and my ears are on fire. I must look like a cobra ready to strike. Lucas looks pretty agitated himself. This is an explosive situation, and the powder keg is close to blowing. I'm right on the edge of my sanity. One more push from Lucas, and I'm not sure I will manage to come back.

* * *

Lucas

How is it possible to be this angry yet so turned on at the same time? Emily's eyes are on fire. Pompei has nothing on her as she stands near the window, her hands balled into fists, glowering at me. Righteous fury never wore a more perfect face.

I'd better get the hell out of this room before I say something I'm going to regret. I don't want to hurt Emily, but if she carries on smart-mouthing me, I may snap back. She's hurt, and I get that, but I'm just a man, and my rev counter is officially in the red.

"Can we stop, please?" I suggest longing to bring this mess back to a discussion rather than a screaming match. "I didn't bring you here to fight with you."

"No. You brought me here to ease your guilty conscience."

"No. I brought you here to keep you safe."

"Like you kept my brother safe?"

"That was below the belt, Emily."

"What's the matter? Does the tough guy gangster have a heart?"

That's it! Emily's gone too far this time. I'll show her who has a heart.

I march up to her and grab her by the wrists. Her eyes are challenging me—stubborn and defiant as ever—but I don't care. This time I'm going to tell her exactly why she should be so lucky that I give a crap about her at all. I mean, I could have left her to go about her life and risk her own safety. She's lucky that I give a damn!

"You are the most infuriating woman I've ever met in my life," I growl at her as I lift her off the ground.

She unexpectedly kicks me in the shin, throwing me off balance for just a moment before I regain my balance.

"You can hit and kick as much as you like, Emily. You are going to remain here until I say otherwise, whether you like it or not. You got that?"

"Fu…" she starts to say, but I don't allow her to finish her insult before I place my mouth over hers.

This time she bites my lips.

"Ouch! Damn it, Emily…"

I'm aroused again. Emily is squirming to get out of my grip, but I hold on for dear life. I kiss her again. She's not fighting me anymore. The feisty woman who a mere second ago was trying to claw out my eyes suddenly stops fighting back, kissing me passionately instead.

My head is swimming as I hold her body close to mine. I can feel her chest heaving from the exertion of fighting me. I have to have her. I refuse to back off this time. I've wanted Emily since the moment I saw her photo on my desk, and now is my chance to show her just how I feel about her.

12

EMILY

This is insane! What am I doing? I don't want to give myself to this man. He's the enemy, for goodness sake. Everything in my mind is screaming at me not to give in, but my body is so not on the same page.

Lucas' body is pressed so firmly up against mine that I'm barely able to expand my lungs. I'm out of breath from fighting back, or is it because my heart is racing out of control from the excitement of being in his arms again?

Lucas is strong. He's holding me off the ground with such ease. I like this way more than I thought I would. I couldn't fight him off if I tried. Not that I have any intentions of being anywhere but in his arms right now.

Lucas stops kissing me and looks into my eyes. What is he waiting for? Permission? I don't want to give it to him. Why not? What's wrong with me? Am I afraid that if I actually say the word yes out loud, the fire will extinguish itself?

When I was a teenager, I'd read the occasional romance novel where a poor young girl would be helpless as the hero ravages her without her spoken consent. Bondage for newbies leaped to mind while I devoured the sex scene pages. Now, here I am, the helpless young thing, desperate for the sexy *bad man* to take me *against my will*.

I close my eyes so that I don't have to deal with the question looming in Lucas' eyes. Rather than speak the word, I kiss him harder. It's the cue my excited lover has been waiting for. Lucas takes off my belt while still holding on to my wrists with his strong hand. Next, he ties my hands together in front of me. I keep my eyes firmly shut. This is new to me and very exciting.

Neither one of us utters a word. Every cell in my body is screaming for my lover's touch, and I'm breathing so fast you'd think I'd just run a marathon. Lucas turns me around so that my back is toward him before he runs his hands along the front of my body, gently squeezing and teasing as he goes.

I'm about ready to scream out for him to take me, but I hold my tongue, afraid to ruin the moment with mere words. The man with the golden fingers pulls the hair tie free, causing my hair to cascade down my back. He takes a handful and puts it to his nose, breathing in the scent.

Lucas moves my hair aside, giving him access to my neck, which he maps out inch by inch with his tongue. My skin breaks out all over with goosebumps. My nipples are hard as pebbles under his fingers as he tweaks them gently. I moan under his firm touch. The sensation is exquisite.

Lucas has me pinned against the cold wall now. He's reaching around me, unbuttoning my shirt, while I'm floating in the sea of darkness behind my fluttering eyelids. I gasp as he pushes my skin against the cold, plastered bricks. My response excites him. I know this because he's grinding his hardness against my back.

Next, my excited lover pushes up my bra, freeing my breasts so that he can explore their nakedness with his fingers. He nibbles on my earlobe, his breath warm and rapid against my skin. The anticipation of having his fingers explore my waiting core is building steadily as Lucas teases me with every subtle movement.

I don't know how much longer I can stand because my legs are fast becoming like jello. Lucas is taking his time. I cannot touch him the way I want to with my wrists tied together. It's deliciously frustrating. Who am I? What is this man doing to me?

I can't bear it any longer. I want him to sink his fingers into my core. I'm desperate for his touch. Lucas, sensing my frustration, pushes my legs apart with his knees and slips his hand down the front of my jeans. He feels around until he finds what he's been looking for since the moment we first kissed.

"Uhhh!" I gasp as his fingers caress and tease.

"You like that, do you?" he whispers.

"Yes," I whisper back, grappling for air.

He pulls away his hand abruptly, leaving me desperate for his touch, while he unbottons my jeans and slides them, together with my panties, to the floor. I step free of the clothes and stand with my legs apart to make room for my lover.

But Lucas isn't done teasing me yet. Instead of sliding into me, he drops to his haunches and uses his tongue to pleasure me. My legs are buckling. I can't stand any longer. The pleasure has me shaky and unsteady on my feet, so Lucas stops, picks me up, and lays me down on the plush rug.

I open my eyes and stare up at the man who has me completely at his mercy. His eyes are on fire as he slowly removes his shirt, then his pants, and finally his underwear. Lucas's body is magnificent. He has a tattoo of an eagle in flight on his left pec and a scar on the side of his belly button.

I cannot look away from his nakedness. His shaft is all I can focus on. He grins proudly at me, enjoying every moment of my desire for him.

He kneels down next to me, hooks his fingers into the belt looped around my wrists, and moves my hands up beyond my head. I'm stretched out as if I'm on a medieval wrack, naked and exposed. I open my legs to make space for his body.

This is it. This is what I've been waiting for. I'm burning with desire for Lucas; all of him.

"Tell me you want me," he purrs.

I'm not ashamed to tell him how much I want him. I'm looking at timidity in the rearview mirror at this point. All I can think about is the throbbing ache that only Lucas can satisfy, so I open my mouth and let out the words.

"I've never wanted anyone more than I want you right now, Lucas," I utter unabashedly.

Before I know it, he's inside of me. The pleasure is indescribable. It's as if I've been asleep all my life, and now I'm awake. Lucas fills every inch of me with his manhood. He moves with such skill that I'm breathless. We're kissing now. I wish I could dig my nails into his flesh as we grind together, but my lover keeps me stretched out. The vulnerability is exciting.

Lucas moves on top of me and takes my nipple into his mouth. Our feverish bodies, wet with perspiration and passion, morph into a single unit, working together in perfect harmony. We move faster and faster until I cannot hold back the wave of orgasm any longer.

"Let it out," Lucas says in a low, thick voice.

It's hard to explain what I'm feeling. It's as if an orgasm that's been stuck inside me for years suddenly bursts out of me with such ferocity that I'm sure my spine will snap as I arch my back. Lucas waits for me, and as soon as I stop jerking, he pushes for the finish line. His orgasm is as earth shattering as mine.

If there was an Olympic event for lovemaking, he and I would surely have just secured gold. I'm too spent to say a word. My deft lover rolls off me and lies next to me as we both try to catch our breath.

I've completely forgotten that my hands are still tied together until Lucas reaches for me and removes the belt. He checks my wrists to make sure that I'm not hurt. He kisses the marks where the belt dug into my flesh.

"I'm sorry. Did I hurt you?"

"No. I'm fine."

It's a little awkward now that I've come to my senses again, and I can't help but wonder where to go from here. I'm naked on a floor in a house where I'm being held against my will. This isn't exactly familiar territory for me.

"That was insane," Lucas says softly.

"A firm first for me. The belt, I mean."

"Yeah, not sure why I did that."

"So, it's not your usual MO, then?"

"No."

"You're an enigma, Lucas."

"Are you still mad at me?"

"Of course. This changes nothing."

"I was afraid you might say that. I really am sorry, Emily."

"Uh-huh. So you keep telling me."

* * *

It's been a week since our crazed session in the studio, and I've settled into a routine of sorts. It's clear to me that I'm a semi-permanent houseguest of Lucas, whether I like it or not, so there's no point in fighting it.

Dominick and his team of merry men keep me fed, and Lucas pops by every now and again to make sure I haven't dug any trenches under the house to escape. I sketch, paint, and go for walks in the garden, and now and again, Dominick lets me off my *leash* so I can walk on the beach.

I keep asking Lucas to contact Dannie to let her know that I'm okay, but he insists that it isn't safe. I'm determined to keep at him until he relents. The conversations get pretty heated.

"No one must know where you are, Emily."

"But you've assured me I'm safe here with you. What's the harm in telling Dannie? She'll be worried sick!"

"Please, Emily. Trust me. It's better for her too."

"How the hell do you figure? She'll be out of her mind with worry. Please, Lucas."

"Fine. I'll get word to her."

"Thank you."

I can't complain, really. Living under Lucas' roof has been less of a prison sentence since he moved me into the cottage. I wonder what David would have thought about the current awkward situation I'm in.

Lucas and I are getting to know each other better. We haven't slept together again. I don't want him to think that I'm that sort of woman. He's going to have to work for it. Besides, the situation is weird enough without complicating it even further by throwing sex into the mix.

I know he wants me, even if he doesn't say it. I can tell from the way Lucas looks at me that he'd be happy to get me out of my clothes if I gave him half the chance. But I must stick to my guns.

It's 6 p.m., and I'm in the kitchen, making spaghetti bolognese. I prefer cooking for myself, even though Lucas' chef is amazing. This way, it feels more like I'm living my own life in my own place.

"Hi."

Lucas startles me.

"Sorry."

"I'm a little jumpy these days," I admit.

"It smells good in here. What are you cooking?"

"An old family recipe."

"Is there enough for two? I'll bring the wine."

"Hmm. Dining with the enemy. Let me think about it."

"Come on. Surely we've made it past that hurdle by now. Haven't we?"

"Just because you've had your way with me doesn't make us friends," I smirk.

"Ouch. You're mean."

"Said the kidnapper to his prey."

"I may be the gangster in this story, but you're as tough as they come, Emily."

"I did tell you that."

"Am I going hungry then?"

"No. You can stay for dinner."

"Thank you. I'll set the table."

"Don't forget the wine."

Before long, we meet at the table—Lucas with a bottle of wine and me with dinner. I dish up while he pours the wine.

"Oh, wow. This is delicious."

"Thank you."

"Chef would be jealous."

"I wouldn't go firing him just yet. This is about the only thing I cook well."

"Noted."

"Any news yet about David's killer?"

"No. I'm sorry, Emily. I know you want to get back to your normal life."

"Thank you for telling Dannie."

"Of course. I just hope that decision won't come back later to bite me in the ass."

"I'm sure you can take care of yourself."

"It's you I'm worried about."

"I'm developing a serious case of cabin fever, Lucas."

"Okay. Let me see what I can do about that."

"Send me home."

"No."

"Then you'd better come up with something before I go stir crazy."

13

LUCAS

"I have to go away for a few days."

"Okay."

Emily looks disappointed. I can't blame her. I imagine it must be very frustrating, not to mention boring, for her here at the cottage. She's been here for nearly a month now, and that's a long time to be pretty much housebound.

"Why don't you come with me?" I suggest on a whim.

"Uh, okay. Where are we going?"

"Do you have a valid passport?"

"Yeah. Why?"

"Paris."

"As in Paris, France?"

"Uh-huh. Have you been?"

"Yeah, sure. My millionaire book club girls and I go there all the time," she scoffs.

"Funny. Would you like to see the Eiffel Tower at night? It's quite spectacular."

"That sounds like something I'd like to see."

"We'll even swing by a few art galleries, if you like."

"Are you trying to ingratiate yourself, Mr. Mobster?"

"Why? Does it show?"

"Maybe."

"Come on. Come with me."

"It's better than staring at the cottage walls, I guess."

"Geez! You're welcome."

"Fine," Emily grins. "Yes, I'd love to go. Thank you. When do we leave?"

"The day after tomorrow."

"I'm going to need a few more items of clothing if I'm to look like a proper tourist."

"Fair enough. I'll take you shopping this afternoon."

"Hang on. Let me check my schedule."

"Are you always this cheeky?"

"Oh, you'll know when I'm being cheeky."

"Good to know. I'll see you in two hours."

"Be sure to bring your black card," she calls after me as I'm leaving the room.

"Fine. I guess I owe you that much."

Emily is playful today. I'm pleased about that. I can't get her out of my head since we slept together. I find myself constantly wondering what she's doing or thinking. It's an unwelcome distraction at this point, but I can't help it. So much for my tough guy facade. Something tells me I'll turn to putty in Emily's hands if I'm not careful.

There's no way I'll be able to focus on business if she's here in LA while I'm in France. Plus, the trip gives me the perfect opportunity to get to know her better. I'm relieved that she agreed to accompany me.

I'm back in the cottage after two hours of negotiating deals with a new supplier. Emily is dressed in jeans and a cashmere top. She has her dark hair up in a bun, accentuating her swan-like neck. I swallow hard when I think about what I'd like to do to her, but now is not the time.

"Here, please, will you wear this?"

"A baseball cap? Seriously?"

"I don't want anyone to recognize you. It's just a precaution. Please."

"Okay, but it's going to ruin my cashmere ensemble," she jests.

"Nothing could ruin your look."

"Hmm. Was that a compliment?"

"Guilty."

"Alright, I'll wear it."

She takes the cap from my hand, lets down her hair, then pulls it into place over her thick hair.

"Go, Lakers!" she chants.

"Ready?"

"Uh-huh."

I made Dominick Emily's personal bodyguard when she arrived at the house. He's been instructed to go wherever she does, so naturally he's in tow while the two of us get into my SUV.

"Follow us, Dominick," I instruct the man-mountain, who nods and gets into a second car.

"He's much sweeter than he looks," Emily says once we're on the road.

"Yeah. Tell that to the men whose kneecaps he's busted."

"Well, he's sweet to me."

"He'd better be if he knows what's good for him."

"What will we be doing in Paris?" Emily asks me after a few moments of silence. "Or is that on a need-to-know basis?"

"I'd prefer it if you didn't ask."

"Illegal, then?"

"Emily, I'm sorry, but I can't discuss my business with you. It's better for you that I don't."

"How did you get into this…profession, anyway? I can't imagine any kid dreaming of one day becoming a gangster."

"Do you always ask the tough questions?"

"It's a quirk. Are you avoiding?"

"No. It's not a simple answer."

"I didn't expect it to be. We have time."

"How about we get to know each other a little better before you roast me over open flames? Okay?"

"Fine."

"I'm taking you to a boutique a friend of mine owns. She'll take good care of you. The store is filled with couture. I'm sure you'll find what you need for the trip."

"Couture, hey?"

"What? You think gangsters don't know about fashion?"

Emily chuckles.

"Is this friend of yours an old girlfriend?"

"Jealous?"

"Don't be ridiculous. I'm just curious."

"No. She and I grew up in the same neighborhood. Sandy is like a sister to me."

I can tell from her expression that the gears in Emily's head are turning at warp speed.

"I know what you're thinking," I smile.

"Oh?"

"Yup. Sandy won't give away any of my secrets, if that's what you were hoping."

"You overestimate my interest in you, Lucas."

"Just saying."

"Noted."

My driver pulls the car into an underground parking area. My bodyguards get out first to scope out the lay of the land while Emily and I wait inside the vehicle.

"It can't be easy," she says.

"What's that?"

"Living like this. Not knowing from one moment to the next if you're going to catch a bullet. Is it worth it?"

"It is what it is. You get used to it."

"I could never."

"You'd be surprised at what one gets accustomed to."

The back door opens.

"Let's go shopping," I say. "After you."

Emily gets out of the car first. I follow closely behind. The store is on the third floor of the building.

"We'll use the private elevator," I say, pointing Emily in the direction of the steel doors.

Sandy is waiting for us.

"Hey, handsome," she says and throws her arms around me. "What's with the long silence?"

"Hey, gorgeous. It's so nice to see you. You look beautiful, as always."

"Oh, you silver tongued devil, you."

Sandy lets go of me and looks across to Emily.

"Oh, good! You brought me a perfect figure. Ah, yes. I have some fabulous outfits for this beauty."

"Emily, this is Sandy. Sandy, meet Emily."

The women exchange pleasantries.

"Can I leave her in your capable hands?" I ask Sandy. "I have to take care of a few things."

"Of course. Emily and I are going to have some serious fun. Aren't we?"

"Definitely," Emily grins.

"Off you go. Take your time," Sandy instructs me.

"Okay. Try not to bankrupt me."

"Oh, please. Nice try. Don't be a miser. Besides, I know what you're worth, Lucas Lucchese."

"That's what I'm afraid of."

I glance in Dominick's direction. He's poised at the door, and gives me a knowing nod before I leave.

"Have fun, Emily."

She manages to give me a smile before Sandy whisks her away.

* * *

"Oh, boy! Those are a lot of bags."

"You did say you wanted Emily to look good in Paris, didn't you? You know my motto, Lucas. Whatever is worth doing at all, is worth doing well," Sandy counters.

"Thank you, Earl of Chesterfield," I laugh.

"Ah, an educated man," Emily grins.

"Oh, yes. Our boy wonder here isn't just a pretty face," Sandy smiles.

"I see," Emily says. "Not a mere jock, then?"

"Oh, no. But I'm not going to give away his secrets," Sandy winks at Emily.

"I have a feeling you've said too much already. Come on, Emily. Let's get you out of here before Sandy gives you the keys to my kingdom."

"Oh, don't be such a bore," Emily smirks. "Thank you, Sandy."

"Only a pleasure, you sweet thing."

Sweet? Wow. I guess I missed quite a bit.

Dominick grabs the bags while Emily and I make our way back to the car.

"What a lovely woman," Emily says.

"Sandy's one of a kind."

"She's very fond of you."

"Of course she is. I'm a great guy."

"And so very modest."

"Did you get everything you need?"

"Yes. Thank you."

"Good. You're welcome."

Emily is quiet for a while.

"I suppose it's only fair that I cook you dinner. You did spend a fortune on my wardrobe."

"It was my pleasure. I don't expect anything in return. But I'll never say no thank you to food."

"Okay. Be at my mansion at 7 p.m. sharp."

"Yes, Ma'am."

***

"Do I need a taster, or is the food safe?"

"This isn't ancient Rome, Caesar. Besides, your watchdog keeps such a close eye on me that I doubt I'd have the opportunity to harvest dodgy ingredients from your back garden," Emily says, pouring the wine I brought.

"Ah, good old Dominick. Here for your protection, as well as mine, it would seem."

"Correct. I hope you're hungry. I tend to serve large portions."

"I am. What are we having? I know it isn't burnt toast. I'd know that smell anywhere."

"Why? Is that your specialty?"

"No. I learned how to cook out of necessity as a young boy. My mother, on the other hand, was a burnt toast specialist."

I don't know why I just revealed a personal detail to Emily. It came so naturally. The words popped out with ease.

"Are your parents still alive?"

Damn it. Now I'm committed to sharing personal details. I walked right into this.

"No."

"Any siblings?"

"Not that I know of."

"That's an odd answer."

"You wouldn't think so if you knew my family."

"I see. A tortured soul. Figures."

"What's that supposed to mean?"

"It's not an insult. A mere observation, if you will."

Emily walks over to the table. She's holding two plates in her hands. She gives me one.

"Roast chicken. I thought you said you only cooked spaghetti bolognaise."

"No. I said that's the only dish I do well. It remains to be seen if this is worth celebrating."

"Okay. Got it."

"Bon appetit."

"Merci beaucoup."

"Do you speak French?"

"A little. You?"

"I do, yes. It was either French or drama at school. There were no decent looking boys to play Romeo, so I chose French."

I can't help laughing. Emily's sense of humor is wickedly good.

"You're going to be an excellent traveling partner, then."

"Yup. I'll be sure to order the hell out of those croissants and French wine."

"Black card?"

"Black card."

I smile and take a bite of the chicken.

"This is delicious. It would seem that you're rapidly expanding your cooking repertoire."

"How nice for me."

"How long will we be staying in Paris?"

"Six days. I will be busy during the day, but we can use the evenings to do some exploring."

"Where are we staying?"

"I own a chateau, so we'll stay there."

"I see. I take it Dominick will be on babysitting duties during the day."

"Yes. I'm sorry, but he goes where you go."

"My very own plus one."

"Free protection," I smirk.

"How long has he been with you?"

"Dominick has worked for me for about six years. He's a good guy."

"One who, on occasion, breaks a knee cap or two."

"Only when it's absolutely necessary. Think of him as a gentle giant who's slow to anger."

"I certainly wouldn't want to be on his enemies list."

"With your sparkling, congenial personality, I can't see that happening."

"Don't you have someone special you'd rather be taking than your *houseguest*?"

"If you're asking me if I have a girlfriend, then no."

"Never been married?"

"Successfully dodged that bullet. How about you? Any proposals?"

"No."

Emily is feeling me out. Her questions aren't mere small talk fodder. I wonder what she thinks of me. Apart from hating my guts over David's death, of course. It's hard to read her.

"So, your mom was a bad cook?" she asks, moving away from my subtle prodding and back to safer waters.

"Awful. Fortunately, she made up for it in other aspects."

"Such as?"

"She loved me fiercely."

"That's sweet."

I want to ask Emily about her parents, but I don't want to pick at a scab, so I leave it alone. I'm sure she'll talk about them when she's good and ready.

"What's in the box?" she asks, pointing toward the kitchen counter.

"I brought dessert."

"What is it?"

"I'll show you once you finish your meal," I tease.

"Funny."

"I hope you're a fan of Italian desserts."

"You had me at sugar."

"Good. Then you'll enjoy my offering."

"I'm sure I will."

"Did you have fun today?"

"Clothes shopping?"

"Yes. And talking to Sandy."

"Yes, to both. She's a lovely person."

"Sandy is very special to me."

"You said you grew up together?"

"We did. She's a few years older than I am, so she appointed herself my protector when we were kids. She's a tough cookie. Don't let her sweet smile fool you. She can whoop ass with the best of them."

Emily laughs. It's good to see her relaxed.

14

EMILY

Have I forgiven Lucas for kidnapping me? A little. I understand now why he did it, but some days are hard. Today, however, isn't one of those days.

I've been awake since 6 a.m. Lucas and I, plus his gang of muscleheads and whoever else he's planning on taking, are flying to Paris today. I've always wanted to visit this romantic city. I can't wait to see the art galleries and the old buildings, and from what Lucas has told me, his chateau overlooks the Eiffel Tower. He says the lights at night over Paris are beautiful and I intend to soak it all in.

I need some fresh inspiration for my work. I haven't painted anything noteworthy since David's death, and I think it's high time I got my mojo back. I know my brother loved my art. He wouldn't want me to waste my talent.

It's 9 a.m. when Dominick knocks on the bedroom door.

"I'll be out in a second."

I'm going to a city where style is king, so I'm wearing a white Chanel suit to celebrate the occasion. It's gorgeous. There certainly are perks to shopping on someone else's dime, especially when it's at a boutique.

Dominick smiles at me when I open the door.

"You look beautiful," he says.

"Thank you, Dom."

"I'll take your bags."

He waits for me to exit the room before he grabs the suitcase I've packed for the trip. I haven't gone overboard. We'll only be there for six days. Mind you, that's plenty of time to collect a few small souvenirs, I'm sure.

"Thanks, Dom."

The flight from Los Angeles to Paris takes ten hours. I imagine that Lucas and I will be traveling first class. Safety is an issue. Who knows how many enemies are out to get us?

"The Boss is meeting us at the airport," Dominick announces, heading for the door.

"Oh, okay."

Dominick opens the black SUV's passenger door for me. I settle in for the trip to the airport.

Dominick sits next to me, behind the driver and co-driver. There are always at least two men with me when I go anywhere. It must be the magic number to keep me from harm. I feel a bit like a pop star with her entourage of hangers on. I half expect the paparazzi to leap out from behind a building.

"What airline are we taking?" I ask Dom.

"The Boss prefers to use his own plane."

Impressive. Lucas' organization must be raking in the cash. I try not to think about the manner in which they make their money. Today is an exciting day, one of almost zero that I've enjoyed in the last few months. I intend on focusing on the bright side.

The driver takes us to a private entrance once we arrive at the airstrip. Lucas is already on board when I board the Gulfstream G650ER.

"Good morning," he smiles.

"Hi. Nice wings."

"Thanks. It gets me where I need to be. Please make yourself comfortable. Would you like a drink?"

"I'd love a coffee, thanks."

"Olivia, would you bring my guest a cup of coffee, please?" Lucas asks the flight attendant.

"Cappuccino?" she asks.

"That would be nice, thank you."

"Have you eaten? Are you hungry?" Lucas adds.

"I'm fine, thanks."

"Well, there's plenty of food onboard. It's a twelve hour flight, depending on the weather."

"Plenty of time to brush up on my French."

"Mais bien sûr."

"Très bien. So, will anyone else be joining us, or is this it?" I ask, looking around the cabin.

"Yes. Andreas is coming along. I'll introduce you."

"Do I get to ask him what he does, or is that also need-to-know?"

"Andreas is my right hand man."

"That's all I'm going to get, isn't it?"

"Clever girl."

"What can I say? I'm a quick study."

"Of that, I have no doubt."

Once we're in the air, Dominick and the other two bodyguards disappear, giving me the illusion that I am once again a free woman. I suppose there isn't much chance of harm coming to me in the air.

Andreas is the stoic sort. I judge him to be more or less the same age as Lucas. He's polite and intelligent. I wonder what exactly it is that he does, but I'm learning to keep my curiosity to myself. I imagine I'll be more likely to stay out of harm's way if I ask as few questions as possible.

Lucas and Andreas leave me behind in the main cabin while they talk in the office. Would Lucas tie me up and gag me if I attempted to use the onboard phone to call Dannie? Probably. I don't want to make waves at this stage of our relationship. We've been getting along so well that I'd hate to overplay my hand and force him to lock me away again.

I enjoy a light lunch while Lucas and Andreas are talking. I'm thankful that it's a private plane because I've never been particularly good at sitting still. After lunch, I walk around the cabin so I can stretch my legs.

"Can I get you anything, ma'am?" the flight attendant asks politely.

"Oh, no thanks, Olivia. I'm stretching out a bit."

"That's a beautiful suit you're wearing."

"Thank you."

"Is it Chanel?"

"It is. You have a good eye, Olivia."

LYDIA HALL

"I'm studying fashion design in my spare time."

"That must be tricky."

"Not really. Mr. Lucchese is very generous, and I get a lot of time off between scheduled flights."

Olivia is very pretty. I can't help but wonder if that has anything to do with Lucas' generosity. What the hell? That thought came out of nowhere. Am I jealous? Surely not. Lucas and I had one crazy sexual encounter. That's it. Why the hell would I be thinking about his other conquests right now?

"How sweet of him," I say nonchalantly.

It's nice to have a conversation with another woman. I feel as if I've been locked away with no one to talk to but Lucas and occasionally Dominick. Not that I feel the need to talk about handbags and pumps, but even so.

Lucas reappears at around 6 p.m. while I'm flipping through a magazine, trying to keep myself occupied.

"Hi. How are you holding up? You're welcome to watch a movie if you like."

"Maybe later."

"Are you bored?"

"No. I know how to entertain myself. You and Andreas have been at it for a long time. How's Operation World Domination coming along?"

"Swimmingly, if you must know. What have you been up to?"

"Oh, not much. Reading, eating, checking the cabin for parachutes."

"Still plotting your escape, are you?" he grins. "Or are you thinking of using the ropes for other, more pleasurable uses?"

Am I blushing? Because it sure feels like I am. My ears are hot, and my face is tingling at Lucas' remark. All I can think about is the belt he used to tie me up while he rocked my world.

"What time is dinner?"

"Nicely sidestepped," he laughs. "We can eat whenever you like."

"Good. All this sitting around is making me hungry."

Lucas is staring at me. His gaze is far too erotic for comfort. I gather from his comment that he too is thinking about sex. I read somewhere once that men think about sex about nineteen times a day on average, and I bet that Lucas is knee deep in one of those times right now.

* * *

It's morning when we land in Paris. I managed to sleep through the night, so I'm well rested. The city is her captivating self as we drive along the streets to Lucas' chateau. I'm happy to be back on land, and I intend to see as much of this stunning place as I can.

"My first meeting is only tomorrow. Are you up for some sightseeing?" Lucas asks as we enter the gates of his chateau.

"Definitely."

"Where would you like to go first?"

"I'd love to visit the Louvre. I've been dreaming of walking its hallowed halls since I was knee high to a grasshopper."

"Le Louvre it is, then."

"I take it we'll have more freedom here."

"Why do you ask?"

"The idea of wearing a baseball cap with this Chanel suit sends shivers down my spine."

Lucas laughs. He's so handsome.

Pull yourself together, Emily. He's still the man responsible for David's death. Don't forget that.

"I think we can dispense with the cap while we're in Paris."

"Magnifique!"

Arriving at the chateau is akin to a scene from a classic French period piece. The staff line the driveway as we pull up outside. Lucas gets out before me and heads for a woman, whom I assume to be the housekeeper. She smiles happily when she sees her master. Good grief! It's as if he's royalty or something.

Dominick opens the door for me. I join Lucas as he talks to the tall woman with the blonde braid.

"Madame Fournier, may I introduce Emily, my houseguest?"

"Au chante, Emily."

"Et vous, Madame."

"No, please, call me Sylvie," she smiles.

"Did you have a pleasant journey, Emily?"

"Yes, thank you. I'm glad to be back on land, though."

"Oui, I'm not a fan of flying," she winks. "Come, let me show you your suite."

"I'll meet you downstairs in half an hour," Lucas says.

"Okay."

My suite has a breathtaking view of the tower and the Seine River. The chateau itself is turn of the century with modern Parisian touches. So chic.

"I will personally take care of your bags for you, Emily."

"Thank you, Sylvi. What a beautiful room."

"Indeed. Mr. Lucchese has impeccable taste."

Is there anything Lucas can't do? A successful businessman with great taste in the finer things in life and a fantastic lover—what am I missing? Oh, yes, there it is. He's in the mob.

"I gather."

"I'll leave you to freshen up,"

"Thank you."

I spend a few minutes looking out over the streets of Paris. I wonder what Dannie would say if she could see me now. It should be one of the best experiences of my life. What a pit it is under such auspicious circumstances. But I did say I was going to focus on the positive, and I'm going to stick to that no matter what.

It's very warm outside, so I change into a summer dress before I meet Lucas downstairs. He's waiting for me and watches me intently as I descend the large staircase. My stomach is awash with butterflies as his bedroom eyes lock on mine.

"You look stunning," he says in a low voice.

"Thank you. Care of Sandy and my benefactor," I smile.

"Ready to see Paris?"

"So ready."

Lucas gives me his left arm, and together we walk to the car. He opens the door for me so I can slip onto the leather seat.

Soon we're on our way to one of the most beautiful museums in the world. I open the window a tad so I can take in the sounds of the romantic city.

"Oh, Lucas! It's absolutely magical," I gasp as the museum comes into view.

"Yes, it's spectacular in the flesh, isn't it?"

"It's so big."

"Wait until you're inside."

"You've been?"

"Yes, once. A long time ago."

I feel like a kid in a candy store. I can't wait to see the art. Being here is surreal, and I have the most unlikely source to thank. Who would have guessed that I'd be here with someone like Lucas?

"If you're a good girl, I'll treat you to a drink in the Tuileries gardens. It's an experience."

"Oh? And what exactly constitutes good, in your opinion?"

"Hey, I'm sure we can work out something," he grins.

"Yeah. I bet you could."

15

LUCAS

I love watching the expression on Emily's face while she walks through the Louvre, stopping at each painting and admiring and scrutinizing the various artists' brush strokes. She's like a kid in a candy store. All bright eyed with wonder.

"This one's a little dark," I comment as Emily stops in front of one of the paintings.

"I know. Isn't it wonderful? It's called The Raft of the Medusa. The artist is depicting the survivors of the Medusa shipwreck calling for help when they see the outline of another ship that could save them in the distance."

"What about those poor bastards?"

"Oh, they're the casualties."

"I suppose there are always casualties."

"You should know," she says, looking at me briefly to check that I can't reach the knife in my back.

LYDIA HALL

"Okay, I deserve that. What's going on here?" I ask, pointing to a painting a few meters away.

"Oh, that. An interesting one. It's Gabrielle d'Estrées and one of her sisters."

"Is it normal for sisters to pinch each other's nipples?"

"Yeah, this painting draws attention for its erotic nature. Some people assume that it also announces the pregnancy of Gabrielle d'Estrées. Her sister's gesture would indicate her future status as a mother."

"Leave it to those cheeky 16th Century artists, hey," I grin.

"Uh-huh."

All this nipple talk is making me horny. Not that I need anymore inspiration in that department. Emily draped in a paper bag would do the trick. I'm aroused at the mere thought of her silky skin under my fingers.

The two of us spend the next hour meandering through the exhibitions—Emily, spellbound by the art, and I, by the stunning woman beside me.

"I could do with a drink," I comment after having had my fill of art.

"Yeah. Art appreciation is thirsty work," Emily smiles.

"Shall we go to one of the restaurants in the garden?"

"That would be nice."

She and I walk for a while when she stops and turns to me.

"Thank you for today, Lucas."

"Does that mean that I'm a little less monstrous in your eyes?"

"Perhaps a little, yes. But don't get carried away. I'm still mad at you."

"Oh, how could I forget?" I smirk.

"How, indeed."

Emily's smile is the kind that can make a man forget anything, including common sense. I know that getting too close to her is potentially a terrible idea for both of us. But how can I stay away? She's like a magnet, pulling me in. I'm helpless when it comes to her charm, even when she isn't even trying to seduce me.

"Are you hungry?" I ask, hoping to distract myself from obsessing about her beautiful body.

"Starving."

"Good. They serve fantastic poached salmon on beet tapenade with crème fraîche and dill."

"Yum. I'm in."

"I thought you might like that."

"How is it that you know so much about what's on the menu?"

"Okay, you got me. I googled it while you were gushing over the art back there."

Emily's laughter fills the garden.

"Clever boy."

"I do have a few redeeming qualities."

"Apparently so. Do you travel to Europe often?" Emily asks once we're seated.

"Yes, quite a bit. We have business interests here, and I've always been the one to meet with our associates."

"You make it all sound so normal."

"Business is business."

"Sure, but not all *trades* are created equal."

"Touché."

"Is it safe? This time around, I mean."

"We have no mortal enemies here, if that's what you're asking."

"Fair enough."

"How long have you been *the boss*?"

"Why do you ask?"

"No reason. Making conversation."

"I'd prefer to talk about something else."

"Fine. Tell me about your childhood."

"What would you like to know?"

"Well, I know you don't have siblings and that your mother was a poor cook. What about your father?"

"Not much to tell, really. Frank Lucchese was a quiet man who believed in hard work and discipline."

"Excellent qualities in a man."

"Yeah. It's a pity his qualities didn't do him any good. He died a mediocre man with a meager pension."

"Is that why you got into your career? More money?"

"I watched my father being used as a doormat all his life. There's no way I'll ever settle for mediocrity."

"One man's mediocrity is another man's peace."

"It seems you missed your calling, young Emily. You should have gone into the field of psychology," I smirk.

"And miss out on all this?" she says, waving her arms around.

"I loved my father. I wish he was still around so I could spoil him with the things he never had."

"I'm sure he'd be proud of your accomplishments."

I'm not entirely sure if Emily is insulting me or if her comment is genuine, but it's been such a lovely afternoon that I decide it's best to let it go. I don't feel like arguing with my beautiful companion.

Lunch is a triumph. The food is perfect, and the company is stimulating. Emily talks to me about her love for art and how she's always wanted to paint since she was a child. Her passion is contagious. I fear I'm starting to have very real feelings toward this enigmatic woman. It's a dangerous place I've put myself in, and I'm not sure I care to stop it from developing into a romantic relationship.

We spend the rest of the afternoon chatting and walking the streets of Paris. I haven't been this relaxed in a long time. Emily is a pill.

"Dinner at the chateau is usually a fancy affair," I say once we're on our way back.

"Oh? It's a good thing I packed my Sunday best," Emily says in a snooty accent.

"The staff have done it for centuries, and I appreciate tradition, so."

"No, I get it. When in Rome…"

"Cute. Are you comfortable in your suite?"

"Hey, it isn't the dungeonesque accommodations I've become accustomed to, but it will do."

"I fear I may be spoiling you," I chuckle, as we drive into the estate.

* * *

Emily is standing at the landing at the top of the staircase. She's wearing a figure hugging, pale yellow evening gown with her hair in a

French braid. I can hardly breathe as she slowly descends the stairs. The woman is magnificent!

"Wow," I say once she's at the bottom, "you look stunning, Emily."

"Thank you, Lucas."

"The dining room is this way."

Emily glides along next to me. I'm wearing a suit and tie.

"A stranger would think that we're dining with royalty," she remarks.

"Well, you do look like a queen tonight."

"You're too kind, sir. Where is Andreas?"

"He's visiting friends in Fontainebleau, so he won't be joining us this evening."

"Romantic dinner for two, then? Should I be on my guard?"

"What? Are you worried that you'll be unable to resist my charm?"

She grins but doesn't answer. My sexy dinner guest is toying with me, and I'm rather enjoying the game.

"Bonsoir, Monsieur Lucchese."

"Good evening, Philipe."

"Madam," the butler says, pulling out Emily's chair.

"Merci beaucoup, Philippe."

Emily is seated across from me. Her beautiful eyes follow my every move. Throughout dinner, I'm completely focused on her every move, and by the time it's over, all I can think about is ripping off her stunning dress.

"What a wonderful meal," she says while I'm escorting her to her suite.

"The chef certainly pulled out all the stops."

The sexual tension is at an all time high by the time we reach her door.

"Would you like to come in for a nightcap?" Emily offers.

Nightcap? No. Frantic sex? Absolutely!

"Is that wise?"

She smiles and enters her suite, leaving the door open. I guess Emily is leaving the ball in my court. How fortunate for both of us that I'm an excellent ball player.

The object of my desire is standing at the window when I enter after her—my sole mission is to conquer. Neither one of us says a word as I shorten the distance between us. I'm moving faster now. I want to be with Emily. My body is crying out for hers.

I remove my tie before I reach Emily. The silky fabric is soft and pliable—perfect for what I have in mind. Tonight I want my lover to enjoy the experience of touch without sight, so I place the tie over her eyes and secure it.

I take Emily by the hand and lead her over to the oak poster bed. Her hand is trembling in mine, and the feeling of being in control of such an exquisite creature is more exciting than anything I've ever experienced before.

"Do you trust me?" I whisper into her ear, nibbling on the lobe.

"Yes," she exhales shakily.

I tear a strip off the silk sheet and fashion it into two ties. Next, I bind each of her hands to the bedpost, taking great care not to chafe her delicate skin. Emily is shaking now. She has goosebumps in the places where I explore her silky flesh with my tongue.

Let's play, my beauty.

I remove my clothes while Emily is still fully clothed. I place my shaft near her mouth, and she instinctively takes me in and caresses me with her warm tongue. I'm careful not to linger inside her mouth for too long, so pull away and start undressing her.

I reach under her dress and pull off her panties. Emily is wet with excitement. I want her bare, so I rip the straps of her dress and slide it off. She gasps at the unexpected action. The only piece of garment left is her bra. It's delicate and tears easily.

Finally, I have her how I've dreamed of ever since our first kiss. Naked and all to myself.

"You are perfect, my darling," I say in a voice thick with desire.

I'm kissing her now, running my fingers along her body, tweaking, caressing, and teasing. Emily moans as soon as I reach her core with my mouth. She tastes so good.

"Please," she whispers. "I want you inside me."

"Patience, my beauty."

I tease her some more with my tongue.

"Open your mouth," I command, and my lover complies without question.

I slide into her mouth once more, reveling in the warmth and tightness it provides.

It's time. I want to be inside this woman. I need to possess every inch of her. Emily spreads her legs as soon as I pull out of her mouth. I know she's ready.

"What do you want?" I whisper.

"You. I want you, Lucas."

I suck on her nipple before I drive into her perfect mound. Emily lets out a muffled cry as I move in and out of her. Her hands are balled into fists as she moves her hips to meet mine with every surge.

I stare at her raptured face as she gasps for air and moans with exquisite pleasure. Our bodies settle into a rhythm as we lose ourselves in the throes of sublime passion.

"Harder!" she moans.

I acquiesce, determined to satisfy my queen. Harder, faster, and deeper. Our bodies are wet with perspiration now as we slide and grind against one another. Emily is close to climaxing. I can sense it by the way she's arching her back.

"Cum for me, my beauty," I command.

My lover cranes her neck and pushes her hips tightly against mine when she climaxes, trembling throughout the duration of her orgasm. I caress her breasts until she stops moving, clearly spent.

Now it's my turn. I don't hold back now that I know my partner is satisfied. I untie the binds so that she can dig her nails into me while I drive hard into her. Emily holds onto my buttocks and pulls me in hard. Is she having another orgasm?

Yes! Together, we ride the beast until it's tamer than a lamb. I collapse onto the bed next to my lover. I've never been this satisfied after sex. This is a new experience for me. One I intend on repeating.

You're playing with fire, Lucas.

Yeah, I know. But some things are beyond my control, and Emily Thornton has just made the top of that list.

16

EMILY

We're back from Paris, but my mind is lost somewhere in the halls and rooms of the chateau. Specifically the suite in which Lucas and I spend our nights, pleasuring each other. I've never had sex like this before. The intensity of my orgasms is so new to me that I'm left wondering if it can possibly last.

Every time Lucas and I make love, I soar to higher heights. I'm hopelessly addicted to my gorgeous lover. I find myself counting the hours until he's in my presence, and I can't focus on anything but my desire for him whenever he touches me.

My mind and my body are at war. I know that falling in love with someone like Lucas can only bring pain and regret, but even so, I can't resist him. I've never been so at odds with myself, and I can't see myself escaping from this dilemma anytime soon.

"That was quite a workout," he chuckles.

We're lying in each other's arms after another killer session of passionate play.

"Hey, you're the one doing all the work," I tease.

"Would you like to change positions? I don't mind if you wish to turn the screws on me, as they say."

"Really? You wouldn't mind if I tied you up?"

"Hell, no. This is the 21st century. Women's lib and all that," he laughs.

"Good to know."

"I'm putty in your hands, my beauty," he smiles, kissing me long and slow.

"You're not afraid I may try and escape?" I tease.

"And miss out on this?" he says, throwing off the sheet so I can gaze upon his impressive erection.

"You're pretty sure of yourself, aren't you?"

"I'm not hearing any complaints," he says, kissing my neck.

"You're very playful tonight. Did you have a good day?"

"I did. And what did my little Van Gogh get up to while I was at the office?"

Lucas must no longer consider me a flight risk because I'm free to roam the estate. We had a good talk when we returned from France, and I agreed to stay with Lucas until such time as he uncovered the identity of the man who murdered David.

These days, I keep myself occupied with painting and cooking. It feels at times as if Lucas and I are a married couple, going about our days in the same way most newlyweds do, coming together at night to create fireworks in the bedroom. It feels more natural than I ever would have anticipated.

"Is it weird that this feels so normal?" I ask him without fear of laying bare my feelings.

"Oh, good. So you feel it too? I thought it was just me."

"No," I say quickly, rolling onto my side so I can see his face. "It's crazy, but I feel as if we have known each other all our lives."

"Kismet, I think they call it. Isn't there a painting somewhere that depicts instances like these?" he teases.

"Yeah, I'm sure if you look closely at The Raft of the Medusa, you'll see us hanging somewhere off the back of the sinking structure."

"And you call my world dark. Why the pessimism?"

"You have to admit that ours isn't your typical love story."

"No, but couples have to start somewhere. Are you not happy?"

"I'm cautiously optimistic."

"Our relationship is as much a surprise to me as it is to you, Emily."

"I know. It does worry me, though."

"What does?"

"Your world. It's a dangerous one, Lucas."

"I know, my love, but I'll protect you. I swear."

"I know you'll try your best to keep me safe. It may not be enough, though."

"Come on, my beauty," he says, kissing my forehead. "Don't dwell on the negative. We have something special. We should celebrate it every day."

"Okay. I'll try."

"I'll help," he says before kissing me passionately.

* * *

"It's time, Lucas," I say one evening after dinner.

"Time?"

"I've done everything you've asked of me. I'm careful when I go outside; I haven't spoken to anyone who knows me, and I haven't tried to *escape* your protection. But there's one thing I want to do."

"I have a feeling I know what you're going to say."

"Please, Lucas. I want to make contact with Dannie. I'll be careful, I promise. She's my best friend. She'll never do anything to put my life in danger."

Lucas stares into space as if he's trying to decide whether to grant my request or not.

"Okay," he says after a long silence. "But, please, Emily, don't tell her where you are. It's for your safety as well as hers."

"I'll be careful."

"Use the burner phone I gave you so the call can't be traced. You never know who's listening."

"I will."

"I love you, Emily."

His words catch me by surprise. Not because I don't feel the same, but because they don't gel with his tough guy persona.

"I love you, too, Lucas."

***

"Emily! I don't believe it…where…where the fuck have you been? I've been out of my mind with worry! I thought you were dead!"

"I'm so sorry, Dannie. I wanted to call you but…"

"Where the hell are you? Are you okay?"

"I'm fine. I'm with a friend."

"Bullshit! I know all your friends, and none of them have the faintest idea where you are. What friend?"

"I can't tell you, Dannie. I'm so sorry. Please forgive me. Are you alright?"

I can hear Dannie's crying. My heart breaks for her.

"Please don't cry, Dannie. I'm so sorry."

"I'm so relieved, Ems. I thought you were dead."

"I would have been if my friend hadn't interceded."

"This must be some friend. Does the friend know who killed David?"

"Not yet, but we're working on it."

"Can I see you?"

"No, not yet. I'll keep in touch and let you know the minute the killer is no longer a threat. I promise."

"What am I supposed to tell the police? They keep checking in with me every so often to find out if I've heard from you."

"Don't talk to the police, please, Dannie. As far as they're concerned, you don't know anything."

"What? Now the cops aren't able to protect you?"

"It's complicated."

"No shit!"

"I don't want to fight with you, my friend. Please, trust me. I'm fine. I miss you."

"I miss you too, you bloody fool. Are you really okay? Promise me you're okay!"

"Yes, I swear. I'm fine."

In fact, I'm better than fine. I'm head over heels in love with Lucas.

* * *

"Sandy told me she had new stock coming in. I'd love to have a peek at it, if you don't mind."

"Hhmm, that sounds expensive," Lucas grins.

"Well, naturally." I smile sweetly, winking. "Oh, come on, babe, I've been stuck indoors for too long. You won't let me see Dannie…"

"It's too dangerous for both of you," Lucas interjects.

"Yeah, I get it. But I need female interaction, or I'll go stir crazy."

"What? Being your bitch isn't working for you anymore?" he purrs, gently biting me on the earlobe.

"Haha," I say sarcastically. "Just because you let me tie you up every now and again doesn't make you good female company."

"Ouch. Now you've hurt my feelings."

"Toughen up, buttercup. Please."

"Oh, alright. I won't be able to come with you. But you'll be okay as long as you take Dominick with you."

"Of course."

"Fine."

"Thanks, babe. I'll pick up a little something for you, too," I coo. "Perhaps something with lace that's easily torn."

"You have me wrapped around your little finger, haven't you, you clever girl?"

"I don't know what you mean," I giggle.

* * *

It's 11 a.m., and I feel like a kid about to take a ride to Willy Wonka's chocolate factory. Dominick is here in all his muscle bound glory to accompany me to Sandy's boutique.

"Are you ready?" he asks.

"Yup. Good to go, Dom. I'll just grab my purse, then we can go."

Dominick has a sidekick today. I guess Lucas wants to make sure that I'm protected to the gills.

There's a new driver, too. Am I surrounded by Lucas' dream team today? I wonder what happened to my regular driver, Ben.

"Good morning, ma'am. My name is Damon," the driver greets me as soon as I'm seated.

"My mother was a ma'am. Please call me Emily."

"It's a pleasure, Emily."

It's odd how one builds up an image in one's head about mobsters. I suppose watching too many Mafia movies will do that. I suppress the urge to laugh out loud at my naivete. I guess there's a lot about the real world that I'm yet to learn. What is that old adage? Fact is stranger than fiction. I'd say.

"Where's Ben? Why haven't I seen you before?" I ask the new driver.

"Ben is visiting family. I've been working for Mr. Lucchese for about four months now. I work mostly the night shift."

"I see."

"Don't worry, ma'...sorry, Emily, I'll take good care of you."

"I'm sure you will."

Damone isn't what I would have expected a driver in the mob to look like. He has a babyface that makes him look as if butter wouldn't melt in his mouth. I've seen tougher looking boy scouts in my time. But I guess he must be good at what he does, or Lucas wouldn't entrust my safety to him.

"Where are you from, Damon?"

"Detroit."

"LA must be quite the change of scenery for you."

"Definitely. I prefer living here. The weather is amazing, and the people are much more relaxed."

"It must be all the fresh air and the smell of sunscreen wafting through the air. It's always summer in La La Land."

"That's the truth."

Dominick doesn't say much. He's his usual stoic self as he sits next to me in the car. His sidekick sits next to Damon, watching the sideroads as we pass by, thoroughly scanning the surroundings.

I'm getting used to my entourage. At first, I was awkward in their presence, but now I hardly notice. Even so, I pray that Lucas finds the killer soon. I don't know if this is the way I want to spend the rest of my life.

Sandy is waiting for me in the store. Her bubbly greeting makes me feel right at home.

"So, how was Paris? I bet you were the best dressed beauty there by far."

"Paris was magical. I'd go back there at the drop of a beret," I grin. "I did feel like a queen, dressed in the gorgeous outfits you chose for me."

"Wait until you see the suits that have just come in. Lucas is going to bust an artery when he sees you in them."

I smile awkwardly. I don't know if talking to Sandy about Lucas and my relationship is wise. I don't know what the two of them have discussed.

"You don't have to play possum, Emily," Sandy grins. "I can see on Lucas' face that he's smitten with you."

"We're getting along," I say, not giving away much.

"Uh-huh," she says, winking. "I haven't seen Lucas 'getting along' with a woman in a while."

Now I'm intrigued.

"Oh?"

"I don't want to speak out of turn, but I have a feeling that my dear friend is in love."

I don't respond.

"You know, Emily. If there's ever anything you need to talk about, you're welcome to chat with me. Lucas and I have been friends our whole lives. Your secrets are safe with me."

"Thank you, Sandy. That's very kind of you."

"I know how it is. Lucas lives in a man's world. There aren't too many women around him. It can be a pretty hostile environment. I just want you to know that I'm here if you need to talk."

"I really appreciate that."

"Good. Enough talk. Let's play dress up. By the way, I received a new shipment of some pretty stunning undergarments too. Just putting it out there."

"It's funny you should mention it," I smirk. "I was thinking of getting a little something for Lucas."

"Honey, I've got just the thing," Sandy laughs.

This is going to be fun. Spending the day with Sandy is just what I need.

17

LUCAS

Emily has been in my life now for six months. My feelings toward her are deepening with each passing day. I can't imagine not having her in my life. We are perfect together. Her incredible wit and intelligence are as attractive as her physical beauty, and I can see myself happily spending the rest of my life with her.

At first, I thought that the age difference would be an issue. But that hasn't made the slightest difference. Emily is wiser than her years, and she brings a fresh, youthful perspective to my life that I find irresistible. I simply can't get enough of her.

My work keeps me busy, though, so I get that my young lover gets bored with her own company. I encouraged her visits with Sandy. First, because I trust my best friend implicitly, and second, because I know that Emily needs female company. Daniella is out of the question, as the enemy is aware of their friendship and is no doubt watching Emily's best friend's moves closely. I can't take that risk.

The friends do talk telephonically, and so far, Emily is satisfied with that arrangement. I'm happy that she trusts me enough to respect my wishes.

"I'm going out of town next week," I say during our late dinner together.

"Can I ask where?"

"Baltimore."

"Okay. I take it I won't be coming along for this trip."

"Sorry, babe. Not this one. I'll be too busy with back to back meetings to spend time with you."

"Plus, it's dangerous. Right?"

"Am I that transparent?"

"No. I've learned to read you, that's all."

"I should have known you'd be this perceptive. It looks like I'm going to have to work on my poker face."

"Your poker face is fine. It's me. I get you."

"Do you, now?"

"Yup."

"Can you tell how much I'm going to miss you?"

"Uh-huh. You're going to be completely miserable," she smiles.

"My little gypsy," I chuckle.

"What will become of me if anything happens to you, Lucas?"

There's a worry line on Emily's face that I haven't seen in a while.

"Why do you think about such things? Has something happened?"

"No. I just worry."

"Nothing is going to happen to me, my love."

"That's what we all think until it's too late. Until we're staring into the face of death."

"Are you okay? This isn't like you, Emily."

"Yeah," she says, shrugging her shoulders. "I'm just having an overly sensitive day, I guess."

I get up and take her by the hand so she can stand, facing me.

"I don't want you to worry about such things, my love. That's my job, and I happen to be pretty good at it."

I kiss my beautiful Emily passionately and hold her in my arms for a while afterward.

"Hormones," she says, wiping away a tear.

"You're okay. We're okay."

"Promise me you'll be careful, Lucas."

"I promise."

* * *

The pilot clicks on the overhead speaker and announces that the plane is descending. Soon we'll be on the runway in Baltimore. I haven't been here in a while. Our expansion is well under way, which is why I decided to meet with Baltimore Capos personally rather than sending one of my generals. It's a sign of respect.

It isn't often that the boss visits, so I believe they've made quite the fuss. I hope it isn't too outlandish. I prefer flying under the radar.

I call Emily from the car once we've landed.

"Hi, my beauty."

"Hi, babe. How was your flight?"

"Pretty boring without you here. What do you have planned for today?"

"Sandy and I are going out to lunch. There's a new restaurant she wants to show me."

"Sounds like fun. Give her my love, will you?"

"Of course."

"Gotta run. I love you."

"I love you too."

*　*　*

Emily

I'm not feeling my vest today. I hate it when Lucas is away. I worry that he will get hurt, and sometimes I entertain the awful thought that he won't come back at all. I know it's not the way to live my life—fear is a destructive force that eats one out from the inside.

I suppose David's death triggered my unconscious fear of loss and abandonment, which took me many years to repress. I thought I'd dealt with all of that after my parents died, but now I'm right back where I started. In fact, I fear that it's worse now that David is dead too.

My fear is starting to manifest itself in my physical being now. I've been nauseous for a few days, and I can only put it down to Lucas' trip away. I've even thought of canceling lunch with Sandy, but it's the only time I get to relax and enjoy a *normal* life.

Come on, Ems. You can do this. You'll feel much better afterward.

"Hello, Emily. How are you today?"

Damon is in the driver's seat. He tips his head in recognition when I get into the back seat.

"Hi, Damon. Yeah, good, thanks. How about you?"

He and I have been chatting for a few months now. Every time he drives me somewhere, we end up having interesting conversations. Ben was lovely, but Damine is closer in age to me, so we have that generational familiarity that a much older Ben and I didn't share.

"You never talk about a partner. Anyone special back in Detroit, Damon?"

"Nope. Too many Custos in my hood."

"Custos?"

"Girls who buy and use recreational drugs from dealers."

"Hm. Yup, not attractive."

"No, ma'am. The women and the dundos here are much better."

"Translate, please," I chuckle.

"Oh, sorry. The money."

"For sure. LA is where it's at. Is your family back there?"

"Yeah. My mom."

"She must miss you."

"She does, but she doesn't complain when I send home the cheque."

"You're a good son, Damon."

"I try. How about your folks?"

"They died when I was a teenager."

"Oh, I'm so sorry. Forgive me."

"It's okay. It seems like a lifetime ago."

"This is none of my business, I know, so please tell me to zip it if I'm overstepping. But I heard about your brother. I'm very sorry for your loss."

I guess the news of David's demise is out there.

"Thank you."

"I know how you must feel. My brother died last year."

"Oh, I'm so sorry, Damon."

"Thanks. It's one of the reasons I left Detroit. Too painful to stick around."

"I know what you mean. Sometimes I feel like running away myself. Somewhere far, where there are no memories of all this death," I say softly, more to myself than to Damon."

"Were the two of you close?"

"Very."

"You?"

"Yes. David was my best friend. I miss him so much."

"I hope Mr. Lucchese finds the man who did it. He should pay."

We drive in silence for the rest of the way to the restaurant. I'm deep in my own thoughts about what the hell I'm doing with someone like Lucas who lives in such a crazy world, and I imagine Damon is battling his own demons.

* * *

"Thank you for a lovely lunch, Sandy."

"My pleasure, darling. Are you okay?"

"Yeah, why?"

"You look a little pale today. I hope you're not coming down with the California two step."

"The what?"

"There's a cheeky little tummy bug doing its rounds again. I blame the tourists. Heaven knows what they drag into town with them while they're here."

"Ugh. I hope not. I have been feeling a little under the weather. I'm sure I'll bounce back."

"Of course, you will. You're young."

"It's not as if you're circling the drain, Sandy," I laugh.

"Darling, compared to you, I'm ancient."

"You're hysterical."

"Sure. Laugh at my pain," she chuckles.

"See you soon, Sandy," I say, kissing her on the cheek.

"See ya, kid."

It's 4 p.m. and the traffic is getting hairy.

"I'll take the backroads," Damon says. "It will be quicker."

"Thanks. Oh, can you stop at the drugstore on the way? I need to pick up something."

"Of course."

Dominick gets out of the car with me once we're at the drugstore. He follows me in and checks around while I talk to the pharmacist.

"Hi, can I help you?"

"Yeah. I'm feeling awful. I think it may be the stomach flu. What do you suggest?" I ask the woman behind the counter, wearing the lab coat.

LYDIA HALL

"Yes, it's a nasty one. Are you pregnant? I have to ask before I can prescribe anything."

Pregnant? Hell no! That would be a complete disaster. I do a quick calculation in my head before I answer her.

Let's see now. It's been…hang on…when did I have my last period? My cycle is one of those that has a mind of its own. It's been that way since I was a teen. I'd get my menses at the worst times—usually when I wasn't anywhere near prepared—and then, just like that, it would stay away for a while.

My doctor told me that stress from my parents' deaths was most likely to blame. Recently, after David's death, it's been acting up again.

"Uhm, I don't think so. I doubt it."

"You need to check. Just to be sure. Here, I'll throw in a pregnancy test into the bag. Just in case. Do the test first before you take these," she says, holding up a bottle filled with tablets.

"Okay. Thanks."

I'm not worried. My periods are so erratic that an accidental pregnancy isn't something I've ever worried about. This is a tummy bug. Plain and simple.

I decide to take the test as soon as I get some so that I can start with the tummy bug meds. The sooner I get this over with, the sooner I'll feel better.

I pee on the stick and place it on the side of the basin while I wash my hands. My cell phone buzzes. It must be a message from Lucas. He promised he'd keep in touch, so I wouldn't worry.

Hey, my beauty. How was lunch with Sandy? I've been stuck in meetings all day. Would rather be there with you. By the way, I'm playing with my tie. Keeps me thinking about you. Haha.

XXX

How adorable.

Hey, you. Lunch was good, thanks. Sandy sends her love. Silk tie. My mind goes wild with possibilities. Wish you were here, too.

XXX

I've all but forgotten the test by the time I make my way back to the bathroom. Are those rings under my eyes, I wonder while I stare at my reflection in the mirror. Man, this bug has me by the short and curlies.

Where did I put the paper bag with the meds? I look around. There it is. Next to the pregnancy test. I'll just…

What the…

No! No, no, no…

This is impossible. No, ridiculous is the right word. It's a dream. It must be. I have to wake up. I pinch myself and yelp at the pain.

There are two lines in the windows on the pregnancy test. I've never seen that before. This is a disaster. It can't be. I'm even more nauseous now, probably from the shock.

F.U.C.K!

What the hell am I going to tell Lucas? I can't have a baby now? This is insane. Shit!

* * *

It's been two days since I discovered that I'm pregnant and my mind has been racing ever since. I don't have the strength to tell Lucas that I'm carrying our child, so I've been avoiding his calls, pretending to be busy.

I know it won't be long before he cottons onto the fact that I'm ghosting him. Damn it, I don't know what to do. I don't want my child born into Lucas' world! What kind of a future will it have, surrounded by gangsters and guns? This wasn't supposed to happen. I wasn't supposed to fall in love with the man who was the cause of my brother's death!

What am I supposed to do now? I know if I tell Lucas he'll want to do the honorable thing and get married. I don't know if I'm ready for that. How will he even feel about it? Does he want children? We haven't gotten to that part of our relationship yet. For all I know Lucas could be vehemently opposed to having kids.

The last thing I want to do is force my lover into some sort of union born out of guilt. I need to think this through for everyone's sake before I make a terrible mistake.

18

EMILY

"Dannie. I have to talk to you."

"Ems! What's wrong? What's happened?"

Dannie's voice is full of trepidation when she hears my tone. My best friend has always known me so well. I need to talk to her about the pregnancy. She'll know what to do.

"I'm pregnant."

"What? How? I mean, who? Who's the father?"

This is gonna sting like hell!

"Lucas."

"Lucas? I don't understand."

"I'm with Lucas. He's the man who took me."

"Woah, back up. The gorgeous Lucas you went on one date with? That Lucas?"

"Yes."

"You're going to have to back up and explain this to me, Ems. Why would Lucas take you?"

"Because he was David's boss."

"What the fuck? You mean his mobster boss?"

"Uh-huh."

"I don't believe this."

"Yes, I know. I was just as shocked as you are when he told me."

"No shit! What's his deal, anyway? Why did he take you?"

"To keep me safe. Lucas told me that David was murdered to get to him. He wants to keep me safe."

"I can't believe you've kept all this from me, Emily! What the hell were you thinking?"

"I know. I know. It's a mess. I never meant for this to happen, Dannie."

"A baby! Man, this is heavy. Do you love him?"

"Yes."

"Holy crap, Ems."

"Yeah."

"Does he love you?"

"He does. But I don't know, Dannie. How can I have a child with a mafia boss?"

"I'm not gonna lie, Emily. This is not ideal. What did he say?"

"I haven't told him yet. Lucas is away on business. I only just found out. I'm so shocked' I'm not sure how I'm going to tell him. I don't think I'm ready."

"Give yourself some time to get used to the idea first. There's no rush. It's early days."

"I can't believe it, Dannie. I'm going to be a mom."

"I know it isn't under the best circumstances, but are you happy?"

"About the baby?"

"Yes."

"I don't know. It's a big step. Life Changing."

"I wish I was there with you, Ems."

"So do I. But Lucas insists that it isn't safe. I have to stay out of sight until he finds David's killer."

"It's been more than six months already, Ems. Is he ever going to find out who did it? You can't hide from the world for the rest of your life. Especially now that you're pregnant."

"You need to be with people who love and support you. People like me."

"I know, Dannie. I miss you so much."

I know she's right. This is no life for me—hiding like a hermit. I want to be free to enjoy this baby. Not hide away in a house, behind locked doors and security fences. I should never have listened to Lucas. I should have gone away with Dannie. But now it's too late. I'm trapped. Why can't Lucas be a regular guy? Why did I fall in love with a mobster?

* * *

I made an appointment with the doctor. I need to know that my baby is okay. It's been such a shock that I'm a ball of nerves. I know that can't be good for a pregnancy.

"Good morning, Dom. I need to go to town this afternoon. Can you arrange the car for me, please?"

"Of course. What time?"

"Let's leave at 2:30."

I have an uneasy feeling. Something's been niggling at me since last night. I can't put my finger on the problem, but I have a sense of foreboding that I simply can't shake.

It's time to go, and Damon has pulled the car around. I get in when Dom opens the door for me.

"Hello, Emily."

"Hi, Damon."

"How are you doing?"

"Okay."

"Just okay? Anything I can do to help?"

"I don't think so."

"Okay. I'm here if you need anything."

"Great. Thanks."

I'm sure you'll be a fantastic help! Do you have a magic wand that will make my nightmare go away? Yeah, I didn't think so.

The OBGYN is running late. Great. More free time to sit around and contemplate the depth of the hole I'm in. I sit and stare out of the window. A pregnant woman walks into the office. She's with her husband. The couple can't keep their hands off each other. They look truly excited about the little bundle. Will Lucas feel that way when I tell him?

"Miss Thornton?"

"Yeah."

"We're ready for you."

"Okay. Thanks."

I follow the assistant to a room where she takes my vitals.

"The doctor will be with you in just a moment," she says, showing me to an examination room.

I nod and take a seat at the desk. The door opens a few minutes later.

"Hello, I'm Dr. Lee. I am pleased to meet you."

"Hi. Emily."

"I see congratulations are in order. How are you feeling, Emily? Is this your first pregnancy?"

"Yes, my first. I'm feeling okay. The nausea is killing me, though."

"Oh, yes. There is that. Don't be too concerned. It will pass soon enough."

"I certainly hope so."

"Do you know how far along you are?"

"Not really. I'm not generally regular when it comes to my menses."

"Okay. That's not a problem. Let's do an ultrasound. That should tell us what we need to know. Won't you get undressed for me, please? You can change into that gown over there."

I do as she asks before I lie down on the examination bed. The doctor does a breast exam before she squirts cold jelly onto my abdomen.

"Sorry, it's always a bit chilly," she smiles. "Okay, let's see what we have here."

I watch the monitor while she moves the transducer around.

"Ah, there we go. Meet your baby, Emily."

I know I should be ecstatic, but I'm stressed. A baby! Wow! There's a tiny human inside of me. Lucas and I are having a baby.

All of a sudden, I'm struggling to breathe.

"Are you alright, Emily?" the doctor asks. "Here, let me help you."

She helps me sit up so I can take a few deep breaths.

"I'll be okay."

"Do you have a support system, Emily? Having a baby can be very daunting if you're trying to do it alone. I can put you in touch with a support network if you like."

"No. That's alright. Thank you, doctor."

"Okay. Please feel free to be honest with me. Whatever we discuss stays between us."

"I know. Thank you. How far along am I?"

"By the size of the embryonic sac, I'd say you're about six weeks along. Give or take a few days."

"When will I start showing?"

"That depends. All women are different. It all depends on your build and the size of the baby. Typically, most women start showing around four months, but that isn't a hard and fast rule."

"Okay."

"Forgive me for asking, but are you in a relationship with the father of your baby?"

"Uh, yes."

"Does he know about the pregnancy?"

"No. I haven't told him yet."

"I see."

"I will. Just not right now."

"I'm here if you need any assistance, Emily. Please call on me if I can help."

"Thank you, Doc. That's very kind of you."

She writes a prescription for pregnancy vitamins and supplements while I get dressed. I thank her and leave.

Now that it's official. I'll have to tell Lucas sooner rather than later.

"Is everything okay?" Damon asks on our drive back to the estate.

"Uh-huh."

"Okay."

He sounds unconvinced. Not surprisingly. I'm not exactly selling it.

He starts to say something, but he's cut short by a sudden, shattering noise. I look to my right in panic. Dominick's full weight is on me, and I'm finding it almost impossible to breathe. What the hell is happening?

"Dom!" I shout, but he doesn't move.

"Stay down, Emily," Damon screams at me over the chaos.

Stay down? I couldn't move if I wanted to. Dominick weighs a ton!

"What's happening, Damon?" I yell out in panic.

Dom is wet and sticky. It's his blood! He's bleeding all over me. Oh, no!

"Dom!" I shout again, hoping he'll respond.

But he isn't moving. Is he dead? Who's shooting at us? This is a nightmare, and I'm terrified. Damine is driving like a maniac. He takes the corner so quickly and sharply that Dom's body is flung off me.

"Hold on!" Damon shouts again. "Stay away from the window!"

I close my eyes and scrunch down as far as I can. It's finally happening. David's killer has found me, and he's determined to kill me too.

"They're following us," Damon shouts again. "I'm going to give them the slip," he shouts. "Hold on."

I bite down hard on my teeth as he snakes the streets of LA, trying to lose the car that's following us.

Damon stops suddenly and jumps out of the car. He opens the back door and pulls Dominick out of the car, so I can get out.

"Are you okay? Are you hurt?" he says, looking me up and down.

"No. I'm fine. Is Dom…"

"He's gone. We have to go, Emily. If we stay here, we'll die."

My first instinct is to stay in the car. But I'm sure Lucas would want me to listen to Damon, so I nod.

I reach into the car for my purse, but Damon pulls me out.

"Leave it. We have to go."

"But I…"

"Leave it, Emily!" Damon yells at me forcefully.

I follow him as he holds my hand. We're running down an alley that's unfamiliar to me. Where the hell are we? My feet are hurting from the heels, so I kick them off and keep running.

"Where are we going?" I puff.

"I know a place where we'll be safe."

"Is it far?"

I'm feeling sick, and I know that if I keep running, I'm bound to throw up.

"Here," he says suddenly, ducking through a door.

We stop running. I'm out of breath and on the verge of hurling. I imagine the pregnancy and the shock of what's just happened are culminating in the mother of all storms inside my body.

"Are you okay, Emily?"

"What's happening? Who shot at us?"

"I don't know."

"We have to call Lucas!"

"We will. But right now, we have to focus on staying out of sight."

"I'm going to be sick."

I move away from him so that I can throw up with a bit of dignity. It feels as if my insides are spilling out. I eventually stop once I reach the dry heaving stage.

Damon is on his cell phone. I don't know who he's talking to, but it doesn't sound good.

"What?" he yells into his mobile. "Are you sure?"

"What's wrong?" I interject, but he holds up his hand to silence me.

"Okay. Call me when it's safe to come back."

Damon hangs up. I'm staring at him in anticipation.

"What is it?"

"There's been an attack on the estate too. It's better if we stay out of sight."

"Oh, Lord. Call Lucas. He'll know what to do."

"You need to trust me, Emily. Mr. Lucchese can't help you now. I'll protect you."

I'm trembling all over. This is exactly what I was afraid of. How did I get myself mixed up in all this? And now I'm carrying a child too. I can't possibly bring my baby into this lifestyle!

Lucas doesn't even know I'm pregnant! This is a disaster.

"Where are we going? We can't stay here. What is this place anyway?"

"It's an old warehouse. Don't worry. I know a place where we can hide out for a while. Do you trust me?"

I'm not sure who to trust right now, but I have no choice, so I nod slowly.

"Come. Let's go."

Damon takes me by the hand. We leave the warehouse and walk a few blocks to another warehouse, where he knocks on the steel rollup door. A man opens, and the two of them speak in hushed voices to each other in Italian. They're talking really fast, so I can't make out what they're saying.

"We'll stay here for tonight," Damon says after a few minutes.

"Here? Where are we?"

"A friend's"

"Will we be safe here?"

"Yes."

Damon must be in shock. His friendly, jovial eyes are darker, and his tone is short. He must be in professional mode. I haven't seen the serious side of him until now. I hope he knows what he's doing.

Damon takes me to a room with a bed and a basin. It's rudimentary at best, but beggars can't be choosers, so I don't complain. I'm alive thanks to his quick thinking and decisive action. I owe Damon my life.

"Rest here. I'll be back a bit later. I have to make a few calls. You'll be safe here; don't worry."

"Please don't leave me alone," I beg, ashamed of my fearful tone.

"I won't be long. I promise."

* * *

Lucas

My cell phone is blowing up with messages, so I excuse myself from the meeting to answer them.

"Lucas, it's Andreas."

"What's up? I'm in the middle of something, here."

"Yeah, I know. But this is important."

"What is it?"

"Emily is missing."

"What do you mean missing?"

"She left for a doctor's appointment this morning, and she isn't back yet. No one can get hold of her on her cell phone, and neither Damon nor Dominick are answering their phones."

Fuck!

"Send out the team to look for her, Andreas. Damn it! I knew something like this was going to happen. I never should have left her alone."

"I'm on it, Lucas. I'll let you know as soon as we have news."

"I'm coming home."

19

EMILY

I must have fallen asleep from sheer exhaustion. I open my eyes when I hear Damon's voice. For a moment, I forget where I am, but soon the memories of the day's terrible events come flooding back to me, so I sit up.

"Can we go home?"

"No. I'm afraid that isn't an option."

"What do you mean?"

"We have to stay away. There's been an attack at the mansion too. It isn't safe."

"I don't understand."

"You have to trust me. I'll get in touch with the boss as soon as I can. But, for now, we have to leave the city."

"Leave the city! Are you crazy?"

"I want to talk to Lucas. Give me your phone, Damon."

"No!" he barks.

His action takes me aback. Why is he being so weird?

"What's going on, Damon? Why can't I call Lucas?"

"It's complicated."

"Explain it to me then."

Damine walks over to where I'm sitting on the bed and sits down next to me. I move away from him, but he moves closer. Something about him is different. His body language is telling me to be on guard. I'm not sure why, but he's creeping me out.

"I want to call Lucas right now, Damon. Right now!"

Damon pulls something from his pocket. Before I have a chance to react, he jams the object into my leg. I squeal as the sharp pain stings my flesh.

"Ouch! What the f…"

The world around me is spinning, and my ears pop. Suddenly, it goes dark as a wave of nausea hits me one more time.

I'm in a small, dark space. It's bumpy. I hit my head against something hard. Am I in the trunk of a car? I call out, and soon the movement stops.

The sunlight streams in as someone opens the lid of the trunk. I get jabbed again before I pass out.

* * *

My mouth is drier than the desert sand, and I have a splitting headache. I open one eye slowly to survey the room, and then the other. Where the hell am I?

Damon! What the hell is he playing at? Why did he drug me? What's going on? I'm in a room that looks like it's seen better days. In fact, that's too kind. It's a shithole, and it smells of stale alcohol and vomit.

"Damon!"

My voice cracks. My throat feels thick.

I get up and move toward the door. I turn the handle, but the door is locked, so I bang on it.

"Damon! Where are you?"

Silence.

"Damon!" I scream one more time, but no one comes to my aid.

The terrible realization that I've been duped starts to dawn on me. Why would Damon do this if he was on my side? Is he even who he says he is? He can't be the bad guy in all this. Surely, Lucas would have vetted him carefully. I don't get this. I have to talk to him, but where is he?

I look out of the window. It's barred up, but I can see the street below. What the hell? This doesn't look like the streets of LA. None that I've ever seen, anyway. Where am I? I open the window so I can hear the street noises. Is that Spanish? Am I in Mexico? No! Can't be!

"Hola!" I shout out of the window at a woman passing by.

She looks up briefly, but then carries on walking.

"Hola!" I shout again. "Excuse me! Where are we?"

The woman looks at me as if I'm crazy, then walks off.

"Wait! Please!"

No joy. I wait until I see another passerby. It's a young boy. I hope he has better manners than the woman.

"Hola!"

The boy stops and looks up, his dirty little face all scrunched up as he looks into the sun.

"Hola!" he shouts and waves.

"Where are we?"

"Qué?"

"Great. He doesn't know what I'm saying."

Come on, Emily. Think. Try to remember the rudimentary Spanish you learned at school.

"Uhm…Dónde estamos?"

"Ah! Tijuana, señora."

Tijuana! What the fuck am I doing in Mexico? Shit! This is worse than I thought.

The little boy waves and runs off before I can talk to him some more. At least I know where I am now. Not that the revelation has done me any favors. Where the hell is Damon?

* * *

It's been a whole day and a night since I've seen Damon. I'm starting to think that I'm going to die here. I'm starving, and I'd kill for a cup of coffee.

There's a rattle outside the door. Keys! Damon!

I jump to my feet, readying myself for whatever lies on the other side of that door.

"You're up."

It's Damon.

"Yes, I'm up! Where the fuck have you been? I'm sick with worry, and I'm starving! Why are we in Mexico, Damon? What the hell are we doing here?"

"Calm down," he says coolly, tossing a plastic wrapped sandwich at me. "Here, eat this."

I want to shove the food back at him and tell him to mind his manners, but I'm too hungry, so I rip open the plastic and inhale the food.

I keep my eyes on the man I once thought of as an ally. He stares coldly at me while I eat. I've made a terrible mistake by trusting this man. Who is he, and what does he want?

"Who are you?" I demand a few bites into the meal.

"I'm Damon. You know who I am."

"Bullshit! No driver of Lucas' would treat me this way. Tell me the truth."

"It's time to grow up, princess," he sneers.

"What?"

"I hope you don't think I'm footing the bill for your accommodations."

"What are you talking about? This place is a dump."

"Well, this is your new address, so you'd better get used to it."

"Damon," I plead. "Please. What's going on? Why won't you let me talk to Lucas?"

"Forget about Lucas Lucchese. He is no longer a part of your life. You belong to me now."

What is he talking about? What does he mean? I belong to him?

"I don't understand."

"I thought you had a good education. You're a little slow."

"Are you kidnapping me?"

"There you go. Now you're getting the picture?"

"So, what now? Are you planning on collecting a handsome ransom from Lucas?"

"Nope. I have other plans for you."

"Other plans?"

"You're worth more to me on a long term basis. Besides, if I hit Lucas up for a ransom, he'll kill me. Although I'm sure we could work something out. Come to an arrangement if you prefer."

I've seen that look before in a man's eyes. If Damon thinks I'm going to have sex with him, he's even crazier than he looks right now.

"No fucking way! I'll claw your eyes out before I let you touch me, you son of a bitch," I snarl.

Lucas smirks.

"Okay, up to you. I'd get used to using that cute little ass of yours if I were you. You're going to need it."

Damon walks toward the door.

"Wait! Where are you going? Damon! Stop!"

He ignores me, slams the door shut, and locks it.

Well, that's it. I'm fucked!

* * *

"Get up."

Damon is standing over me. I didn't hear him entering the room. I leap to my feet.

"What?" I stammer, still half asleep.

I'm feeling weak and shaky, as I haven't eaten much in three days. I wish I could push my way past him, but I'm too wobbly on my feet.

"Put this on," he says, handing me a set of clothes.

I unfold the items.

"This is completely inappropriate. I'm not wearing this. I'll look like a slut."

"You *will* wear it, or I'll rip off what you're wearing and dress you myself."

"Asshole," I mumble under my breath. "Can I have some privacy, please?"

"No."

"Can you at least turn around?"

"Just get on with it. We don't have all day."

I'm spitting mad, but something warns me not to push it with Damon. He's not the sweet guy I thought he was.

I change, staring defiantly at him.

"Did you enjoy that?" I snipe.

"Don't flatter yourself. Come on. Let's go."

"Where are we going?"

"You have a job interview."

"What? Looking like this!"

"Yeah."

"Damon, please. Take me back right now, and I'll tell Lucas I ran away. He never has to know that you took me. I swear. Come on. I thought you and I were friends."

"A guy like me could never be friends with someone like you, Emily. Don't be naive."

"What would your mother say if she knew what you were doing to me? You're such a good son. Why don't you think about this?"

"My mother was a bitch, and she's dead."

"So, was everything you told me a lie?"

"Shut up and get in the car."

Damon opens the door and shoves me into the passenger seat. I don't know where he plans on taking me, but it can't be good. Whatever I may have thought about this man is now in tatters. He is *not* on my side.

There's no point in talking to this asshole. He clearly has no intention of answering my questions. We drive into the city center, where he stops outside a dodgy looking club. My stomach is in a knot. The gravity of the situation I'm in is slowly dawning on me. We're parked outside of what looks to be a strip club, and I'm dressed like a tart. It doesn't take a genius to work this one out.

"No. Please, Damon. I can't."

"You can and you will."

He grabs my arm, and frog marches me to the front door.

"You're hurting me," I snarl.

"Behave, or you'll find out what real pain is," Damon threatens under his breath.

I bite my lip and keep walking.

I've never been in a strip club before, but this is pretty much the way I pictured it. There are a host of poles on elevated platforms around the large open room, with half naked women swinging listlessly around them.

A rotund, well dressed man sits at the bar counter. He's staring me up and down as Damon and I approach. His lecherous glare makes my skin crawl.

"Hello, Damon. What did you bring me?"

"A new star."

"I see. Yes. Very nice," he says, staring at my body. "Can you dance, honey?" he asks me.

I don't say a word.

"The man is talking to you, Emily. Answer him."

"Fuck off," retort.

I don't see the blow coming until it's too late. I'm sure the back hand has left red welts on my cheek. I touch the spot where the skin is burning.

"Now, now, Damon. Don't ruin that pretty face. Leave the young lady with me. I'll have a nice chat with her."

"No! Damon! Don't leave me here!" I call after him as he walks away.

"We're square now, Paolo," he calls to the man beside me as he gets to the front door.

"Yeah!" the man calls back before he turns his attention to me.

"So, we're not going to have a repeat of what just happened, are we?" he grins. "If you behave, I won't have to discipline you. Okay?"

What choice do I have? I'm in deep shit here. If I give this guy any lip, I'll probably end up on the receiving end of a fist again, and I don't want that.

I nod.

"Good. Come, let's go talk in my office," he says, gets up, and motions for me to follow him.

I want to make a dash for the door. Run out into the street and call for help. But I don't have any money, I don't have a phone, and, most importantly, I don't know who I can trust. So, I follow him while my mind is churning.

The women who work there are staring at me. They don't look friendly at all, even though they probably don't want to be here either.

So much for comradery. Paolo leads me down a narrow passage into an office.

He sits down behind his desk and points to a chair.

"Sit. Let's chat."

Marvelous.

20

LUCAS

"What the fuck! I trust you to watch over Emily, and this happens. Where is she?"

I'm yelling at my staff. They are petrified while I scream and shout like a madman, but I don't care. They'll be lucky if they leave this room without a bullet in their asses.

"We found the car in an alley. Dominick is dead, and Emily and the driver are missing."

Dominick was one of my best men. I'm furious that someone would have the gall to ambush one of my vehicles. First David, and now this.

"This is unacceptable! I want answers!"

"Yes, Boss."

"Are you alright, Lucas?" Andreas asks me when the soldiers have left the room.

"No, I'm not alright, damn it! Emily is out there somewhere, and I have no idea if she's alive or... I swore to her I would protect her, Andreas! I swore it."

I rake my fingers through my hair while pacing the office floor.

"And what's the story with Damon? Where is he? Can we trust him? I thought you checked him out, Andreas."

"I did. He was clean. There are no known associations with local or other gangs. We don't know enough yet to assume the worst about him. He wasn't even supposed to be on duty when this happened. There was some sort of mix up and he stepped in to help. He was supposed to be in Detroit visiting his mother."

"Something stinks, Andreas. I'm tired of being on the receiving end of these attacks. This is the last straw. It's bullshit! Aren't there any witnesses who saw what happened? Someone must have seen something."

"We're doing all we can, Lucas."

"Well, it isn't enough! Find Emily, Andreas. Do it now!"

Andreas nods and leaves the room. I'm too upset to care that I'm taking it out on the wrong man. I'll talk to him when I've cooled down. What the fuck is happening around here?

* * *

It's been two days since the incident, and I'm at my wit's end. Emily and Damon have simply vanished into thin air. No one saw anything, and there's no talk on the street. I know in my gut that this has something to do with that scumbag, Gallo. He's been a thorn in my side for too long, and I intend to do something about it sooner rather than later.

But first, I have to find Emily. She must be terrified. I can't believe I let this happen. I'm so unbelievably pissed off with myself.

Then it hits me. Perhaps Daniella knows something. It's a longshot, but I've exhausted all other avenues. I dial her number.

"Hello."

"Daniella? It's Lucas."

"Lucas? Is everything okay?"

"Something has happened. Have you heard from Emily?"

"What! What do you mean, something has happened? What are you talking about? Where's Emily? Is she okay?"

Daniella is talking so fast that I can barely make out what she's saying.

"I was out of town and…"

"I knew this was a bad idea. Damn it! I told Emily to come home. Where is she?"

"I don't know. I was hoping she would have reached out to you."

"Oh, no. No, no, no! This is a disaster. She needs us, Lucas! Especially now that…"

Daniella stops talking. Her silence is deafening.

"Now that? What were you going to say?"

"You don't know?"

"Know what?"

"The baby."

My legs are suddenly quite infirm, so I lean against the edge of my desk. Baby? What is she talking about?

"What baby?"

"Emily didn't tell you."

"No."

Holy shit! Emily is pregnant. Fuck!

"You have to find her, Lucas."

"I know. Please call me if you hear from her, will you?"

"Sure. I think it's time to call the cops. Don't you?"

"No. They can't help. I'll find her. I swear it."

* * *

Emily

I haven't seen Damon since he dumped me at the strip club five days ago. I can't believe how stupid I was to trust that bastard the way I did. I should have been more careful, but Damon did his level best to manipulate me and take full advantage of my naivete. I feel like a bloody fool.

To be fair, he fooled us all. Lucas sure as shit would never have let Damon anywhere near me if he thought there was a possibility of the driver kidnapping me.

Poor Dom. My heart breaks when I think about his terrible ending. He was nothing but kind to me. His only crime was that he worked in the wrong business. It's so easy to judge people when you're on the outside looking in. I did exactly that the first time I laid eyes on Dom. But he turned out to be a gem. And now he's dead.

Damon's parting words to Paolo were telling. I imagine he owed the man money or some sort of favor, as I am his payback. Slimy son of a bitch! I hope Lucas finds him and rips him limb from bloody limb, the snake.

My talk with Paolo went pretty much as expected. He talked, and I kept my mouth shut. There is no democracy when it comes to strippers and the boss of the club.

So, this is my new life. Lucas has no idea where I am; Damon has left me here to rot; and Paolo expects me to entertain the clientele by dancing half naked on a stage and occasionally swinging from a bloody pole like a cheap whore.

My morning sickness isn't helping my situation. I spend half the morning hanging over the toilet bowl and the rest of the time sleeping off the exhaustion from dancing into the early hours of the morning. This is so fucking humiliating, but I daren't go against my boss.

I've seen what happens when his *girls* don't perform to his satisfaction. I watched as Paolo slapped the cheek right out of one of the strippers when she dared to smartmouth him. The poor girl has been covering up a nasty shiner with makeup for three days now. I can't afford bodily injury. I have to be extra careful for the sake of my baby.

My room is a shithole. The bed has seen better days and the kitchen, if one can even call it that, was chaotic when I first moved in. It took me the better part of a day to clean and make the place look like something.

I don't have access to a phone, and Paolo's men watch me like hawks. It would seem that everywhere I go these days, a man is watching me. I dance, I sleep, I wake up, I throw up, I eat, I go back to sleep, and then I prepare myself for a long night of work.

The men who come here are an interesting mix. I have a feeling that the business may be a front for other illegal activities. The place has a distinctly illegal feel about it, something I've become an expert at spotting.

The Mexican police don't seem to care much about what happens inside here, either. Patrons openly use cocaine and other drugs to enhance the seedy mood that practically drips from the blood red walls. Alcohol abuse is another problem with frequent bust ups between the bouncers and the men who grab at the dancers.

My thoughts are interrupted by a bang on my door.

"Open up!"

It's Paolo. Ugh! What the hell does he want? I really don't want to see him. He's so creepy.

"What is it?" I call through the door.

"Open the door!"

Fuck.

I open the door to find him standing there in all his glory—shirt open, thick gold chain barely visible in the mat of dark hair on his chest. As if holding onto my breakfast isn't hard enough.

"What is it?"

"I have a VIP coming this evening. I want you to look your best. And you'd better behave. I'm sure I don't have to tell you what will happen if I'm not happy with your performance."

"Yes, you've made it perfectly clear," is all I can say. My response is much too polite for the likes of him, but I'm trying to be smart here.

"Good."

A VIP. Wonderful. Translation, scum with more money than the rest.

Paolo ogles me briefly before he turns and walks away. Thank God he hasn't tried anything with me. Not yet, anyway. I pray that it stays that way. I'm not sure why, but Paolo treats me just a tad better than he does the rest of the women here. Does my new boss know who I am? I get the feeling he knows about my connection with Lucas. It would explain a lot.

Lucas. Oh, where are you? This is exactly the kind of consequence I've dreaded from the start. I should have listened to that little voice urging me to stay the hell away from Lucas and his gangster lifestyle. Now, here I am, pregnant and destitute!

There must be a way to get my hands on a phone. Prisoners do it every day, so why is it so hard for me? The girl with the shiner seems to be the one in the group with the most street smarts. Surely she can help me. I just have to figure out how I can get to talk to her privately without Paolo's meatheads reporting back to their boss.

I'll talk to the girl tonight. Hopefully, she won't rat me out. It's a chance I have to take. This is no life for me and my baby.

※ ※ ※

I'm in a large private room at the club, waiting for the VIP. The meatheads are outside, watching the door. I've been hoping to bump into the young stripper all day, but she's nowhere to be found. I have to talk to her.

The door opens, and in slinks Paolo, followed by a tall man dressed immaculately. He carries himself as if he's somebody, and I can tell by the way Paolo is kissing his ass that the VIP has the upper hand.

"This is the woman," Paolo says in a muted tone, barely audible, but I manage to catch it.

The tall man looks me over and nods at Paolo, who takes his cue and leaves. Now I'm alone with the stranger, and I'm nervous. What does he want from me?

He checks me out before he sits down. I wish he would say something. His stare is disconcerting as hell. The man has the coldest eyes I've ever seen.

"So, you're Emily Thornton," he says slowly in a deep, gruff voice.

What? How does he know my name?

I'm too shaken to answer.

"I heard you were a stunner."

What does he want?

"We have a mutual acquaintance," he says in a manner that makes my skin crawl.

I hold my tongue.

"Can you guess?"

Is this man talking about Damon? He doesn't seem like the type who would hang around with lowly drivers. But who else could he mean?

Come on, Emily. You're a clever girl. Can't you guess?

"Lucas?"

"Very good. Beautiful and smart."

"Who are you?"

"My friends call me Vince."

"Are we friends?"

"We could be, if you play your cards right," he grins.

"I have all the friends I need, thank you."

"I see. Feisty. I like it."

The door opens. It's Paolo.

"I'm sorry for interrupting, Mr. Gallo. It's urgent."

Vince stares at me for a few seconds before he gets up.

"We'll continue this discussion later."

"You. Get back to work," Paolo says as soon as the tall man is out of the room. "I don't pay you to stand around here looking pretty."

You don't pay me at all, you bastard, I want to say, but then think better of it.

I spend the rest of the night wondering what Vince Gallo has to do with Lucas. They can't be on good terms, or Vince would do the right thing and get word to Lucas about my fate. No. I get the feeling that Vince Gallo is the reason I'm here. In fact, I wouldn't be at all surprised if he has something to do with my brother's death.

I have to get the hell out of here before it's too late! Damn it, Lucas! Where are you?

21

LUCAS

"We found Damon," Andreas says as he storms into my office.

"What?" Where? What does he have to say for himself?"

"He says he was knocked unconscious when he tried to escape the car with Emily. He looks like he's taken quite a beating."

"Where is he now?"

"He's downstairs."

"Well, bring him here, for fuck's sake! I want to talk to him."

"Sure."

At last. Something is finally going my way for a change. I'm going to question Damon properly until I'm satisfied that he doesn't have a hand in this. God help him if he does, because I'll gut him like a fish.

I'm surprised when he enters the room. He looks like he's been through the mill.

"Where the hell have you been, Damon?" I demand. "Where is Emily?"

"I'm so sorry, Boss. I've been laying low for a few days. I was afraid the men who jumped us were out looking for me."

"What men? Where is Emily?"

"I don't know, Boss. I'm so sorry. I tried my best to protect her. I swear! I thought they were going to beat me to death."

"Tell me exactly what happened."

"They ambushed us when we were on our way home. Poor Dominick was taken out immediately. I instructed Emily to stay down while I drove through the streets trying to shake them."

"Where is Emily, Damon?"

"I don't know, Boss. We were running when they jumped us. Someone knocked me out. They must have kicked the shit out of me when I was on the ground. When I came to, she was gone."

"And it never occurred to you to call me?" I thunder in frustration.

Damon looks down at his shoes.

"I'm truly sorry, Boss. I was afraid for my life so I stayed out of sight. Please forgive me."

"Who got the jump on you?"

"I didn't recognize them."

I suppress the urge to wrap my hands around Damon's neck so I can squeeze the life out of his useless ass. I'm not convinced yet of his story. Let's face it, he wouldn't be the first gangster to get a buddy to whip the snot out of him so that he can substantiate a bullshit lie, and he won't be the last. But I have to keep in mind that either way, he's my only link to Emily right now, so it would behoove me to keep him close.

Damon is sweating. Is it guilt or is he nervous? I'd be nervous too if I were him. In fact I'd be downright petrified. His life depends on how he answers my questions. If I suspect even for a second that he's bullshitting me, it's, as the Red Queen once said, off with his head!

"Just get out," I sigh. "Don't leave the estate."

I have to be alone for a moment so I can figure out what to do next. Damon leaves the room.

"What do you think?" I ask Andreas.

"Something isn't right," he answers.

"Yeah. I thought so too. His story is far too polished."

"I'll keep an eye on him. Follow him around. If he's lying, I'll find out for sure."

"I hope for his sake he's telling the truth. I'm sure I don't have to spell out what I'm going to do to him if he had anything to do with Emily's disappearance."

"You'll have to get in line, Lucas. I'll happily put him down."

"Do me a favor. You've got a connection with the phone company. Right?"

"Yeah."

"Good. Buy old Vanessa a box of candy and ask her to get us a copy of Damon's text messages, will you? If he's dirty we should get what we need that way."

"Good idea. I'm on it."

Andreas heads for the door but stops before he leaves.

"I'm truly sorry, Lucas. This is my fault. I should have dug a little deeper into his past."

"Andreas, you've been a loyal friend and an excellent employee for many years. We're good."

"Thanks, Boss," he says without looking at me before he leaves the room.

There's no point in taking out my frustrations on Andreas. He's helped me out of many jams before and without him I'd probably be dead already. If Damon is dirty he'll get what's coming to him.

* * *

Emily

Vince didn't come back. I assume he had better things to do. His visit did at least have one small silver lining, as my dancing time was cut in half. Woop!

My morning sickness is subsiding, thank God. I'm so tired of spending the better half of my day praying to the great white porcelain god with the gaping mouth. I've lost far too much weight. My only saving grace is that the weight loss will hide signs of my pregnancy for a while longer.

I've been in this hellhole for a month already. How time flies when you're swinging from a pole like a cursed circus animal. Paolo is beyond creepy. I'm very surprised that he hasn't made the moves on me. He seems to help himself to the other women in the club, but not when it comes to me. I wonder if Vince Gallo has anything to do with it.

The young stripper with the streetsmarts has been missing in action for a few weeks. I hope she's okay. That girl's mouth is her greatest enemy. I have to give it to her—she's a tough cookie. I reckon she's one of those women who grew up on the streets, using her looks and smarts to keep her from starvation.

Life on the streets of Tijuana can't be easy. It's a lawless place, if the stories I hear from the other girls are anything to go by. Then again, any city has it's underbelly, so why would Mexico be any different.

It saddens me when I look around at the women who are here with me. Most, if not all, of them are hooked on drugs. I guess they use it to numb the pain of their existence. I honestly can't say for sure if I'd be immune to the temptation were it not for the little baby growing inside me. Lucas' baby.

I'm gutted that he hasn't found me yet. For all his promises, he's let me down. How does someone like Damon pull the wool over Lucas' eyes? He must have been planning this for a very long time. It takes time to establish a backstory. Andreas would have checked Damon out for sure. How the hell did he manage to pull the wool over everyone's eyes?

It makes me wonder if he had help. Big help. Big, like Gallo. Is it possible? Is that why I'm the only woman in here who doesn't have to constantly watch her back and fend off sexual advances? It's possible.

"Hey, bitches. Guess who's back."

What? I don;t believe it. Smartmouth is back. Battered and bruised, but alive.

"Elena! Where have you been?" I blurt out. "I was worried about you."

Elena looks at me with complete surprise.

"Why would you concern yourself with me, Gringo? And what are you still doing here? I thought you were too good for the likes of us."

Wow! I had no idea the other women felt this way about me. I just say, it hurts.

"I'm a prisoner here just like everyone else, Elena. And, no. I don't think I'm better than any of you. Shouldn't we stand together? Isn't that what women do?"

Elena laughs out loud.

"Oh, please. You white women all think your shit doesn't stink."

"Elena, please. I'm not like that. You'd know if you gave me a chance before judging me."

"Yeah. Whatever."

"I'm glad you're alright," I say, walking away.

"Hey! Emily, is it?"

"Yes."

"I'm sorry. I've had a crappy day."

"It's okay. I really am glad you're safe."

"Thanks. I just wish I wasn't stuck back here again. I was so close to being free."

"Where did you go?"

"I got as far as the border before Paolo's men found me and dragged me back. But not before they *taught me a lesson.*"

"Bastards," I sigh. "Are you alright?"

"Hey, it's nothing every man in my life has ever done to me. I'll live."

"I'm so sorry, Elena."

"Hey, it's cool. Next time I'll cross the border. I came closer this time than ever before."

"You've done this before?"

"Hell, yeah! Many times. Why do you think Paolo hates me so much? I make him look bad. I'm lucky I'm still alive," she grins, as if what she's saying is nothing.

"I wanted to ask you something, Elena."

LYDIA HALL

"What?"

"I need access to a phone. Any ideas?"

"Yeah. Forget about it."

"Come on. I asked around. They tell me you've been here the longest. Surely, you would know."

"It isn't worth it. If Paolo catches you, he's going to kill you."

"So, there is a way."

"Listen, Emily. I'd love to help you. I really would. But I have enough strikes against me. If Paolo finds out I helped you, they will be singing and dancing on my grave before the day is out. I'm sorry."

Damn it! Elena was my best hope at escaping. What the hell am I supposed to do now?

"Please, Elena."

I don't want to tell her that I'm pregnant. Would she even care if she knew? I can't risk Paolo finding out or he'll surely force me into generating money for him in other ways. And I'm thinking waitressing isn't it. My only hope is if Elena helps me to get word to someone back home.

If only I could make one phone call. Either to Lucas or Dannie. One of them will make a plan to get me the fuck out of here. I don't know how much longer I'll be able to stand it. I hate this awful place with its dirty rooms and even dirtier minds. My skin crawls everytime someone looks at me. How the hell will I bring a child into this world?

Elena leaves the room. I'll give her a few days to settle in before I try again. I know she'll help me if I persist. I have a feeling that she'd love to get one over on Paolo. If I get away, he'll no doubt get an ass whooping from Gallo. My only regret is that I won't be here to see it.

It's been two days since Elena's return and she's her prickly self once more. I hear chatting when I walk past her room one morning. I recognise the four voices, so I knock on the door and announce myself.

Elena calls for me to enter. She and three strippers are sitting on her floor doing girly things. One is having her hair brushed, the other is painting her nails, and Elena and the fourth girl are paging through old magazines.

"What's up, Gringo?"

"Nothing much," I answer, trying to blend in.

"Do you know how to braid hair?" one of the girls asks me.

"Sure. You want me to braid your hair for you?"

She nods, so I walk over to where she's sitting and take the hair brush.

"You have such gorgeous hair, Maria."

I hope these women stop seeing me as an outsider. Sure, I'm American and they're locals, but we're all in the same sinking ship here.

"Maria used to win all the local beauty pageants."

"Really?"

"Yeah, before her drunkass father sold her to Paolo."

"You're kidding!" I say with genuine shock.

"It's true," Maria confirms.

"How the hell is that okay? Don't you have other family? Anyone who can help you?"

"No. My mother died when I was young."

"This is outrageous," I say, disgust dripping from my lips.

"We live in the real world, honey. Not the one you're used to," Elena chirps.

"My life hasn't been smooth sailing either, Elena."

"Oh, come on. Look at you. Everything about you screams money and privilege. Has anyone ever beaten the shit out of you?"

"No, but there are other ways to hurt someone."

"Like what?" Elena insists.

"Well, my parents died when I was a young girl, and my brother was murdered a few months ago. And, now I'm here with you. Not exactly the dream life, is it?"

I have four sets of eyes on me now and for the first time I don't see abject loathing and judgment in them.

"I'm sorry that happened to you, Emily," Maria says.

"Thank you, Maria. I'm sorry about your mother."

"My uncle raped me for years before I ran away," one of the other women says softly.

"Hey, we all have sad stories," Elena crows. "No point in feeling sorry for ourselves. It will only make us weak."

"There must be something we can do if we work together," I say with renewed conviction.

"Yeah? Like what? Paolo's men watch us 24/7."

"That didn't stop you from running away, Elena," I insist.

"Yet, here I am again. Back where I started."

"You can't give up, Elena," Maria pleads. "You can get us help once you're free."

"So can I," I insist. "But I'll need help."

"Stop it! This kind of talk will get us all killed," Elena barks.

The rest of the women clearly see her as the leader, so they stop talking. I can see that the discussion is done for today.

22

EMILY

Another day in hell. It's early, and I'm awake despite the long night of dancing and dodging grubby paws. I have to talk to Elena again. It is vital that I explain my situation to her without giving away the fact that I'm pregnant. I can't have Paolo find out. Not yet, anyway. Not until I've figured out a way to escape this nightmare.

It's going to take a miracle to get out from under the watchful eyes of the bouncers and bodyguards, but I'm determined to do something to save myself. Seeing as the father of my child has failed me.

Perhaps I'll host a little party in my room tonight. Let's call it a little soiree for my fellow strippers. We'll all be wired after the night's dancing anyway. The barman is well disposed toward me. I'll ask him to *donate* a bottle or two of wine and some bar snacks toward my cause. I'm sure he won't mind. I'll mention it in passing to the women who were in Elena's room yesterday. They seem to be a tight unit, and they trust each other.

It's lunchtime when I bump into Elena and Maria on my way to the kitchen.

"Hi. I was wondering if you ladies were in the mood for a little party after work tonight."

"Party?" Elena asks.

"Yeah. In my room. I've arranged a little wine," I whisper, hoping to entice the duo.

"Ooh, yes. I could do with a little fun," Maria beams. "I'll bring my CD player."

"CD player? What, have you gone mad?" Elena sneers. "Paolo will shit himself if we drink on the sly."

"What? Since when are you afraid of bending the rules?" I challenge her.

"Fine. But if anything goes wrong, it's on you," she snaps and walks off.

Maria winks at me before she too walks away. Yes! My plan is in motion. I'll be out of here before long.

It's 3 p.m., and the girls are in my room. The barman came through for me, and I'm pleased with my attempts at catering on a budget. I even managed to get some chocolate. I had to sell one of my bracelets to sweeten the deal, but it's worth it if I can get out of here.

"Welcome, ladies," I greet my posse when they arrive. "Wine?"

"Wow! I can't believe you pulled it off, Emily," Maria grins happily.

"Uh-huh. I thought you could all use a bit of a break. Come in. Help yourselves."

"Is that chocolate?" Elena gasps.

"Go ahead. Eat as much as you like."

Before long, the room is abuzz with chatter and laughter. The girls are relaxed, and I'm thankful to have an audience. I'll wait until they've all had a few glasses of wine before I casually drop a few hints about trying to escape.

"How did you end up here, Emily?" Maria asks.

"I trusted a man. How else?"

"Why do we do that?" she sighs. "They're always fucking us over."

"Well, this one was a *trusted* man. Or so I thought."

"Oh, please. The only trustworthy man is a dead man," Elena snaps. "They're all useless."

"Not every man," Maria says softly. "My Diego was a good man."

"Who's Diego?" I ask.

"We were engaged. He's dead now."

"Oh, Maria. I'm so sorry. What happened?"

"He got involved with the wrong people."

"I know all about that," I answer. "My brother died the same way."

""Was he a good man?"

"The best. He took care of me after our parents died. David was a wonderful person."

"How did he die?" Maria asks, her eyes tearing.

"He was murdered."

"Who did it?"

"That's the worst of it. I don't know."

"And the man who dumped you here?" Elena asks.

"Him. That bastard was working for my boyfriend. Damon betrayed us both."

"Damon?" Elena asks, looking around at the rest of the women.

"Yeah. Do you know him?"

"Yeah, we know him. That fucker dumps girls here all the time. He's connected to Paolo somehow. I think they have the same boss."

"Vince Gallo?" I ask, hoping to put together the pieces of the puzzle.

"Yeah, that's the one. He owns this club," Maria says. "He's a big time criminal. A very bad man."

"I wouldn't be surprised if they had something to do with your brother's death. Damon is a nasty son of a bitch."

Could it be? No! I would know, wouldn't I? I would have picked up on his vibes.

Sure, you would have. You didn't even see Lucas for who he was, you fool. You're out of your depth with these men, Emily.

"Why hasn't your boyfriend come to save you yet?" Elena snarks. "He's probably an asshole too. All men are."

"To be honest, Elena, I don't know. I thought I could depend on him, but now I'm not so sure anymore. I don't know anything. Except that I have to get out of here before…"

"Before what?" Maria encourages me.

Can I trust these women to keep their mouths shut? What choice do I really have? It's a matter of weeks before my belly will start to show. What then? Perhaps they'll take pity on me if they know I'm pregnant.

"Before what, Emily?" Elena chimes in.

"Before it's too late," I answer.

"Too late for what?" Elena pushes.

"You're pregnant, aren't you?" Maria says softly.

A hush falls over the group. They're staring at me, waiting for an answer. Oh, what the hell do I have to lose?

"Yes."

"How far along are you?" Elena asks after an awkward silence.

"Far enough to be showing soon."

"Fuck!" Elena says and slams down her glass.

"What?" I ask.

"You know what Paolo will do to you if he finds out, right?"

"What?"

"Elena!" Maria chastises her smartmouth friend.

"What? She needs to know. It's for her own good," Elena snaps back.

"Tell me, Elena. What will he do?"

"If you can't dance, you'll have to bring in money some other way," one of the other women interjects.

"Like what?"

"Prostitution," Elena announces. "You'll have to earn your keep the old fashioned way. On your back."

"No," I whisper. "I can't. I won't."

"You won't have a say. Look around you. This isn't a democracy, Emily. Men don't come here to hold your hand and talk. You're just a piece of ass like the rest of us."

"Why are you being so mean, Elena," Maria snaps at her friend.

"Would you rather Emily find out the hard way? We could help you get rid of the kid. I know someone who will arrange it," one of the other women suggests.

"No! I could never," I say quickly.

"Suit yourself. But, trust me," Elena says, "nothing good will come of this pregnancy. Besides, Paolo will never let you keep the baby, even if you do carry to term and deliver."

I haven't thought that far ahead, but Elena's words ignite a new fear inside me. This is no place for a baby. How will I take care of a child in this hell?

"Please, Elena. You have to help me. Please. I swear I'll come back for you all. I swear it."

"Oh, really?" she scoffs. "And how will you do that? You have no money, I'm guessing you don't have a passport, and your boyfriend has clearly forgotten all about you and your petty-ass problems. How are you going to help us?"

She's right. Even if I escape this club, how will I get back home? I'm an illegal alien. They'll throw me in prison if they catch me.

"Oh, and if you're thinking of asking the cops for help, don't bother. Paolo has them in his pockets. They'll drag your skinny ass right back here before they help you," Elena reinforces her point.

"Then why do you keep running?" I ask her.

"I'm a local. I know this town better than any of you. I have connections on the outside."

"I have money, Elena. Back in the US. My boyfriend is loaded. I know he'll help us if he knows where I am."

"Pfff! Wake up, Emily. You're on your own," Elena says, getting up. "I'm going to hit the sack. It's been a long night."

"She's not as mean as she appears," Maria says after Elena has left the room. "She's just had a hard life."

"Will you talk to her, please, Maria? Please?"

"Sure. Thank you for tonight."

"My pleasure, Maria."

The women leave me alone with my thoughts. Have I accomplished anything? Who knows? At least I tried. And I'll keep trying until I find a way out of here.

I touch my belly.

"I'll get us out of here, baby," I whisper before I turn off the lights.

I know I'm dreaming, but I can't wake myself up. Lucas is standing in a field, and I'm running toward him. But no matter how fast I run, I cannot get to him. David is standing next to him. He has tears in his eyes, and his arms are open, beckoning me.

Paolo and Damon are chasing me. They're so close now that I can hear their labored breathing. My legs are lame as I run. I'm slowing down, and Lucas and David seem to be moving further away with each step that I take.

"No! Wait for me!" I hear myself screaming, but it's no use.

Lucas is gaining on me. He's right behind me now. I turn just as he reaches for me. He grabs me by the arm and shakes me.

No! Please. No!

"Emily! Wake up. You're screaming."

It's Maria. She's standing over me. I sit up, drenched in sweat.

"Are you okay?" she asks me. "You were having a nightmare. I heard your screams all the way down the hall."

"Oh. Maria. I had a terrible dream."

"It's okay," she whispers once I have my breath back. "I'm going to help you."

"What? Really?"

"Yes. I'll find a way."

"Oh, Maria," I say, grabbing onto her and hold her tightly. "Thank you."

"Don't thank me yet. It's going to be difficult. But I think I know how to get you out of here."

"I promise I'll come back for you, Maria. I promise."

"I'm coming with you."

"Are you sure?"

"Yes. I don't want to be here anymore than you do, Emily. I have family in Troncones. No one will find me if I go there. My cousin works there at a seaside resort. She'll help me if I can get to her."

"Do you have any money?"

"I've been hiding a few bills here and there over the last two years. I have just enough for a bus ticket."

"Then it's a deal. You get us out of here, and I'll make sure you get to your family. I can have money wired to us as soon as I can make a phone call."

"Okay."

"Maria, you're amazing. Thank you."

"Let's get out of here first before you thank me. Don't tell anyone what we're planning, Emily. Some of the women in here will sell you out for a shot of tequila."

"Okay. I won't."

"Good. How are you feeling? How's the baby?"

"Much better now that I have something to look forward to. The baby is fine. I'm so sorry about Diego."

"Thank you. I'm sorry about your brother."

"He'd be here if he were alive. David was a good man. He made a terrible mistake, working for the wrong people. He'd be horrified if he knew what his bad decision had sparked."

"Diego would be too. If he were alive, we'd be married now, living in a small village with our son."

"Son?"

"Yes, we had a son."

"Had?"

"He was killed in the car accident along with Diego."

"Oh, Maria. I'm so sorry."

"That's why I'm helping you, Emily. I can't stand by and watch another innocent child hurt by these bastards."

"Thank you, Maria. I'll make it up to you. I promise."

23

LUCAS

I can't sleep. I can't eat. I can't focus on anything else but my racing thoughts about Emily. I think I've aged ten years since she disappeared. The news that I'm about to be a father isn't helping my situation one bit. The worst is that I have no idea whether the woman of my dreams, my soulmate, is alive or dead.

I'm a fucking mafia boss! How can I not find one woman? This is ridiculous. How far can she get without a passport?

No matter where I turn, I end up at a dead end. I'm at the end of my rope when Andreas enters my office late one night.

"I think you'd better have a look at this," he says, handing me an envelope.

"What is it?"

"A printout of Damon's text messages for the last six months. He deleted most of them off his device, but the messages were backed up."

I open the envelope and take out the printed pages. My heart is pumping hard while I glance over the texts. I look up at Andreas halfway through. He has the same dark cloud around him as I do.

"Where is he?"

"Downstairs. I had him picked up."

"Bring the little fucker to the gym, will you?"

Andreas nods and leaves the room. I can't believe what I'm reading. It's a veritable treasure trove of damning information. One name stands out. I know this name. He's a capo in Gallo's camp. It can't be a coincidence.

Damon is in the gym, tied to a chair, by the time I get there. I'm spitting mad as I glare at him, but I know I must keep my cool until I get the information on Emily's location. Once I have that, I'm going to make Damon suffer the way he's made me suffer.

Damon isn't saying a word. He's motionless on the chair, blinking occasionally and staring ahead into space. So he's acting tough, is he? Okay. Two can play this game.

I walk up to him calmly, of course, and give him a backhand. Damon and the chair he's tied to topple to the floor. Andreas picks up the chair and Damon with it and places him upright again. A small gash on Damon's lip is wet with blood. A thin stream trickles down his chin and drips onto his white shirt.

"Where is Emily?" I growl at him.

"I don't know," he says defiantly before I punch him.

Damon spits out a mouthful of blood. I hit him with my fist the second time around, so he's bleeding profusely now. I don't care. I'll hit him as many times as I have to to get the truth out of him. I'm not above killing this man for Emily's sake.

"I see you've been rather chatty," I say, throwing down the printout I got from Andreas.

Damon's expression reveals a brief moment of panic before he puts on his tough guy act once again. It won't be too long before he'll be begging me to kill him.

"Where is Emily?"

"I don't know."

This little bastard is tough. Time to up the ante. I nod at Andreas, who takes out a small bag and places it on a table next to Damon.

"I'm going to give you one more chance, Damon."

He glares at me defiantly and then down at his shoes. Andreas unzips the bag and lays it open on the table. Damon looks at the contents of the bag. He's sweating profusely now.

"I hear it's pretty painful. Losing your fingernails, that is. I haven't had the misfortune of experiencing it, but I must say that most men I've witnessed who have endured this procedure weren't happy."

Damon blinks faster.

"I don't know where she is."

"Are you sure?" Andreas asks, picking up the shiny pliers and twisting them in the light.

"I think we need to make sure that we have young Damon here's full attention, Andreas. What do you think?"

"I think it's a good idea. Just to be sure. I hear pain is a fantastic memory trigger," Andreas agrees. "Eenie, meenie, miney, mo," he says, then grabs Damon's right hand and settles on the baby finger.

"We'll start with this one," he says, yanking at the nail.

Damon yelps, then bites down on his lip. He can't move, though, because his arms and feet are tied to the chair.

"I don't like doing this, Damon. I'm not a violent man. But understand me. I will do anything to get Emily back. Anything, Damon. Including taking you apart piece by piece."

"I can't," he growls through his teeth.

"Yes, you can. Gallo can't save you now."

He flinches at the mention of Gallo's name.

"What? Did you imagine that I wouldn't find out about your little dalliance with the enemy? Have you forgotten who I am, Damon?"

"He'll kill me."

I throw back my head and laugh out loud.

"And you think I won't?"

He goes quiet again. Clearly, he's afraid of Gallo. This infuriates me further.

"Tell me what I want to know!" I bark.

"You killed David Thornton, didn't you?" Andreas announces.

Damon looks up and stares at him. Bingo!

"Why?" I ask.

"Come on, man! Can't you guess?" he sneers, causing Andreas to punch him in the mouth.

Damon throws back his head and laughs. Does this guy have a death wish? Well, he can taunt me as much as he likes. I'm not going to kill him until I know where Emily is.

"I've got all day," I sigh and nod at Andreas, who gets a firm grip on another fingernail and yanks.

"Fuck!" Damon yells out in pain.

"Eight little piggies to go, bro," Andreas says calmly.

"Eighteen, if we're counting toes," I interject.

"Fine! Gallo is pissed off because you succeeded the old man. He wanted David dead so you would lose control of the finances."

"What difference does it make to Vince who takes over our organization? He has his own family," I comment.

"He wants the whole of LA."

"And with me out of the way, Gallo figures he'll swoop in and save the day, does he?"

"I guess."

"I see. So, when that didn't work, he took Emily to bring me to my knees. Is that it? Does Gallo really think that I'll bow out and give him the business? The man is a fucking idiot. The men would never allow that anyway."

"Are you sure?" Damon grins.

Is he bluffing, or are there other rats in my family?

"Nice try, Damon," Andreas barks and yanks out another nail. "Burns, doesn't it?"

"Oh, well," I say, "you may as well shoot him in the head. We know Gallo has Emily, so we don't need this little turd anymore. Thanks for playing, Damon, but you're out."

Andreas pulls out his gun and starts to screw on the silencer before he points it at Damon's head.

"Wait!" he yells.

"What was that? Did you suddenly remember something important, young man?" I smirk.

"She's in Mexico. Emily is in Mexico."

"Mexico?" I say.

"Where in Mexico?" Andreas says, pushing the edge of the silencer into Damon's temple. "It's a big country."

"I'll tell you if you let me go."

"No. You'll tell me, and then I'll decide what to do with you."

Andreas pulls back the hammer on the gun. Damon is openly panicking now, squirming in the chair.

"Okay," he shouts. "Okay, I'll tell you."

"Start talking!" Andreas roars.

"Tijuana. Emily is in Tijuana."

How the hell did they get her out of the country? This is bad. Mexico is no place for someone like Emily. I imagine that wherever Gallo is holding Emily, it probably isn't the Ritz.

"Where?" I demand.

"I'll take you there. You won't get past the front door unless I do."

Andreas knocks Damon on the side of his head with the butt of the gun. He's lights out.

"What do you think, Lucas? Is he bullshitting us? Can we trust that this rat won't lead us straight into a trap?" Andreas asks once Damon is out cold.

"I don't see too many alternative choices here, my friend. We have to get to Emily before Gallo decides to use her against me."

"I know you don't want to hear this, Lucas, and I'm really sorry for even bringing it up. But what if Damon's full of shit? What if Emily is dead and he's lying to lure us into a trap?"

"Gallo is a bastard, but he's cunning. He won't hurt Emily if he thinks he can use her against me. No, Emily is alive and in Mexico. Once this bastard wakes up, we'll start working on a plan."

LYDIA HALL

"Okay, Boss."

"You did good, Andreas."

"Thanks, Lucas."

"There's one more thing," I say before I leave Andreas to deal with Damon. "We can't drag our feet on this one. We have to get to Emily sooner rather than later. She's carrying my child."

* * *

"He's awake, and he's singing like a canary," Andreas smiles.

"Is he now? I guess Damon is smarter than he looks."

"Forget Ginkgo Biloba. Nothing is quite as effective for memory loss as a silencer to the temple."

"Isn't that the truth?" I snort. "Where in Tijuana is Emily?"

"I feel I have to prepare you. You're not going to like this, Lucas."

"Where is she?"

"Gallo owns a club down there. A strip club."

"She's not…"

"I'm afraid so, Lucas. I'm sorry. Damon dumped Emily there in the care of a guy named Paolo. Apparently, he did so under Gallo's orders. They are keeping her there until Gallo sets his takeover plan in motion."

"That fucking son of a bitch! I'll kill him! I'll kill them all! Starting with Damon!"

"Wait, Lucas. Calm down. We need him. I agree the little worm needs to be taught a lesson, but after we find Emily. Okay?"

Andreas is blocking the door to my office. He probably fears that I'll storm out and put a bullet in Damon's head. He's not far off.

"Fine! I'll deal with the bastard later. Have you put together a team to go with us to Mexico?"

"Us? Oh, no. You're not going. The boys and I are leaving tonight."

"Andreas, I know you mean well and that you're being a good friend. But there's no way in hell I'm staying here while Emily is at the mercy of Gallo. No fucking way! I'm going, and that's final."

Andreas sighs. He's frustrated with me, but I don't give two shits. Emily is in trouble, and the last thing I need is to sit around like a spare part while others save the woman I love. There's zero chance of that happening.

"Okay. I'll make sure we have enough muscle. Gallo will certainly try to take you out. You're not dying on my watch, Boss."

The next few hours are a blur. The mansion looks like a platoon's barracks, with our mercenaries assembling to go over the plan that Andreas had laid out. There is no shortage of weaponry and men capable of starting an invasion. But we have to be careful how we approach this mission.

We don't know who's in Gallo's pocket in Mexico. The federales are easily bribed. Crossing the border is the trickiest part of this whole mission, so I leave it up to Andreas to arrange. This isn't his first rodeo when it comes to smuggling men and weapons through the border post, so I have complete confidence in him.

It's 11 p.m. when we set off for the border. It's a two hour drive, so we should be in Tijuana by 1 a.m., give or take a few minutes to get through customs. That is usually the time of night when the strip club will be at its busiest. A good time to sneak in and snatch Emily back without being noticed.

My mind keeps straying to places where I don't want it to. The what ifs are driving me to distraction. I have to believe that Emily is okay. The idea of her being forced to strip or dance on a bloody pole like a tart makes my blood boil. She is far too classy and innocent for the situation she's in. I feel awful for protecting her against Gallo and his scumbag entourage.

Damon glances sheepishly in my direction the entire time we're on our way to the border. I insisted that he stay right by my side the whole way. If he's going to try anything, I want to be there to whip the shit out of him.

Hang in there, Emily, my love. I'm coming.

I sincerely hope that Gallo is there too. It's about time the two of us had a little chat.

24

EMILY

"You're pregnant, aren't you? I thought you could put one over on me, did you, you little bitch?"

Paolo is furious. His face is red, and his eyes are darting to and fro as he stares a whole through my abdomen.

I was afraid this would happen. How long did I imagine I could hide my belly? I wear a bikini every night. It doesn't exactly hide much.

"Well, I hope you're as good at giving blowjobs as you are at dancing," he snaps, "because that is going to be your new profession."

"No! Please, Paolo. I'll do anything else. Please, not that," I beg.

"Shut up, you whore! You're going to earn money on your back and knees from now on. It costs money to keep you bitches fed and clothed."

He storms out of my room and slams the door. I have to tell Maria. This is a disaster!

I find her alone in her room.

"He knows, Maria," I say through tears. "Paolo knows I'm pregnant. We have to go."

Maria looks stressed.

"Mierda! Okay, leave it with me. Let me see if I can move our plans forward."

"I'm sorry, Maria. I haven't eaten much in the last few months, but the baby is starting to show anyway."

"It's okay, Emily. Don't cry. I'll sort something out."

"Thank you, my friend," I whisper, hugging her closely.

* * *

"Tonight," Maria whispers as we pass each other in the hall of the rundown apartment block where all the strippers are supposed to play house. "Meet me in my room after your shift."

I nod and keep walking. My stomach is in a knot at the thought of getting out of here and the possible shitstorm that lies ahead for Maria and me if we're caught. But it's too far down the track now to turn back. I imagine Maria has gone out on a very shaky limb to arrange this. I truly hope that all will go smoothly.

I'm distracted while I dance. Who can focus when your life is literally on the line? I know I'm struggling to keep a poker face. I can only imagine what poor Maria is feeling right now.

The minute hand is taking its sweet time ticking its way around the face of the clock. Ugh! If only I wasn't pregnant. I could do with a stiff drink right about now to settle my nerves.

Paolo is watching me. Fuck, I hate those bug eyes of his. Is he walking over to talk to me or the girl next to me? Please let it not be me. Shit! He's coming over to me. I keep dancing, hoping he'll change direction and leave me in hell alone.

"Emily," he says, waiting for me to look at him.

I nod.

"Our VIP is back. He wants to see you later tonight. Don't disappear after your shift."

My legs go a little lame. Oh, no! I can't do this. Why tonight of all nights? Shit!

I look over to where poor Maria is fending off a drunkard's unwelcome advances. Did she see Paolo talking to me? Damned place!

It's 2 p.m. when we finally get our break. I rush over to Maria and share my news with her.

"We have to go now, Maria. I don't want to be in the same room as Vince Gallo. He is a bad man. I just know it. Please, we have to leave right now."

"Okay. Just give me five minutes."

Maria disappears from the break room while I try my best not to run for the front door, screaming like a banshee. I check the clock on the wall. Maria's been gone for what feels like a lifetime. What is she doing? I can't wait much longer. It's now or never. Come on, Maria! Where are you?

"Let's go," she says, rushing back into the room.

"I need to collect my cash from the room," I say.

"No time. I have enough for both of us."

"Oh, okay."

"Here," she says, handing me a set of clothes and sneakers. "Put this on. Come on. Follow me. Stay close and be quiet. Don't talk, no matter what. You got me?"

"Uhm, okay."

LYDIA HALL

"I mean it. Not a word!"

"Okay."

Maria takes my hand and walks so fast I can barely keep up. We walk into a part of the club I've never seen before, then out through the kitchen and into a car that is waiting for us. As soon as we're inside, the driver speeds off.

I want to ask Maria who we're with and where we're going, but I promised to keep my mouth shut, so that's what I do. We race past other cars, past street parties and fireworks, past dilapidated apartment buildings, into the darkness.

I have no idea where we're going, but I trust Maria. She has as much to lose here as I have. She and I are ducking down behind the driver and passenger seats like kids playing hide and seek. I'm holding onto her hand so tightly that I'm probably cutting off her circulation.

The man in the front seat starts talking to Maria. He's talking pretty fast, but I manage to catch every few words. He's saying something about a fee. Maria reaches into her hoodie pocket and hands him a wad of notes. They look like they've seen better days, so I guess she's been squireling them away for a while now.

The man hands the money over to his co driver who counts the notes and then nods. I look at Maria, who places her finger over her lips, reinforcing her previous command for me to keep quiet. I nod.

It's been at least half an hour, and my legs are cramping in the small space on the floor behind the passenger seat. But my discomfort is a small price compared to the freedom I'm racing toward.

The car slows down and comes to a stop. The driver speaks to Maria, who gets up. She pulls me from my compact hiding spot.

"Come," she whispers.

She doesn't have to tell me twice. The car doors open, and we get out. Where are we?

The car speeds off as soon as we're out. Maria takes me by the hand again and leads me toward a motel.

"You can talk now."

"Oh, thank God. Where are we?"

"On the outskirts of Tijuana. We'll be safe here."

"Why did you tell me not to talk?"

"If those guys knew you were American, they would have charged me double the price to get us out of there."

"I see. That makes sense."

Maria takes out a key.

"Where did you get that?"

"The driver booked us a room. I told him not to tell the owner who the room is for. It's better if we stay out of sight."

"Maria, you're a lifesaver! I can't believe we made it."

"We're not out of the woods yet. You'd better get hold of your friends as soon as possible so we can leave this place altogether."

"Of course."

Maria and I stop outside room number fourteen. The place is run down and smells like it's seen its fair share of travelers. But it's not the strip club and it's in better shape than the rooms we are used to staying in.

I make a beeline for the phone. Thank God, I know Dannie's number by heart. I don't care that it's the middle of the night. I reach for the receiver and place it a short distance from my ear. Who knows what kind of germs and grime have attached themselves to the piece of plastic? Yuk!

"Oh, fuck! The phone's dead."

I fiddle with the phone a few times without any success. There's no dial tone.

"What are we going to do now?" I say in exasperation and plonk myself down on the bed.

"I think I spotted a payphone down the block. Come, let's go," Maria says.

We leave the room and lock the door behind us.

"There," she says, heading for the phone booth.

"Well, this is just fucking fantastic," I gasp when we get closer. "The receiver is lying on top of the call box, severed from the wire."

"Fuck," Maria whispers.

"This is typical. Cell phones have taken over the world. No respect for other forms of communication," I whine.

"We'll find one. Don't worry," she sighs.

"I'm so hungry."

"I saw a vending machine outside. Room service is out of the question, I'm afraid," Maria insists.

"Hey, I'll eat anything right now."

"Here, take some cash."

"Thank you. Can I get you anything?"

"Yeah, grab me a packet of crisps and a Coke. I'll walk a little farther and see if I can find another phone booth."

"You got it."

"I'll meet you back in the room. Don't open for anyone but me. Okay?" she says and walks off.

I make my way to the vending machine and buy as many snacks as I can afford, after which I return to our motel room. Maria returns after about ten minutes.

"Did you find a phone?"

"No. We'll have more luck in the daylight. I'm exhausted. I need sleep."

"Okay. I could do with a few hours of sleep myself. Thank you, Maria. I will always be in your debt."

"Just get us the cash we need to travel, and we'll call it quits," she smiles.

"You got it."

"Oh, my goodness," I say a few minutes later while we're digging into the snacks I scored from the vending machine. "Junk food has never tasted this good. I can't believe there's beef jerky in that machine."

Maria chuckles as I shove more food into my mouth.

"I guess the baby is hungry too."

"Yeah, I guess so."

"I wonder if it's a boy or a girl."

"Me too. What's it like to be a mother, Maria?"

"Wonderful. Scary."

"I'm so sorry about your family, Maria. I cannot imagine the heartache you've had to endure."

"Thank you, Emily. That's why I want to go to my cousin's house. I want to start over. It will be good for me."

"Well, if there's anything I can do to help you, just ask."

"What does the father of your baby do?"

This isn't a question I'm prepared for. Will Maria still help me if she knows what Lucas does for a living? I wouldn't if I were her. The mafia is the reason she and I are in this mess in the first place. How do I explain to her that I've fallen in love with the enemy? It's too complicated to even contemplate.

"He's a businessman," I say instead.

"Is he rich?"

"Yes. But I don't care about that," I add quickly.

"It's nice when you have money."

"I guess. But even rich people have problems."

"We're all just human."

"True. I'm so tired. I think I'll close my eyes for a few minutes. Do you mind?"

"No. You sleep. I'll keep watch."

"Okay."

I'm utterly exhausted. I'm sure I'll sleep for a month once I'm home. I'm not in the clear yet, but once morning comes, Maria and I can get to a working phone so I can call Dannie. I'll just close my eyes for a bit so that I'm not the walking dead in the morning.

* * *

What was that? I sit bolt upright in bed.

"Maria," I whisper.

"Shhh," she says.

She's standing at the window, peeping through a slit in the curtains. I don't like the look on her face. There's trouble outside, and if I were a betting woman, I'd say it has something to do with us.

"What is it?" I whisper.

"There are men outside with guns. They're busting down doors," she says in a panic.

"Is there a backway out of here?" I ask.

"I don't think so," Maria says with a look of pure terror in her eyes.

"I'll check the bathroom."

I jump out of bed and rush over to the bathroom. There's a small window above the toilet. I'm sure Maris and I will squeeze through it if we try hard enough.

"Come," I call to her from the bathroom. "There's a small window. I'm sure we'll fit."

I watch as Maria crosses the floor toward me. But before she can reach the bathroom door, the front door flies open. Shards of wood fly all over the place as the lock shatters. A heavy set man with a gun moves at lightning speed and grabs Maria by the hair as she tries to get away. She screams and squirms to break free, but it's no use.

I slam the bathroom door shut and turn the lock. Will I have enough time to squeeze through the window before he can get to me? I scamper onto the toilet and reach for the window. But as I do so, my food slips, and I fall backward and hit my head against the bath. I'm overcome by a wave of nausea before I pass out. I guess there will be no escape for me today.

25

LUCAS

Our car is second in line to get through the border post. We've patched Damon's face to look a little less beaten up so that he doesn't attract too much attention from the guards.

"Keep your mouth shut," I instruct him as we move forward.

He looks at me defeatedly and nods. I'd play along too if I were him. He's lucky he's still drawing breath. The only reason Damon isn't fish food is because he's agreed to take us to Gallo's club and show us the backway into the seedy joint.

The border patrol guard looks at our passports and gives Damon a side glance.

Damon smirks and says, "Boxing. You should see the other guy."

The guard grins and nods before he returns the documents to us and waves us through.

"Resourceful," I say. "Keep it up, and you may live to see another day."

Another forty-five minutes, and we'll be in Tijuana. The streets are bound to be teeming with tourists and partygoers at this time of the morning, which is good for us. The more people around us, the better.

"So, this Paolo guy. Tell me more about him," I bark at Damon.

"He runs Gallo's strip joints."

"Does he have muscle?"

"Yes."

"How many?"

"About ten guys inside the club."

"Is that where Emily is?"

"That's where I left her."

"Well, you'd better pray that I find her there, safe and sound."

I can only imagine how scared Emily must be. What an awful place to land up in. The town itself is known for its unsavory nightlife, amongst other things. I have no idea what condition my poor Emily will be in once I find her. I can only pray that she forgives me for my failure to protect her. I wouldn't be at all shocked if she never wants to see me again once this is over. Who could blame her?

Damon gives the driver directions as soon as we enter the city limits. We drive by the club once to check it out before we park a distance away.

"Okay," Andreas says as the men who have joined us for this mission exit their vehicles and stand around for the briefing. "This is a diagram of the inside of the club. According to young Damon over here, Paolo's office is over here."

Andreas points to a spot on the diagram and maps out the route for each of the men.

"Eddie, you and two of the men are coming with me and Mr. Lucchese. We're going to head straight for Paolo's office. Sunny, you and the rest of the crew are in charge of creating a distraction so we can slip in unseen. Does everyone know what to do?"

The men nod.

"Good. Let's go."

All of us are armed to the teeth. We're not taking any chances. This isn't a picnic, and we're not dealing with ordinary men here. Gallo's men are notoriously violent and low class. He seems to troll the gutters for his minions.

Andreas, Damon, Eddie, and a few chosen men, and I hang back until the shit hits the fan. As soon as it's safe to slip past the occupied bouncers at the front door, we head straight for Paolo's office. Eddie kicks the door down, and we rush him.

Paolo is stunned at our intrusion. The unfortunate young woman is servicing her fat boss under the desk and screams as we burst in and raise our weapons.

"Get out!" I yell at her. "Andreas, lock the door."

The girl scampers while trying to get her top back on.

"Who the fuck are you?" Paolo demands, zipping up his pants. "Damon, what's going on?"

Andreas hits him in the face with the butt of his machine gun, causing the fat bastard to collapse backwards onto his chair.

"Where's Gallo?" I ask, irritated that he isn't here.

I was looking forward to kicking his ass, but I guess that will have to wait now. My first priority is finding Emily.

"That's none of your fucking business," Paolo snaps.

Clearly, Paolo's enjoyed far too many years during which he's been the one calling the shots. It would seem that picking on defenseless women has given him a false sense of importance. Well, I'm about to slap that illusion right out of him, the prick.

"I asked you a question, you fat fuck!"

"Who are you?" he asks again.

"I'm your worst nightmare, Paolo," I growl.

Paolo looks confused for a moment. I think he was under the impression that this was a robbery. Now that he realizes it's something more serious, he looks nervous.

"Where is Gallo?" Andreas barks.

"He isn't here."

"Where is Emily?" I demand.

Andreas points the machine gun at Paolo's knee.

"Perhaps he needs a bit of prompting, Boss. How about it, Paolo? Which knee cap are you less fond of?"

"Wait! The whore isn't here either."

I'm fuming at his derogatory comment, so I walk over to him and punch him in the face.

"Don't you call her that! Where is she, you bastard?" I demand in a low, threatening voice.

Paolo's mouth is bleeding. He wipes at it and glares up at me with disdain. "You'd better start talking, or you're a dead man!"

He doesn't say anything.

"Mr. Lucchese isn't fucking around, Paolo. You'd better tell him where his woman is," Damon interjects.

Paolo's eyes widen at the mention of my name. Clearly, he's heard of me. I watch closely as the gears in his head start spinning. How long before he realizes that he's in deep trouble?

"I'd start talking if I were you," I smirk. "Gallo isn't going to save your ass. You're far too replaceable, Paolo. Don't be an idiot. Save yourself while you still can. Do it while I'm feeling generous."

"She's not here," he pouts, fed up that we have the upper hand in this situation.

"Where is she?"

"Paolo, I'm warning you. I'm losing my patience, and trust me, you don't want that."

Andreas pushes the barrel of his gun down hard onto Paolo's right knee cap. He flinches and groans.

"Okay, okay. She's at the safehouse. The little b…"

Clearly, he's rethinking his words more carefully before he carries on. "She ran away. We caught her and locked her up."

"Where?" I urge him, tiring of his stalling tactics.

"Damon knows where."

I look from Paolo to Damon. I guess Paolo reckons that if Damon spills the beans, Gallo will let him off the hook. I don't care which one of these clowns takes me to Emily, as long as I get to her.

"Damon?" Andreas barks.

"Yeah, I think I know the place."

"Take us there right now," I order him loudly.

I turn to leave Paolo's fate to Andreas when I catch a glimpse of a shiny object out of the corner of my eye. It's a knife. Paolo must have pulled it from somewhere while Andreas was focusing on Damon.

"Andreas!" I shout at my friend. "Look out!"

There's no time to wrestle the weapon away from Paolo, so I point my weapon at him and pull the trigger. Paolo goes down like a fat kid on a seesaw in a hail of bullets as Eddie joins in and fires at him.

"Stupid man," Andreas says as he watches the life draining from Paolo.

"Come on, Damon," I say, rushing to the door. "There's no time to waste. Take me to the safe house."

It's absolute chaos inside the club. Gunfire, punters rushing about trying to escape the club without getting shot, and terrified strippers running for the exit.

"Burn it to the ground, Eddie," I yell as we reach the exit.

"Yes, Boss!"

I hope Gallo hears about this, and it spoils his fucking day. I'm so tired of the bastard meddling in my affairs that I'll do anything to get rid of him. He can count himself extremely lucky that he isn't here tonight, or he'd be going up in flames along with his seedy club and all the brutes that work for him.

I may be in the criminal world, but I've never condoned human trafficking. It's despicable, and I refuse to be a part of that cancer eating away at society. It warms my heart to see Gallo's dancers running for their freedom.

The club is going up in flames as we drive away, the blaze visible in my rearview mirror.

"I hope that asshole chokes on the news when he wakes up later today," Andreas comments.

"It's about time someone holds Gallo accountable for all the pain he causes people," I agree. "Okay, Damon. Where are we going?"

"It's not far from here. Paolo likes to keep his girls close."

"You'd better pray that he hasn't done anything to harm Emily," I seethe.

"I was only doing what I was ordered to," he mumbles.

"You'd better shut your piehole, Damon," Andreas warns the man, who is teetering on the edge of a severe beating.

"Have you still not learned anything? Listen to Andreas," I agree.

Damon shows the driver which roads to navigate, and after ten minutes, he tells the driver to stop.

My nerves are shot. I don't know what I'll find inside the house that looks like it could use a good dose of TLC.

I'm here, my love. I'm here.

26

EMILY

When I come to I'm no longer in the bathroom, where I was so desperately trying to escape the man with the gun. How the hell did they find us? Where's Maria? Oh, Lord, please let her be alright.

I sit up. What fresh hell is this? I'm chained to a bed. I look around the room to find Maria on another bed in the corner of the room. She isn't moving and is also chained like a dog. What kind of people are these? How can human life be so cheap to them? Have they no shame?

I mean, I've read about situations like these in magazines and books, but you never actually think it could happen to you. This is unbelievable!

"Maria," I call out, trying not to be too loud. Who knows who's listening and what they're planning on doing to Maria and me?

Maria stirs, but she doesn't sit up just yet. I hope she doesn't have any serious injuries. I was out like a light after I hit my head on the tub, so I have no idea what to expect.

"Maria. Are you okay? Can you move?" I whisper now that I know she can hear me.

"Ugh…" she groans.

"Oh, thank God! Are you okay? Can you move?"

"I feel like a truck hit me. What happened? Where are we?"

"I don't know. How the hell did they find us, Maria?"

She sits up slowly, holding her head.

"I don't know. Are you okay, Emily?"

"I'm alright. I can't believe this is happening to us. How the hell did they know where we were? Do you think one of the guys who helped us escape talked? Did they double cross you, Maria?"

"Who the hell knows? I guess we're not going anywhere now," she says, tugging at the chain attached to her ankle.

"I can't do this again, Maria," I whimper, tears welling in my eyes.

"We're just going to have to find another way, Emily. You can't give up now. You have to stay strong for your baby's sake."

Maria's stern voice reminds me that I'm not alone in this nightmare. My baby's life depends on me keeping my wits about me. Maria's right. This is no time to fall apart.

"Okay," I say, sniffing back the tears that are threatening to spill over. "How are we going to get out of this one, my friend?"

"I don't have a clue, but we're going to try."

"I'll see if I can find something I can use to get this chain off me."

I look around the floor to see if I can find a hairpin or something sharp that I can use to jimmy the lock on the chain. The place is a mess. Dust and dead bugs are scattered everywhere. I shudder to think about what these dirty walls have witnessed through the years.

"What are you looking for?" Maria asks.

"A pin or a piece of wire."

"Why?"

"I'm going to try and get this lock open. It's our best chance out of here."

"Here," she says, pulling a pin from her hair. "Use this."

Maria throws the hairpin in my direction. It lands just out of my reach.

"Shit! Sorry. Can you reach it?"

"No. Hang on, I'll try. Ugh! Almost."

I stretch out as far as the chain will allow, but I'm still a few inches short.

"Use the blanket," Maria suggests.

"Good idea."

The blanket next to me is filthy. I wish I didn't have to touch it, but what other choice do I have? I'll worry about diseases later. Now is not the time to be squeamish.

"Do you know how to open a lock?"

"My brother and I used to do it when we were kids. He loved illusions and magic, so we played with a set we got for Christmas. I hope I can remember how to do it."

"Hey, it's like riding a bike, right?" Maria smiles.

"Let's hope so."

I pull the dirty blanket off the bed and throw it across the floor. It covers the part of the floor where the pin is.

"Here goes," I say, pulling the blanket gently toward me.

"Did it work? Have you got it?"

"Got it!"

I straighten the hair pin and gently push it into the lock. It makes a scraping sound as metal scrapes against metal. I know I can do this. I know I can.

"Shhh! Stop! I hear someone coming," Maria says suddenly.

"Fuck," I mumble, shoving the hairpin into my bra.

"Lie down. Pretend you're still sleeping," Maria whispers.

The door opens slowly. I keep my eyes closed, and I don't move a muscle. Oh, please just go away! I can't deal with this right now. I'm tired and sore from the fall, and quite frankly, I'm due for a fucking break!

Whoever is at the door stays in the doorway. The door closes. Is the person in the room or has he left? I'm not taking any chances, so I keep still. After a few minutes of deathly silence, I open my eyes to check. We're alone.

"Who was that?" I whisper.

"I caught a glimpse. It's the same man who brought us here."

"Son of a bitch! Did he say anything back at the motel? Do you know who he is?"

"No. He just threw us into the car and told me to shut my mouth."

"Such charming people, aren't they? I must remember to invite them to my summer house for a barbeque."

Maria laughs hysterically at my attempt to lighten the mood. Laughter is better than tears, I guess, so I smile and retrieve the pin from my bra.

"Okay, let's see if I can do this."

"I think that asshole must have ripped a handful of hair out when he grabbed me. I'm so tired of men thinking that they can do whatever they like with us."

"I tell you, Maria, I haven't been here for as long as you have, but I feel like I've taken a lifetime of crap from bullies. We're going to make these men pay for what they've done to us and to others like us. That, I promise you."

"Agreed. How's it going over there? Any luck?"

"Not yet, but it's coming back to me. Tell me about your cousin's place," I suggest to keep our minds off the hail Mary pass I'm attempting with the hairpin.

"It's beautiful. The resort is right on the beach. My family used to meet there for the holidays when I was a child. My cousins and I would play until it was dark outside. We'd swim and roll down the sand dunes for hours. Sometimes I wonder why we have to grow up."

"Yeah. Adulthood isn't exactly a walk in the park, is it?"

"Not from where I'm sitting, no. How about you? It must have been awful for you, losing both your parents like that."

"It was. But David made it all seem bearable. I miss him so much."

"I miss my mom. She was the one who kept the family together. My father is a bastard. He didn't used to be."

"Do you have siblings?"

"I have an older brother. I don't know where he is now."

"Were you guys close growing up?"

"Not really. He's much older than I am. He got involved in drugs after my mother died. I don't even know if he's still alive."

"That's too bad."

"Yeah. The men in my family aren't worth much. They do more harm than good. What about your baby's father? What's he like?"

That's an excellent question. I used to think that Lucas was the most amazing man I'd ever met. I trusted him with my life. Now, I'm not so sure.

"Honestly, Maria. I'm not sure anymore. It seems that he's brought nothing but pain and loss into my life."

"I know the type. Do you think he's looking for you?"

"I hope so. If he isn't, I'm pretty screwed."

"We don't need men. We'll figure this out."

I'm about to answer Maria when there's a loud crashing sound outside the window. I have such a fright that I drop the pin.

"What the hell was that?" Maria gasps. "Can you see anything outside?"

"No. The window is too far away."

"What else can go wrong?"

"This could be a good thing. The commotion may give us a chance to slip out unseen. If only I can get this bloody lock…"

Against all odds, the lock pops open.

"Wow! You've got this, Emily," Maria shouts above the chaos.

I pull free from the chain and move over to Maria so I can start working on her lock. I'm eerily calm, which is crazy considering the situation I'm in. Perhaps I'm just fed up with being afraid. And, most of all, I'm pissed off! I'm pissed off with David for dying, beyond pissed off with Damon for betraying me, and most of all, I'm pissed off with Lucas for leaving me out to dry.

The second lock clicks open.

"Okay. Let's figure out a way to get the hell out of here," I say.

"Check over at the window. What's happening out there?"

"Not much to see on this side," I say, my heart beating out of my chest. "It's an alley."

"Fuck! So I guess we won't be sneaking out the window."

The noise outside is getting louder, and I imagine that whatever is going on is escalating. I have to get Maria and myself out of here before we end up hurt or worse.

"Is the door locked?" I ask Maria, thinking that because we were securely chained, our captor wouldn't have bothered to lock the door.

Maria goes over to the door and turns the knob. The door doesn't budge. Damn it!

"No, we're not getting out of this so easily," she says.

Oh, come on! One break. Just one small break from the universe would be so much appreciated around about now! Just one!

The door flies open, and in runs a man with a gun. Maria and I are terrified. Who is he? Friend or foe? These days, it seems impossible to tell at face value. I get my answer soon enough when the man rushes toward me and grabs me by the hair.

"Ouch!" I scream as he shoves me around like a rag doll. "Let go!" I scream at him, but it's no use.

He's afraid of something—or someone.

Maria is yelling at him in Spanish to let me go. She's pleading, but he yells obscenities at her and tells her to shut up. What happens next makes my heart leap into my throat. A man rushes into the room and points a gun at the miscreant pulling at my hair.

It's a face I'd recognize anywhere. It's Lucas! Can it be? Am I hallucinating? Nothing at this point would surprise me. They say the human mind does crazy things when under intense stress. This certainly qualifies as one of those situations. I mean, what is more stressful than having a gun jammed into the back of your head while a brutish Mexican is screaming profanities?

I close my eyes tightly and open them again. I blink a few times too, just for good measure. It *is* Lucas! It really is him. Oh, thank you, God! I've never been so happy to see someone as happy as I am at this very moment. But I'm far from safe with this gorilla manhandling me.

Lucas shouts at the man, ordering him to let me go. The brute swears at Lucas and pulls me closer against his sweaty body. I know he'll never let me go, and if he gets any more nervous, he may pull the trigger by accident and shoot me in the head.

The only solution I can think of on the spot is to whip back my head in the hopes that I'll break his nose or, at the very least, startle the oaf. So, that's what I do. I throw back my head as fast and hard as I can. The pain from connecting the man's hard head hurts like hell, but he is startled and lets go of my hair.

I drop to the floor so that I'm out of his reach. At the same time, Lucas fires a shot that sends the brute stumbling backward. He lands on the floor next to the bed. He isn't moving. Is he dead? Am I safe?

I'm not going to wait around to find out. Lucas is next to me in a flash. He pulls me to my feet, gives me a quick once over to ensure that I'm not wounded in any way, then grabs me in a bear hug.

I have no words. I'm crying like a baby.

"Come, my love. Let's get you out of here," Lucas says, letting me go.

"Maria!" I yell. "Where's Maria?"

"I'm here," I hear my friend calling from the corner of the room.

"Come, Maria. Let's go."

"Stay close, Emily," Lucas says, moving his body in front of mine.

Oh, I intend to. In fact, I may never leave your side again!

"Andreas!" Lucas yells at the top of his lungs. "I found them!"

Andreas appears in the doorway.

"I'll get Eddie to clear a path," he says from the doorway.

Andreas takes Maria's hand and keeps her close to protect her from the chaos surrounding us. We move very slowly out of the room and into the hallway. We step over bodies and navigate through a maze of passages until we're finally outside.

Lucas and Andreas escort Maria and me safely to an idling car.

"Quickly! Get in. Stay down," Lucas instructs us.

Lucas jumps out of the car. I shout after him, begging for him to come back. But he's gone.

27

LUCAS

Emily looks so vulnerable. All I want to do is hold her in my arms, as close to my chest as possible. But now is not the time. I have to make sure that we're out of danger first. Emily is screaming for me to get back into the car, but there's something I have to take care of before I leave. Damon!

The slimy bastard leaped at his chance to break free from Andreas and me as soon as the shooting started. He even tried to stab me with a knife he found on the floor inside the house, but I was too quick for him. I punched him hard, and he fell to the ground. I have to find the little rat and teach him a final lesson.

I return to the spot where he lay when I punched his lights out. He's gone. Damn it! There's no way I'll rest until Damon is no longer a threat to Emily. I know his sort. He's a vindictive scumbag.

"Eddie. Where's Damon?"

"I don't know, Boss."

"Well, find him!"

Eddie nods and disappears. Damon is the only man who knows what's happened here tonight. I have to silence him if we're going to get across the border without the authorities hunting us down like dogs.

A sharp pain in my bicep spins me around. What the hell? It's Damon. He's standing behind me with the face of a madman. He's holding up a knife.

"Come on, Lucchese," he spits, "let's see what you're made of."

"You pathetic little guttersnipe! You think you can kill me? Okay, let's play," I say.

"It isn't fair if you have a gun," he snaps.

"I don't need a gun," I seethe. "I'll kick your ass the old fashioned way. Let's see what you're made of when my back isn't turned, you coward."

Damon lunges at me. But he's too slow. I hit him on the forearm. The blow is hard, and he drops the knife. Now it's a fair fight.

"Come on, you bastard! Come at me," I taunt him.

Damon circles me a few times before he lunges at me. I grab him in a headlock and squeeze as hard as I can. Damon kicks and squirms to get out of my grip, but I hold on for dear life.

"This is for David, Emily, and all the women you've ever sold into slavery, you fuck!" I growl, throttling the life out of this terrible human being.

I'm not proud of myself for doing this, but sometimes life requires us to do terrible things in order to keep others safe. I won't lose any sleep knowing that Damon is dead.

I stop when he stops struggling. Blood is pouring from the cut on my arm, turning my shirt crimson. I'll have to make a plan to stop the bleeding before we attempt to leave Mexico, or the guards will be suspicious.

"You're bleeding!" Emily cries when I get into the car.

"It's alright, my love. It's worse than it looks."

"We'd better get that bleeding under control, Boss," Andreas says as we speed away from the house.

The drive pulls into a side street when we're at a safe distance from the chaos.

"Are you okay? I ask a trembling Emily.

"I'm fine."

Andreas pulls a clean shirt from the trunk of the car and fashions a bandage from pieces of the old shirt he rips free.

"Are you okay, Maria?" I ask the woman with Emily.

She nods. I imagine she's too scared to speak. I would be too, I suppose. I'm just another stranger to her.

"Oh, Maria, this is Lucas," Emily says. "Lucas, this is Maria. If it weren't for her, I'd probably be dead by now."

"It's a pleasure meeting you, Maria. How can we ever thank you?"

"Maria needs money to get to her family, Lucas. I don't have access to any cash right now. Could you help her?"

"Of course. Anything you need, Maria."

"That's so generous. Thank you," Maria smiles.

"I could never repay you for your kindness, Maria," Emily says, hugging her.

"Get me to the bus station and buy me a ticket. We'll call it quits after that," Maria smiles.

"Andreas, get us to a bus stop," I instruct.

"Sure."

We drive out of town to the nearest bus stop. There, Andreas buys Maria a ticket and gives her a wad of cash. I watch from a distance while Emily and Maria say a teary goodbye. I cannot imagine what these two women have been through together.

"We have to go, Lucas," Andreas urges.

"I know. Let's give them a few more minutes.

"Okay, but the sooner we cross the border back into the US, the better."

I know he's right. But this woman was there for Emily when I wasn't, so I let them have their tearful farewell.

"She's going to be fine," I assure Emily once she returns to the car.

"I hope they don't capture her again, Lucas."

"I know, my love. I know. Come, we have to get going. I'm sorry, but we're going to have to smuggle you out of Mexico. I'm apologizing in advance for hiding you in the trunk of our car."

"I guess I'll leave the country in the same way I entered."

"I'm so sorry, my love."

"We're going to have to have a long talk when we get back home, Lucas."

Emily's words leave a pit in my stomach. Is she going to tell me that she never wants to see me again? Is this the end of the road for us? I can't imagine my life without this woman. I love Emily with every fiber of my being. But there's no time to think about that now, so I nod.

"Are you ready?" Andreas asks us.

"Yeah, let's go home."

"How are we going to manage this, Lucas?" Emily asks with a look of grave concern on her face.

"Well, I'm not going to lie. It's not going to be easy or comfortable, but I have a plan."

"O.k.a.y.," she says slowly.

"I know you have no reason to, taking into consideration that I've failed you so miserably, but please trust me one more time, Emily. I'll get you out of here."

"Okay."

"Andreas, do you have that blanket handy?"

"Yeah. It's in the trunk. I'll get it."

"My love, you have to be very quiet. It doesn't matter what you hear; don't make a sound."

She nods.

Emily's belly is starting to show. She instinctively rests her hands on her abdomen. I want to tell her that I know about our baby, but I'll wait until we're safely out of Mexico before I tell her. We have more than enough on our plate for the moment.

Andreas hands me a blanket.

"Take out the false bottom in the trunk. I'll wrap Emily up in the blanket in the meantime," I tell him.

Emily is trembling again. I wrap the blanket around her body and pull her in for a hug.

"You're okay," I whisper in her ear. "I've got you."

I want to tell her how sorry I am and that I love her endlessly, but now is not the time, so I just hold her tightly instead.

"Ready, Boss," Andreas says.

"Here we go. We're about a ten minute drive from the border. I'm going to wrap you up and cover you with a board in the trunk."

"I don't know if I can do this, Lucas."

"Yes, you can. We're so close to freedom, my love. So close."

Emily is shaking violently now, but she nods.

I pick her up and gently place her in the small space. When she signals to me that she's comfortable, I place the board over her and put the luggage on top of the board. No one will suspect a thing. The trunk looks just like any other.

"I hope this works," Andreas says as he starts the engine.

"It has to. I'd hate to have to shoot my way out of Mexico."

"You and me both, Lucas."

* * *

"It's crazy busy. That's a good thing," I say when we wait in line at the post with the engine idling.

"We're here, Emily," I say loudly enough so she can hear me under all the luggage. "Don't make a sound until I tell you it's safe."

I'm glad it's a chilly morning, or the poor thing would be overheating back there. It's our turn, so we pull up and open the window. It's the same guard we saw the night before.

"Where is your friend, the boxer?" he asks as he looks at our documents.

"He's got a fight tomorrow, so he stayed behind," Andreas offers.

"Open the trunk for me, please," the guard says after looking at us for a few moments.

Fuck! I hope he doesn't dig around in there. Not only will he find Emily, but he'll find my handgun too.

"Sure, Officer."

Andreas keeps his cool and gets out of the car. The two men walk around to the back of the vehicle. I don't move a muscle. My heart is racing, but I'm determined to keep a straight face.

I can see the guard in the side mirror as he steps closer to the trunk and rummages through the luggage. Andreas is cooler than a cucumber while the border guard goes about his business. What takes him mere minutes seems like hours.

The guard slams the trunk shut.

"Okay, you're good to go."

Andreas gets back in the car and gives me a knowing look. One that screams relief. We start up the engine as soon as we have the green light and drive back into the US.

"Stop the car," I order Andreas once we're at a safe distance from the guards.

Emily is a ball of nerves when I get her out of the trunk. She throws her arms around my neck and bursts into tears.

"Oh, Lucas. I was so scared. I can't do this anymore. I'm so tired. Take me home."

"It's over, my love. We're home now."

"No! I want to go home, Lucas. My home! I want to forget this nightmare. I'm done!"

It feels like my heart has just been ripped from my chest. The pain is excruciating.

"There's one more thing I have to do before I can take you home, Emily."

"No, Lucas! Please. I want to go home."

"The man who is behind your abduction is still out there. Once I've dealt with him, I'll take you wherever you want to go. I promise."

There's no point in making the case now for our relationship or that I want her to stay with me so that we can raise our child together. Emily is too upset right now to think rationally, so I'll placate her.

"You know who killed David, don't you?"

"Yes, I do."

'Who is it?'

"I'll tell you everything once we get safely to my place. Please, Emily. Let's get you home. My arm is killing me."

"Oh, yes, I'm sorry. I forgot about that."

"It's okay. You've been through a terrible ordeal. Come, you'll feel better once you've had a bath and a decent meal. We'll talk then."

Emily relents and gets back into the car. Ten minutes into the drive, she's fast asleep on my shoulder. I can't begin to imagine what she's seen and experienced since she was taken. All I can do to keep my own sanity is to imagine that no one man handled Emily or took advantage of her in the most vial way. I couldn't live with myself if I thought that the woman I love, the mother of my child, suffered physical abuse at another's hand. It's bad enough that she had to fear for her life.

She's still out for the count by the time we get home, so I carry her to my bedroom, place her gently on the bed, and cover her with a blanket. I watch her chest as it moves up and down. I'm so grateful to have this woman back. I love Emily so much. I thought I'd never see her again when Paolo said she had run away.

"Sleep well, my love. You're safe now," I whisper, closing the bedroom door.

28

EMILY

It wasn't a dream. I'm back in Lucas' bed. I sit up and look around me, soothing my soul with the knowledge that this is real.

Maria. I suddenly think of the brave woman who risked her own life to help me escape. It doesn't matter that we weren't entirely successful on our own. What matters is that she took a chance on me. I'll wait until tomorrow and then call the resort her cousin works at to find out if Maria made it there safely.

Dannie! I have to call my best friend and tell her that I'm home safely. Poor Daniella must be worried sick about me. What a terrible year it's been. I have to wonder what David would have done had he known what destruction his choices have led to.

One thing is for sure. If Lucas wants to be a part of my life and that of his child's he's going to have to give his career choices a good evaluation. I don't want to be with a man who lives like this. I can't. It's too hard. I love Lucas very much, but I have a child to think of now. I'm going to be a mother soon and no matter what happens, my child's needs will always be my main priority.

The door opens and Lucas peeks into the room.

"Oh, hi, You're awake. How are you feeling?"

"Like I could sleep for a month and still take frequent naps after that."

"I'm not surprised. Are you hungry? Chef will be happy to whip something delicious for you. Anything you like. Just name it."

"Sounds wonderful. I think I'll have a bath first."

"Your clothes are in the closet and there are fresh towels on the tub."

"Thank you, Lucas."

"Anytime, my love."

"We should talk after I've had a bite to eat."

"Okay. What can I get you to eat?"

"Don't laugh, but I'd kill for a cheeseburger."

"And a cheeseburger is exactly what you'll have."

I get up as soon as Lucas has left the room and head for the bathroom. I can't wait to soak away the dirt from my body. The stench of Tijuana's strip club and safe house clings to me like shit to a blanket. I'll have to wash my hair a few times to get the smell out, I'm sure.

I add as many fragrant bath balls to the water as I can stand before I slip into a heavenly tub filled with warm water. Oh! Who would have guessed that something so simple as a bath would hold so much pleasure. The room in Tijuana was small and the bathroom wasn't anything more than a glorified hose over an open drain.

I close my eyes, allowing the steam to open up my pores. I hope it will flush out the awful memories as well as the clogged pores on my face. The perfect tranquility is disturbed by one tiny thing. The baby is moving and it's the first time I can feel it.

LYDIA HALL

I move my fingers to the spot where I feel the light flutters of a tiny baby's limbs touching my insides. It's an odd sensation, like something tickling me very softly.

"We made it, sweetheart. We're home."

I'm so happy. But it isn't the sort of joy that can last forever. Not if Lucas refuses to hear me out. I pray that he'll listen to what I plan on saying to him because I refuse to put this precious new life at risk again. Once was enough.

"You look so peaceful."

I jerk at the sudden interruption. Lucas is standing next to the tub. I open my eyes and stare at his handsome face.

"Oh, sorry, babe. I didn't mean to startle you."

"I'm thinking it will be wise for the foreseeable future to not sneak up on me."

"Got it. My bad."

"This is arguably the best bath I've ever had," I sigh, settling back into Nirvana.

"Well, you'll be glad to know that it will be followed by the best cheeseburger you've ever had."

"I can't wait."

I open my eyes again and stare at Lucas for a while before I speak.

"Lucas, we have to talk."

He looks worried.

"I know about the baby," he says.

"What? How?"

"Dannie told me. She thought I needed to know. Also, your belly is much rounder than it was when we first met, and I'm guessing it isn't from the taco diet."

"That would be funny if it wasn't too soon."

"Again. Foot in mouth disease. Sorry."

"And?"

"And, I'm incredibly happy. I cannot imagine having a child with anyone else but you, my love."

"Really?"

"Of course! I love you, Emily. And I love our baby too."

"But it's so soon. We've only been together for a short time."

"That doesn't make the slightest difference to my feelings for you, my love. Don't you know yet how I feel about you? Can;t you tell when we're together?"

"I don't know what to think anymore, Lucas. I'm exhausted and I'm a ball of nerves at the thought of being a mom. And you…"

"What about me?"

"Lucas, you know how I feel about the life you're in. I don;t want this for you…for us."

"But, it's over now, Emily."

"For now, yes. But what about the next time? And the one after that? This isn;t the life I want for our child."

"What are you saying, Emily?"

"I'm saying that I'm not sure we have a future together if you choose to stay in this business, Lucas. I refuse to subject our child to this kind of violence. I love you, Lucas, but I don't know if I can do this again. No. I know I can't. I don't want to!"

* * *

LYDIA HALL

Lucas

She's ripping my heart from my chest and she doesn't even know it. How do I explain to my soulmate that being in the mafia isn't something from which you just bow out gracefully? Once you're in, that's it! There's no resigning, for goodness sake!

But, here we are, at the crossroads. I don;t know what to say in response to her firm demands.

"I'll see what's keeping the chef," I say, bowing out of the discussion like a coward.

"We're not done talking about this, Lucas."

"I know."

When did my life become so complicated? You'd think I'd be cruising. I'm at the pinnacle of success; I have more money than I know what to do with; I'm respected amongst my peers and competitors. How do I give that up? Why should I? I've worked hard my whole life to get here. Sure, I'm not saving lives or curing cancer, but I'm proud of my success.

But nothing is worth shit if I don't get to share it with the woman I love. Also, what kind of a father will I be if I stay? Fuck! This is hard!

"What's eating you, Lucas?"

"Andreas. I didn't see you there."

"Are you okay? Is Emily alright?"

"Yeah, she's fine."

"Come on, Out with it. Yours is not the face of a man who just pulled the fat out of the fire. What's wrong?"

"It's a mess, Andreas. A bloody mess. Women. They're complicated."

"Uh-huh. So, what's the trouble with yours?"

"Emily is worried about my *lifestyle*."

Andreas chuckles.

"I've never heard it called that before."

"Makes two of us."

"Sorry, I didn't mean to laugh. So, what are you going to do?"

"That's the million dollar question, isn't it? I can't just hand in my keys and sail off into the sunset, can I? I have responsibilities. This organization depends on me."

"I hear you."

"It's a fucking nightmare, buddy."

"Not to throw a second cat amongst the pigeons, Lucas, but I get where Emily's coming from. She's pregnant and recently rescued from a strip club in Mexico. I'd be shocked if she weren't about to do a runner."

"You're not helping."

"I'm just saying, Look at this from her point of view."

"Go away."

"Yeah, yeah. I'll leave you in peace. But you're going to have to think about this one, Boss. I don't envy you."

I pass the chef in the hallway, carrying the tray. It's unusual for him to deliver the food himself, but I know he's fond of Emily. Everyone is. She's an amazing woman. I can't lose her.

* * *

"What was that?"

Emily is sitting upright in bed. The noise outside woke me up too, so I go over to the window to investigate.

LYDIA HALL

There's a fire at the gatehouse and men are running from all directions.

"Stay here!" I tell Emily before I pull on my pants and a sweater and slip into the loafers alongside the bed.

"What is it, Lucas?"

Emily's eyes are filled with terror. This is not what I need right now.

"I'll be back in a bit. Stay here, my love. Lock the door behind me and don;t open it for anyone but me. Okay?"

She nods.

"It's going to be fine, baby," I say and kiss her before I leave the room.

I wait until I hear the key turning in the lock before I storm down the hall and downstairs. I run into Andreas. He's carrying two machine guns and hands me one.

"I was just coming to find you," he says over the noise.

"What the hell is going on?"

"Gallo's men are attacking us."

"That fucker! I'm so done with that man. Tonight is the night I rid the world of one more waste of space. Come on."

Together we run toward the entrance hall where a group of men are already gathered with weapons. Andreas and I assign them to teams.

"Is Gallo with them?" I ask Andreas.

"Are you kidding? And risk getting his hands dirty? I doubt it. He's probably at home torturing small animals."

"Well, not tonight. I have an idea."

"I don't know if I like the sound of that," Andreas says with a look of concern.

"Come on, Andreas. Where;s your sense of adventure? You've been living too cushie a life, I see."

"You're not calling me chicken are you?" he grins.

"Come on. Let's go. We're going to need more ammo."

Twenty minutes later, Andreas and I pull up outside Gallo's place.

"He'll never expect me to come here in person to kick his ass," I say as we watch the guard house from a distance.

"It is a crazy move, so no, probably not. Are you sure you want to do this?"

"Oh, yeah. It's long overdue."

"Alright, you crazy son of a bitch. Let's go kick his ass."

"That's the spirit. How many guards have you counted?"

"Four."

"Yeah. Okay. Let's pop 'em."

Andreas used to be in the armed forces. His sharp shooting abilities are legendary. I trust him to take out the guards before they know what's hit them. The silencer on his weapon gives us the upper hand here. Gallo won't hear us coming.

"Okay," he says once the guards are down, "open the gate."

Cracking safes and keypads are a little hobby of mine. I spent many years honing my skills while I was climbing the ladder.

"Once I open the gate, we're going to have to move our asses."

"Ready when you are, Boss."

We're inside the estate. Andreas and I make a beeline for Gallo's section of the main house. His sexual escapades are infamous, so I'm willing to bet that he's in his bedroom working on a pre-victory celebration with his hookers.

Sure enough, that's where we find him. Andreas took out a few more of Gallo's men on the way in, leaving me a clear run to the big cojones.

I slip into the room and watch for a few seconds while Andreas is giving the busty blonde his all.

"Celebrating prematurely, I see," I say out loud.

Gallo throws the blonde off him and reaches for his nightstand.

"I don't think so!" I yell. "One more move and I'll blow you to Kingdom come, you scumbag!"

Gallo looks at me. He's furious.

"You! What the hell do you think you're doing?"

"What I should have done years ago, you asshole."

"You won't kill me. You can't be that stupid."

"Oh, but I can. And I will."

"What? Is this about your girlfriend? Did she enjoy her new career as a stripper? Short lived, I know, but I'm sure she picked up a few handy tips. You should be thanking me."

I can feel the rage bubbling up from my gut. Gallo is stalling, getting a few digs in while he no doubt waits for the cavalry to save him.

They're not coming, asshole. It's just you and me.

"Why don't you leave the boys to have a little talk, sweetheart?" I say to the blonde covering in the corner of the room.

She grabs her dress and runs past me toward the door. I close it and lock.

"Okay, Gallo. Let's have a heart to heart."

29

EMILY

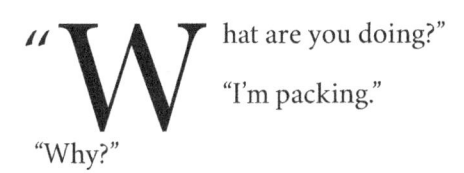

"What are you doing?"

"I'm packing."

"Why?"

"I need a break, Lucas. I can't think in this house. I don't feel safe with you. I'm going to Dannie."

"Please, babe. Don't go. It's over. Gallo is dead."

"It's never going to be over! Don't you get that?" I yell at him.

"Please, Emily. Don't go."

"I need time to think. Please don't try to stop me. I'm begging you. Just let me go."

Lucas is hurt. I can see that my words are stabbing at him. But I need time. I cannot stay here one more minute.

"I'll be fine with Dannie. Besides, if Gallo is dead, there's no reason for you to protect me anymore. Right?"

"I'll drop you off," he says, clearly defeated.

*　*　*

"Are you okay, Ems?"

"Not really. I'm a mess, Dannie. What the hell am I going to do? How did I get myself into this jam?"

"You did have help."

"Poor David. If only he knew what he started."

"It's not just David. I wish Lucas would listen to reason."

"I'm not going to make excuses for him. I'm pissed off as hell with that man. But I know he loves you very much."

"Sometimes love just isn't enough, Dannie."

"Don't say that, Ems. You've never been so happy as when you were with Lucas. Why do you think I didn't call the feds on him? I could hear from the way you talked about your relationship with him that you really love him. You can't throw in the towel now."

"What am I supposed to do, Dannie?"

"Fight for your man. If you believe in your heart that Lucas is the man for you, then make him understand that. Don't let anything stand in the way of your happiness. Do you know what I would give to have a love like yours? I'd move heaven and earth! Don't blow it, Ems."

"Wow. Where did you pull that bit of sage advice from? Did you do a guru's course on happiness while I was away?" I chuckle.

"You bet your ass! All kidding aside, my friend. Make him listen."

"Okay, I'll do my best."

Dannie is right. I've been feeling sorry for myself—wallowing in self pity even. And why? Because everyone around me is dying. Or that's all I see. What a terrible reason to give up on living! I have to make Lucas understand that if he wants to be happy with his own little family, he must give up his false sense of security. This baby and I are his security. This is where his joy lies—with us, not in the mafia world of wealth and perceived power.

"So, are you going to call him?"

"Yes."

* * *

"I'm so glad you called me, my love."

Lucas is sitting across from me in the apartment I share with Dannie. He looks nervous. I can only imagine what's going on in his head. He has a lot to lose. As do I.

"I want to talk to you about our future, Lucas."

"I…"

"Please, let me finish. This is hard enough without interruptions."

"Okay. Go ahead."

"I love you, Lucas. I hope you know that. And I'm so happy that we are going to have a baby together."

I take a deep breath before I carry on. I'm just as nervous as Lucas. What if he doesn't agree to my terms? I don't know if I'll be able to handle that. Thankfully, he doesn't interrupt me. If he does, I'll surely lose my nerve.

"Babe, listen. You have to get out of the mafia if you want to be a part of your child's life. I cannot, in good conscience, expose an innocent to your world."

"And you? Will I be a part of your life?"

"Yes. We're a package deal."

"I don't know if what you're asking is even possible, Emily. This is the mafia. You don't just resign and ride off into the sunset. And how will I provide for you and our baby if I don't have an income?"

"I don't care if we have to pick fruit in a field for money, babe. All I want is to live a normal life. I don't care about the money."

"That's a noble idea. But you have no idea what it's like to scrape by."

"I have more than enough for both of us, Lucas. David left me plenty. We'll be fine."

"I don't want to live off of my wife."

Wife? The word sounds so foreign.

"Yes, I plan on making you my wife. If you agree, of course," he smiles.

"You'll find a way. I know you will, Lucas. You at what you've accomplished already. I have faith in you."

"What you're asking me to do isn't going to be easy, my love."

"I know."

Lucas stares off into space. I know his mind is working overtime. I can see it. I keep my silence, as I've said what I wanted to say. Now, the ball is in his court.

"Okay," he says after a very long pause. "Let me see what I can do."

"Thank you. I mean it."

"Don't thank me yet."

* * *

Lucas

"You're what?"

"I'm going to hand the baton to you, Andreas."

"Have you lost your mind, Lucas?"

"I must have. But this is what Emily wants, and I cannot say that deep down I haven't thought about it myself."

"And how do you propose to get out?"

"That's where you come in."

"How so?"

"I need you to help me fake my death."

"Bloody hell, Lucas. That's a big ask. And I don't know if I'm ready to take over from you."

"Nonsense. You've always been ready. You've controlled your ambition because you're a decent human being. If you weren't, you would have pipped me at the post a long time ago."

"Bloody hell, Lucas. Thanks for dropping the bombshell on me so early in the day."

"I wouldn't ask if it wasn't so important to me, Andreas."

"What will you do?"

"Whatever it takes to make Emily and my child happy."

Andreas is more than a little thrown by my announcement. I cannot say that I blame him. It's almost unheard of for a boss to leave behind everything he's worked so hard to achieve. Unheard of, but not impossible.

"Okay," he says after a long silence. "How do you propose to do this?"

"I have enough money stashed away. I've been saving for a long time. For a rainy day, you know."

"Well, it's pouring now, buddy."

"Torrential shit, man."

"If we're going to do this, we'd better make it believable. I'm thinking a car bomb or something like that. It must be big or no one will believe it."

"Agreed."

"I'll see what I can come up with with regards to a body. This has to be believable and a wreck without a body is usually a dead giveaway."

"Better get a few. It's not like I travel alone."

"I'm on it."

"Thank you, Andreas. You're a good friend."

"Of course, Lucas. Not sure if I'm ready for this."

"Can one ever be? I have faith in you. I can't think of a better successor than you."

"I'm sure Peter will disagree with you. He's not too charmed about my career choice either. But, at least there aren't any children to gum up the works," he winks.

"Yeah, kids are the next level when it comes to complicated things, bud."

"Sounds to me like a you-problem, Mr. Heterosexual."

"You missed your calling, my friend. I'm thinking standup comedian."

* * *

"You're going to what?"

Emily's face tells me she isn't exactly thrilled with my plan.

"I have to, my love. This is the only way out of this."

"But, it sounds incredibly dangerous."

"It's risky, I'll give you that."

"I suppose Andreas knows what he's doing. Right?"

"Absolutely. I wouldn't trust anyone else with my life."

"Oh, Lucas. I'm beginning to think this is a bridge too far."

"I'll be fine, my love. Trust me. I have the tickets here. I'll meet you at the airport at exactly 4 p.m."

Emily's hands are trembling as she takes the tickets from me. It's been two weeks since Andreas and I hatched the plans, and tomorrow is D-Day. I'm a ball of nerves, but this is the only way I can think of to get out safely. Lucas Lucchese must die. No other option will truly free me from the life I'm living.

"Can I tell Dannie?"

"Sure. But you can't tell her where we're going. Okay?"

"This again."

"Yes, this again. I'm sorry, babe, but this is what you wanted."

"I know."

"Okay. I'll see you tomorrow. I love you."

"I love you too. Please be safe."

"It will be all over the news, I imagine. Don't stress."

"Easy for you to say."

"Hey, I'm the one who has to go up in flames, darling."

"Don't you dare."

I hug my Emily and kiss her passionately before I leave. This is it. My last day of being Lucas Lucchese, Mafia Boss. I'd better make it count.

* * *

Emily

I can't breathe properly. In fact, I haven't drawn a decent breath in days. Today is the day that I explain to Dannie that we will no longer see each other. I'm about to change my name and everything about me will be as if it never was.

My only consolation is that I have no family left who will mourn my loss. I'm starting my own family now, and that's all that matters to me. Nevertheless, this is going to hurt deeply.

I've loved Dannie for a long time. She's my best friend. Others have come and gone from my life. People like Maria, who were there for a season, but Dannie is special. She and I are soul sisters. That is what makes this so hard. I don't want to hurt her.

"Dannie, we have to talk," I say at dinner.

"Sounds heavy. Are you breaking up with me?" she grins.

"Kinda."

"What do you mean?"

"I have to go away, my friend."

"Hey, you've gone away before. What's different now? Are you planning on becoming a nun? They are allowed visitors, you know."

"Haha. No. I have to disappear."

"Disappear?"

"Yes. The only way Lucas can extricate himself from the mafia is if he's dead. Or appears to be, anyway. Therefore, I have to disappear, too."

Dannie is silent. She's processing while I'm aching to change something I'm powerless to.

"I'm so sorry, Dannie. You know that I would move heaven and earth if I thought I could do this any other way. Right?"

"I know that. It doesn't make this hurt any less. Where will you go?"

"I can't tell you that."

"Will I ever see you again?"

"I don't know."

"Oh, Ems," she says, tears rolling down her cheeks.

"I know. This is so fucking unfair," I sob.

"I was looking forward to having our families together. Watching our kids grow up. Barbeques in the backyard. How is it possible that we won't share any of that now?"

"I'm so sorry, Dannie. I don't know what to say. I love you so much. Please forgive me."

Both of us are balling now. The pain is excruciating.

"I will think of you every day for the rest of my life. I swear it."

"You'd better, or I'll haunt you."

"It won't be forever, Dannie. A few years, and then they'll forget all about Lucas."

"Yeah, sure. Because the mob forgets," she sniffs.

"Oh, shut up, you fool."

"I love you."

"I love you more."

***

Lucas

"Are you ready?"

"No. But let's do it anyway," I smirk at Andreas.

"Promise me you'll get word to me one day. I need to know that all of this wasn't for nothing."

"Andreas, I plan on living to a ripe old age. We'll laugh about this some day."

"I hope so. Now, get in the car and let's get you dead."

"Such sweet words. Take care of yourself, Andreas."

"Love you, brother."

"Ditto."

30

EMILY

"It's all over the papers, hon. Can you believe the fuss? I guess you used to be a big deal, Mr. Miller."

"Any regrets?"

"Not a one, my love. I'm so proud of you, Luke. Hmm. Luke. I'm getting the hang of this. Soon I won't even remember what our names used to be." I chuckle.

"I know what you mean, Ella," Lucas grins.

We live in a beautiful little coastal town in South Africa now. We've been here for a few months, and I'm about to pop. The baby is healthy and growing like a weed. It must be all the fresh air and a lack of mobsters.

Life here is so tranquil. Lucas thought that leaving the American continent would be the best thing for our new family, and I must say, I agree. The little village we're in is stunningly beautiful. We spend our days taking long walks along the ocean and watching the whales frolic and give birth just a few feet from the beach. It's quiet, but that's what I've always wanted, so no complaints here.

I feel and look very similar to the whales in the distance. My stomach is round and large. Lucas says I'm glowing. I think he's being kind under the circumstances. He's so sweet. Or he could be a little afraid. I'm like a yoyo at the moment. I pivot from hoy to tears at the drop of a hat. Man! Having a baby is something else.

"There's something I wanted to talk to you about, my love," Lucas says as we're shuffling along the sand.

"If it's about my speed, or my fat ankles, you're wasting your breath."

"You're funny. No. That isn't it."

"Good. Go ahead."

"I'm never going to love anyone else. You're it for me, my beauty."

"That's good news."

"That said," Lucas says and stops. "Will you do me the honor of being my wife, Emily Thornton?"

Lucas drops to his knees and opens a little velvet box. Inside is the most perfect ring I've ever seen.

"Lucas!"

"Is that a yes?"

"It's a hell yes!"

He takes the ring from the box and slides it onto my finger.

"There you go. Perfect fit."

"It's beautiful, Lucas. I can't believe it fits. My fingers feel like sausages. How did you guess the size?"

"When you're good, you're good."

"Uh-huh," I snort.

"Okay. I may have measured your little sausages while you were taking a nap."

"Once a criminal, always a criminal," I chuckle.

"Excuse me! You cheeky little…"

I stare at the ring while Lucas feigns emotional distress.

"I love you, Lucas."

"I love you right back, you gorgeous creature."

"I suppose Miller is easier to spell than Lucchese," I tease.

* * *

I wake up in a puddle. Lucas is fast asleep next to me. He's been so calm since our escape from LA. He sleeps like the dead these days. I nudge him.

"Babe, I think it's time."

"What?" he mumbles, half asleep.

"The baby. It's time."

I've never seen a man move so fast. He's up and out of bed in a flash. Lucas is dressed and on the phone to first the doula and then the midwife in no time.

We decided that a homebirth was the best option for us. I hate hospitals. Okay, to be fair, I should say that I hate them because that's where the morgue is. I cannot face starting my child's life in a place of death.

Lucas was skeptical at first until I explained to him that women have been having babies since the beginning of time, and that with the right assistance, I'd be just fine. Joanna and Ester sat us down and explained to us exactly what the process was all about. I have complete faith in their ability and experience. This won't be their first rock around the birthing pool.

"The girls are on their way, babe," he says. "Don't even think of dropping that baby before they get here."

My labor pains have started, so I nod between contractions.

"Breathe, my love. Breathe."

"I am breathing," I snap. "Sorry, I didn't mean to take a chunk out of you. Man, this hurts."

"Are you sure you don't want to do this at the hospital? There's still time."

"No. Absolutely not. Our baby will be home from the moment it draws breath."

"Okay."

"Will you prepare the bath for me, please?"

"Of course."

"And don't look so terrified. I've got this."

I'm upbeat in front of Lucas. But secretly, I'm shitting myself. The doula and the midwife better get here asap.

I'm about ready to do a cartwheel of joy when I hear the doorbell. Oh, thank you, God! They're here.

"Hi, Ella!"

It's so strange to hear people calling me by that name. But it's a necessary precaution. Emily and Lucas died back in America.

"Hi. Ouch! Here comes another one," I grimace.

"Okay, let's take a look," Ester, the midwife, says, gently touching my shoulder.

"Hi, Ella. I'm right here," Joanne says, squeezing my hand.

"Okay, sweety, your cervix is dilated by about eight centimeters. You're doing great."

"How long before I can push?"

"It depends. Not all women are the same. I'd say anywhere from thirty minutes to two hours," Ester replies.

"Ugh! Two hours. This is going to be a hoot, isn't it? My lower back is killing me," I moan.

"Let's get you in the pool. The warm water will help soothe you," Joanne smiles.

"Hey, no arguments here," I mumble.

An hour has passed since the women arrived, and the pain has intensified.

"That's it, Ella; breathe through it, my love. You've got this," Lucas says, kissing me on the forehead.

I'm blowing and moaning, moaning and blowing. Lucas reminds me to keep breathing, but honestly, I feel as if I'm about to leap out of this tub and run this little one out.

"Okay. You're fully dilated, Ella. It's time to push. Are you ready?"

"Are you kidding? I've been ready for two months," I groan.

"Okay, at the next contraction, I want you to give me a good push. Okay?"

"Uh-huh!"

"Okay, here we go. Push!"

The noises coming out of me take even me by surprise. I guess childbirth isn't for the fainthearted. Oh, how I wish my mom was here to hold my hand. Lucas is being so sweet, but honestly, the pain is overwhelming right now, and I don't want to be touched.

I bear down with every ounce of strength I have.

"Good, you're doing great, Ella. Your baby is crowning."

"Uhhh!" I moan and take a deep breath until the next contraction.

"Ready for the next one?"

"I guess!"

"Nice big push, Ella."

I close my eyes and push.

"There you go. The head is out. Just one more push, sweetheart," Ester encourages me.

"Won't our baby drown in the water?" Lucas asks, clearly freaking out.

"No, the baby is fine. Don't worry, Luke. Just hold Ella's hand and encourage her," Joanne says gently.

"Okay. If you're sure," he says shakily.

"One more, Ella."

I bite down and give it the old heave ho.

"Ahhhh! Ouch!"

"There you go! Well done, Ella. Sit up and meet your baby."

"Is it over?" Lucas asks.

"Yes, meet your son."

"It's a boy, my love!" Lucas grins from ear to ear. "We have a son!"

"Let me see him," I cry.

Ester puts our son on my chest. He's beautiful. He looks just like his daddy.

"Look at all that hair!" Lucas grins. "Oh, darling, he's exquisite."

"Isn't he?" I agree.

"Hi, baby," Lucas coos. "Welcome to the family."

"Luka, will you hold him while we see to his mommy, please?" Loanne says, handing Lucas our son.

"Of course."

"Come, Ella. Let's get you out of the birthing tub. You'll be pushing out the placenta soon."

"Oh, goody. More contractions."

"Don't worry. It's not as painful."

"Luacs, would you like to cut the umbilical cord?"

"Sure."

"Now you're a full fledged member of the dad's club," Ester chuckles.

"Proud to be," he grins.

"What does he weigh?" I ask.

"Seven pounds, fourteen ounces."

"Well done, my love," Lucas coos. "I'm so proud of you."

"What is his name?" Ester asks.

Lucas looks at me before he answers.

"His name is David."

* * *

Lucas

Our son is beautiful. It was my idea to call him David. Afterall. I have David to thank for the amazing life I now have. I often think about him when I look at Emily. What started off as a terrible tragedy has culminated in such profound joy. I will be eternally grateful for his sacrifice.

Our David is growing so fast. It's been nine months filled with new discoveries and the kind of love I was always too afraid to hope for. Emily is an amazing mom. She dotes on little Davie and lights up whenever he is in the room. He too is besotted with his mother. I am beyond blessed and I owe it all to Emily.

"I think it's time we tied the knot, young lady," I announce one day while Davie is having his afternoon nap.

"I was wondering how long this engagement was going to be before you locked me down," Emily smiles.

"So, what do you say? Shall we have a small ceremony next month?"

"Yeah. We can invite our new friends. Oh, and Joanne and Ester."

"Perfect."

"I've always wanted a beach wedding," Emily sighs as we're lying on the beach, Davie fast asleep on the blanket with his thumb in his mouth.

"We can get married wherever you like, my love."

Emily's face is bright but I can see the pain in her eyes. I know what she's trying to hide. I feel it too.

"I'm sorry your family won't be here with us to celebrate with us," I say, squeezing her hand.

"I wonder if it will ever stop hurting."

"I don't know the answer to that. But I do have an idea that may cheer you up."

"You do?"

"Yup."

"You're not going to make me drag it out of you, are you?"

"I might."

"Oh, come on. Spill it!"

"Shhh. You'll wake our son."

"Oh, please. He sleeps dead like his daddy. Come on. Out with it."

"How about I see if I can arrange a VIP on the day?"

"Oh? Do I get a vote?"

"Absolutely not."

"Tell you what. Let's discuss it later tonight. I'll let you tie me up so you can torture it out of me."

"It's a deal!" I laugh. "You're such a bad boy."

"Well, I guess you'd better punish me later."

"You bet."

* * *

Emily

"You look stunning, Ems!"

"Why, thank you, Dannie. How's Davie holding up?"

"Ester says he's just fine. Shoving anything and everything into his chubby little cheeks. He's so adorable, Ems. I could just gobble him up."

"I still can't believe you're here, Dannie."

"Yup. Lucas did good. Oh, sorry, I meant to say Luka."

"It's so weird, Dannie. I keep forgetting. The other day, someone called my name about five times before I responded. The locals must just think I'm a bit of a snob."

"Let them think what they like. You're safe, and that's all that matters. Lucas is amazing, Ems. You look so happy."

"I am."

"Do you miss home?"

"No, not really. It feels good to have new memories. A fresh start is good for the soul. Nothing here reminds me of the chaos and pain I left behind in LA. I do miss you, though. Very much."

"Lucas looks different."

"He's happy. There's a lot to be said for not living the life of a mafia boss. He's more relaxed. And he adores Davie. He's such a good dad. He even changes the little guy's smelly diapers."

"Geez! He's a keeper."

"I know, right."

"Who would have ever guessed? I'm so happy for you, Ems."

"How are things back home? Anyone special in your life?"

"As a matter of fact."

"What? Who is he?"

"His name is Adam. He's a math professor."

"He must be so intimidated by you," I smirk.

"Oh, totally. I mean, I am the smartest math nerd on the West Coast," Dannie grins.

"Correction. You're the horniest math nerd on the West Coast."

"You got me."

"I'm sorry you couldn't bring him along to the wedding, Dannie."

"That's okay. I understand. As it is, I had to do quite a bit of globe trotting to get here. Talk about zig zagging. No one would ever have guessed where I was going."

"Yeah, we're being careful."

"Hey, I'm not complaining. I love traveling. Gotta use up those frequent flier miles somehow, right?"

"Is my veil okay?"

"Stop faffing. You look gorgeous. Lucas is going to trip over his tongue when he sees you in this dress."

"Ah, thanks, Dannie."

"Okay, ladies. It's showtime," says Joanne. "The sunset is upon us. Oh, my word, Ella. You are a vision."

Dannie and I share a quick glance.

"Let's go, *Ella*," Dannie teases as soon as Joanne is out of earshot. "Time to make an honest woman out of you."

* * *

"Welcome to your new home, gorgeous," Lucas says as he pulls off my blindfold and carries me across the threshold of the most beautiful house on the beach.

"What? How did you manage to sneak this one past me?" I cry out in delight.

"I get up to all sorts of things while you and Davie have your naps."

"Oh, wow, Lucas! It's beautiful."

"I thought we needed a fresh start. And what's fresher than a brand new home for our little family?"

LYDIA HALL

"Oh, Lucas. You're so adorable."

"Wait until you see the main bedroom. It has a stunning view of the ocean. You can watch the whales and dolphins from the comfort of our bedroom now."

"Thank you, my love. For everything. Thank you for loving me enough to leave LA behind. Thank you for bridging Dannie to our wedding. Thank you for a beautiful baby boy. And thank you for this. I love it."

"It's nothing compared to the joy you give me, my love. I'd do anything for you and Davie. I can't imagine loving anyone more than I do you and our son."

"Yeah, about that," I say as he's carrying me upstairs.

"Hang on. Let me get you onto our new bed. Man, this dress is heavy," he groans.

"It's not just the dress," I say when he places me on the bed.

"Must be those fabulous boobs of yours, then. I must say, I like your new look," he grins. "Who knew breastfeeding would agree with me?" he laughs.

"Well, I have a little confession to make," I smile as he stands over me, grinning like a Cheshire cat.

"What's that?"

"I hope there's enough space in the nursery for a second crib."

It takes him a few seconds to register, but when he does, Lucas' mouth is agape.

"Really?"

"Uh-huh."

"You're pregnant? Again?"

"What can I say? You're a baby making machine, Lucchese. I'm too scared to tie my shoelaces around you."

"I can't believe it. Another baby!"

"Are you happy?"

"Are you kidding? Am I happy? Can't you tell?"

"Well, you're a little pale, so…"

"Hey, I just carried two people and a wedding dress up a flight of stairs. Of course I'm pale."

"Oh, good. I was worried," I giggle.

"How are you feeling?"

"I feel great. Davie's going to have a sidekick soon, so we'd better form a united front or we're toast."

"Oh, crap. We're never going to have sex again, are we?" Lucas says, raking his hands through his hair. "Not with two kids who possess sex radar!"

"Hey, we did pretty well with one around. Exhibit A, you honor," I say, pointing to my belly.

"Get out of that dress this instant, Mrs. Lucchese. I'm going to ravish you every day until the new baby comes."

"Thank goodness I can't get any more pregnant," I laugh as Lucas buries his head in my cleavage and blows.

"Wanna bet?"

My husband helps me out of my dress and lays it gently over the white chaise lounge near the window. Next, he shimmies me out of my panties and unclips my bra.

"Hm, delicious," he groans as he takes one of my nipples into his mouth. "You are so very yummy, mummy."

I can't help but laugh at his silly antics. My husband is so gorgeous, he takes my breath away.

Lucas stands back and watches me as I lie on the bed, naked and ready. He slowly loosens his tie and slips it over his head.

"It's silk," he grins.

"I know."

Lucas holds the tie between his teeth while he takes off his jacket and then his shirt. Next, he unzips his pants and slides it off. His erection is standing proud, threatening to poke a hole in his boxers. Finally, he slips them off. Lucas is naked. I love looking at his perfect body.

Each move he makes causes a series of muscles to ripple beneath his blemish free, olive colored skin.

"You are so gorgeous, my love," I breathe hard.

"I'm all yours, my love. Wanna play a little game?"

"Oh, yes, please," I gasp as he kisses my kneecap and trails his tongue along the inside of my thigh.

Lucas stops just short of my sex and looks at me tauntingly before he ties my hand together with the silk tie and wraps it around the bedpost.

"Close your eyes, my gorgeous," he commands, his voice thick with desire.

I do as I'm asked.

"Keep them closed," he says.

I can feel him getting off the bed as I lie there in anticipation. The next sensation is one that makes me jump.

"Keep them closed," he chuckles.

"Wow! That's cold," I gasp.

Lucas drags an ice block across my belly and around my breasts. The cold makes my nipples rock hard. Lucas sucks on them until they warm up and then repeats the ice treatment.

I'm so turned on, I can scream, but I keep my eyes patiently closed while my lover explores my body with the ice block and his warm tongue.

My husband slips a blindfold over my eyes. I can't see anything now. Even the light that was there a moment ago has now gone. I'm in total darkness as he takes complete control of me. This is pure ecstasy.

I open my mouth to moan, but he covers it with his while his hands roam freely.

"Take me," I beg when he moves away from my lips.

"Tell me what you want, beautiful," he teases.

"I want you inside me, Lucas," I moan.

"What was that?"

"I want your beautiful, hard cock inside me, Lucas."

I can tell from his breathing that he wants me too. But he's teasing me. I love it and I hate it. I cannot take what I want because I'm tied to the bed. Lucas knows this, so he teases me a little more until I'm ready to gnaw my way out of my restraints.

That's when he teases me with his tongue. Lucas licks and sucks and plays with my sex until I'm crying out for release.

"You like that, do you?" he coos.

"Oh, yes! Yes! I want more."

"Then you shall have more, my perfect little peach."

With one smooth motion, Lucas drives his hardness into me and starts to move inside me. It's Heaven! Oh, I long for this every waking moment. My lover is inside me, and we are moving as one.

I want to pull at his perfect cheeks, but I can't, so I move my hips off the bed to meet his perfect body. My orgasm creeps ever closer with each heave of my hips. I'm so close to falling off the edge.

"Harder!" I shout.

Lucas obeys my command and pushes further into me. He's touching me now in the deepest place. It's pure pleasure.

"I love you, Lucas!" I shout as I climax uncontrollably, my breath catching in my throat and my toes curled under.

"Cum for me, my perfect wife," he breathes hard.

I shudder and tremble. I'm in the midst of a powerful force that spills out of me like a raging river.

Lucas holds on until I'm spent before he follows. He flips me onto my stomach, digs his teeth gently into my shoulder, and rides the wave. He comes hard and long. His orgasm is intense.

When he's spent, my lover falls down on my back.

"I love you, Emily," he gasps for breath.

We lie together, perfectly still, utterly spent, and completely happy.

"This is the first time we've been alone since Davie was born," I whisper.

"And it won't be the last time today that I'll ravish you, my sweet woman," he says.

"If we carry on like this, we'll have twins for sure," I laugh.

"Baby, you couldn't scare me, even if you have triplets."

"That's an awful lot of dirty diapers to look forward to, Braveheart."

"Darling, with you by my side, I'll clean diapers all day long."

"I'm going to remember you said that," I giggle.

"I guess the very expensive French champagne I bought for today is wasted on you, isn't it?" Lucas sighs.

"I'm afraid so, my darling. You could keep it for after the new clan member arrives."

"Anything for you, my love. Anything for you."

31

EXCERPT: DANGEROUS SECRETS

He's been tasked to kill me... but I love him.

A woman like me is never meant to fall in love. My love is the kiss of death for everyone that comes near me. Except this time, I might wind up dead myself.

As soon as I meet mafia assassin Roman Gusev, sparks fly and the urge to stop fighting temptation sizzles within me.

I want what I can't have.

And what I can't have is him - mysterious, dark, cruel Rome who can only be soft for me.

Rome has been tasked with killing an assassin terrorizing the underworld. A shadowy figure who will never pledge allegiance to Rome's mafia family.

The problem?

Rome has no idea that assasin is the woman in his bed…

Me.

DANGEROUS SECRETS is the fifth book of The Corrupt Bloodlines series of interconnected standalones.

This sizzling, spicy dark mafia romance can be read on its own, or binged along with the rest of the interconnected series!

Rome

The club is quiet. I'm parked out back, half a block away and watching the back door. The man I'm hunting is supposed to be here tonight, at least based on the intel given by our detective friend. This bastard has it coming too. He's killed at least seven of our men over the past year and just as his name suggests, he is a shadow. L'ombra is elusive and incognito. In fact, I don't even have enough intel to judge whether I'm hunting a man or a woman, though with his stealth and accuracy, and the strength he has displayed when seen on camera, I can only suspect I'm facing one of the most dangerous assassins in the world.

I light a cigarette, inhaling deeply and exhaling slowly, watching as the smoke dances in front of me. The night is still and the only sounds I hear are the faint whispers of cars a block or more away. I check my watch; it's almost ten, and the club will be overflowing soon. I know I need to make my move before my target slips away again.

Suddenly, I see movement out of the corner of my eye. A figure in all black emerges from the shadows, swiftly followed by several others. My hand automatically reaches for my gun, but I pause when I see their faces. They're not here to attack me; they're paying customers, dressed in suits and dresses. They laugh raucously as they cross the dark alley and hug the side of the building, vanishing around the front.

I exhale the last puff of my cigarette and flick it onto the pavement. My nerves are on edge, and the sudden appearance of a van makes me more suspicious of my surroundings than ever. I've been tracking L'ombra for months, and he's never been so careless as to let anyone get close without knowing exactly who they are. The panel van has no windows; it's an early model too. It turns into the alley and stops near the back door, exactly how I'd suspect an assassin to travel.

I wait a few more minutes, scanning the area for any other signs of movement. When I'm convinced that the coast is clear, I slide out of the car and make my way to the back of the van, hand on my gun. If I can take the assassin out quickly and quietly, I will, but if not, I can at least catch a glimpse of his face, find out what he looks like. So, I make sure no one can see me, then peek around the end of the van. Two men, large and black-clad, escort a third, smaller person toward the door. My chance is now, and if I don't take it, I may not get another.

I leap out from behind the van, gun drawn and aimed at the trio. "Freeze!" I order them, my voice carrying through the silent night. The two men turn to face me, their hands reaching for their own weapons.

But the smaller figure, the one they're escorting, freezes in place. I can see their shoulders square. They're waiting for a signal, waiting for my move.

I keep my gun steady, finger on the trigger. "Who are you?" I demand, keeping my eyes trained on the two larger figures. They're both well-built, with muscles straining against their clothes. They're henchmen, no doubt, but I'm not afraid of them. Both of them have anger scrawled over their faces, furrowed brows, narrowed eyes.

"You need to walk away, buddy," the taller one says, and in barely perceptible movements, the third one takes a step toward the building.

"You're going to find more than you bargained for if you don't get lost." The second one draws his weapon. I'm not looking to make this war any worse than it already is. I'm not here for the goons, I'm here for L'ombra and if my suspicions are correct, the smaller third man is the assassin.

"Just step away from your friend there, and we won't have a problem." I flick the tip of my weapon in a gesture to indicate they need to leave, but one of them lunges at me. I fire off a round that slices into his shoulder, but he keeps coming like a freight train. He's fast and he's hurt, but when he slams into me, I find myself being smashed between his refrigerator-sized body and the side of the van. My gun discharges again before I realize I'm still gripping the trigger. I bring my hand around in a right hook and clock the guy on the jaw. His buddy charges at me too, both fists bared.

I hear the distinct bang of the door slamming shut as the first man drops to his knees, leaving space for his friend to come in with the butt of his gun. It comes down hard on my head, and I clench my eyes shut as I swing my left hand out, grasping for him. It's a miss; I can't make purchase, and I can't open my eyes. Pain shoots down my neck into my shoulders and I drop to my knees next to the injured goon.

"I said you should leave. You didn't listen," the second man says, giving me a swift kick to my gut. I catch his foot and pull, toppling him, then quickly stand and return the favor of a boot in the stomach.

If the assassin was here, he isn't anymore, at least not in this alley. Neither one of these idiots fights like a trained killer. They're hired muscle and nothing more. I stare down at the one who is bleeding while the other coughs and sputters, rolling on the ground. I'll never get in through the back door, so I head back to my car to gather my thoughts and make a new plan.

Bianca is in that club right now, maybe even starting her set. The problem is, I can't very well hunt an assassin under all those lights, and she'll have her eyes on me the instant I walk in. Any more work tonight will only be reconnaissance, but it's all I can do. My oldest brother and leader of our family, Dominic, won't be happy. That's a tomorrow problem.

I use the dome light and the rearview mirror to assess my injuries. There is a gash near my hairline that has left a trickle of blood down the left side of my face, and I feel tender on the chest where the first man's shoulder hit me hard. Other than that, I'm no worse for wear. I use my handkerchief to dry the blood and pour some water on it to wipe the dried blood off my cheek. When I'm presentable, I safety my weapon and slide it into my glovebox. I have to get in that club and scout the place, even if all I do is memorize faces.

Inside I make my way through the crowd, scanning faces and trying to remain inconspicuous. I don't want to draw any unwanted attention to myself. I spot a booth in the corner and head toward it, slipping into the seat and ordering a drink from the waitress. I watch as the crowd grows larger, people pouring in from the street and filling up the tables and booths. The spotlight on the ceiling is directed at the pianist playing a little tune.

There's no sign of Bianca yet—I must be early—or the assassin. So, I sit and sip and watch. Waitresses clad in short black skirts and low-cut white tops carry drinks and drink orders. A few men stand around the bar, blocking my view of the bartender, but I know him. He's been here for years and he's not harmless, so my eyes refocus on the crowd. I ignore the regulars, whom I see every week, and I pay particular attention to a table where there are four men seated. I easily see two of their faces; one of them I can only see the profile, but one of them has his back to me.

If only they were sleeveless. I know L'ombra has a tattoo on his arm—a triangle with an all-seeing eye inside of it. It's his trademark and he leaves his calling card nearby whenever he claims a victim. But I can't just walk over there and tear their suits apart.

Lights begin to dim, and a hush begins in the front of the dining room nearest the stage. The red velvet curtains are drawn as soft jazz music replaces the sound of acoustic piano. Bianca is on now. Any second they will open those curtains and she will be staring back at me. My window for finding the assassin tonight is closing quickly, and I have only put a few faces to memory now. Without thinking, I draw my phone from my pocket and ensure the flash feature for its camera is turned off, then start snapping pictures. Our tech guy, Lenny, will be able to isolate faces and run them through his facial recognition software. At the very least, we'll know who frequents the club.

When the curtains' part and the spotlight grow bright, I am forced to put my phone away. It's so dark in here, except for the stage, that no one can get a picture. The warm melodic tones of the piano are joined by a hiss and tap of some drums and Bianca takes the stage dazzling everyone.

Jet-black ringlets drape across her creamy shoulders, bared all the way to her plunging sleeveless neckline. Long white gloves rise all the way past her elbows; her dress sparkles with each of her movements. Her voice rises in a husky alto, sending goosebumps across my flesh. Every eye in this place is on her, and so is the spotlight, as she belts out her song and sways her hips.

LYDIA HALL

Her gaze scans the crowd as she sings the love song—a ballad about a woman who has to seduce her man to bring him home from a bar. It's a signature song, and she is a classy woman. She spots me, a half-smirk quirking her lips. Then she steps down from the stage carefully and works the crowd as she heads my direction. Her hand drapes across shoulders, smooths down backs, and cups a few cheeks as the spotlight follows her, and when she gets to me, she goes all out.

Her arms wrap around my shoulders, careful to keep her microphone in range of her breathy voice. She straddles me and the slit on her dress rides up, revealing the garter belt high on her right thigh. I'm tempted to touch her, hold her as if she belongs to me because in my mind she does. We've done this very tango alone in her dressing room dozens of times. But tonight, she is just a singer entertaining the crowd as she fusses my hair and leaves lipstick stains on my cheek.

And then she's gone, headed to the next poor schmuck who thinks she's flirting. I know it's all an act, but some of these men think they have a chance with her. The only thing they have is the right to fuck off and keep their dirty fingers away from my property.

I straighten my tie and smooth my hair, but before I can even have another sip of my drink in hopes that the raging erection swollen within the confines of my trousers will go away, the two goons from out back are here. One of them grabs me by the bicep and hauls me to my feet while I raise my hands in surrender. The other pulls a gun and puts it in my ribcage.

"I thought you learned your lesson, fellas," I snicker but I'm forced to comply with them. I can't blow my cover if L'ombra is watching. To him and anyone else watching, I am an unruly or unwanted patron at this establishment, and I have to obey the hounds.

They walk me toward the front entrance and one of them opens the door. They smell like body odor and pipe tobacco. The man holding me gives me a hard shove, while the second one strikes the back of my knees collapsing me on the pavement.

"Stay the fuck out. Don't even think about coming back." The door shuts behind me and I push myself off the walk, then dust my hands. I may not have gotten very far in my pursuit of the assassin tonight, but I learned one interesting thing. An assassin needs bodyguards, or at least some extra muscle now and then, and he is comfortable enough with this club that he enters the rear exit without even so much as knocking, which means he is somehow connected to this business.

Heading back to my car with my tidbit of intel, I feel the blood beginning to trickle down my face again. I hope Bianca didn't see it, or she will chastise me again next time we're together. Whenever that may be. Now that I've been outed from this nightclub, I'll have a more difficult time getting back in, at least when those idiots are working.

That's another problem for another day. For now, I need to get back to Dominic and report what's going on, then check on my dying father. After that, I can worry about Bianca and the next time we'll rendezvous.

Read the complete story here!

SUBSCRIBE TO MY EXCLUSIVE NEWSLETTER

I hope you enjoyed reading this book.

If you want to stay updated on my upcoming releases, price promotions, and any ARC opportunities, then I would love to have you on my mailing list.

Subscribe yourself to my exclusive mailing list using the below link!

Subscribe to Lydia Hall's Exclusive Newsletter

Made in United States
North Haven, CT
21 February 2024